"Take me to Planet Margo," said Krinata.

AND SHE LOOKED DEEP INTO THE MIND OF THE DUSHAU

An awesome three-dimensional image formed in the green haze of the debriefing cone. A sheer cliff of red marble rose to a magenta and silver sky. A frothy white waterfall crashed downward.

Krinata's imagination transported her into a waking dream. She <u>became</u> one of the Dushau Oliat officers walking the surface of the new planet. An image of a hillside farm etched through her mind and she was there. Oliat perceptions extended; she walked toward the farmhouse. But a part of her mind complained she was sinking too deeply into the dream state and searched out a question: <u>What dangers lurk here in the wilderness?</u>

Suddenly the sky was swept with darkness as purple, black and yellow clouds boiled along the horizon. A funnel cloud dipped down and ripped a channel across the harvested field, its deafening roar shaking the earth as it corkscrewed toward her, gathering dirt and chaff—and several human bodies.

"NO!" Krinata screamed, as the battering monster violently sucked her up...

THE DUSHAU TRILOGY #1
DUSHAU

JACQUELINE LICHTENBERG

POPULAR LIBRARY

An Imprint of Warner Books, Inc.

A Warner Communications Company

POPULAR LIBRARY EDITION

Cover art by Ken Barr

Popular Library books are published by
Warner Books, Inc.
666 Fifth Avenue
New York, N.Y. 10103

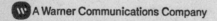 A Warner Communications Company

Printed in the United States of America

First Printing: May, 1985

10   9   8   7   6   5   4   3   2   1

To Andre Norton, for writing *Star Rangers*, a.k.a. *Last Planet*, but not the sequel I felt it desperately needed, and for not being mad at me for threatening her, as she stood among the lovely flowers in her front yard, that I'd do it myself.

To Jean Airey for hours spent on my back porch enthusing about *Doctor Who* until I lit up, too.

To Judy Bemis and the many fans who've gone out of their way to show me tapes of *Doctor Who*. You may not see the derivation of Jindigar from The Doctor, or you may feel it's spoiled by the admixture with *Star Rangers*, but to me, it seems Zacathans and Time Lords share the same Tailored Effects with Dushau.

To Don, Elsie and Betsy—for the spark that lit the conflagration (and for a lovely breakfast at Chicon IV).

To Marion Zimmer Bradley, for introducing me to Russ Galen.

To Russ Galen, for temerity, perspicacity, and audacity, as well as finesse.

To Nansey Neiman, for sheer nerve.

ACKNOWLEDGEMENTS

Here must be mentioned those who contributed actively to the preparation of this book.

Katie Filipowicz, editor of *Zeor Forum*, one of the fanzines devoted to my Sime/Gen universe, and creator of the Sime/Gen chronology published in the Playboy paperback edition of *First Channel*, made Stephen Kimmel's world-building program work on my computer. She also acquired for me several Ravi Shankar records on which I've based my concept of Dushau music. All this in addition to customizing Wordstar so I could learn the darn thing! She's one of those "without whom..."

Jean Lorrah, my sometimes collaborator and now independent author in my Sime/Gen universe, suffered through the rough draft of *Dushau* despite her own crushing schedule to produce two books—her first independent Sime/Gen, *Ambrov Keon*, and her first professional STAR TREK, *The Vulcan Academy Murders*—from scratch within 8 months. She showed herself to be a true friend and a magnificent critic.

Anne Pinzow, Executive Editor of *Ambrov Zeor*, the oldest of the Sime/Gen fanzines, and Roberta Mendelson, of many talents, Gail Lichtenberg and Susan De-Guardiola, all read and reacted to the rough draft.

There is no way to thank such people except to pray the finished product justifies their investment of self.

Further information about any or all of the above, or about forthcoming Dushau, Sime/Gen or Kren novels or 'zines is available by sending a SELF-ADDRESSED STAMPED ENVELOPE with your request to:

> Ambrov Zeor
> Dept. D.
> P.O.B. 290
> Monsey, N.Y. 10952

Contents

FOURTH OBSERVATION OF SHOSHUNRI

"It is incumbent upon The Incarnate to discern the Policy behind the Laws of Nature so They can anticipate results of action/motivation during a Cyclical Hiatus when there is no evidence to reveal even the existence of such Policy."

FIFTH OBSERVATION OF SHOSHUNRI

"Disregarding the Fourth Observation is a capital offense."

From : *Purpose and Method*
By: Shoshunri, Observing Priest of Aliom

ONE

Heraldry Rampant

> THE KAMMINTH OLIAT HAS RETURNED, AND IS SCHEDULED TO RECEIVE COLONIZABLE PLANET DISCOVERY HONORS. IN THE NAME OF EMPEROR RANTAN, ALL SURVEY BASE PERSONNEL ARE COMMANDED TO ATTEND THE AFTERNOON AUDIENCE.

The words crawled onto Krinata Zavaronne's desk screen and refused to be banished: an imperial command.

She swore. As a programming ecologist she was "Survey Base Personnel." The new Emperor would not allow her to put duty above protocol, even though with the food riots and threats of whole species seceding from the Allegiancy Empire, her work was more critical than ever. The Emperor obviously hoped pomp and ceremony would whip up a sentimental loyalty to carry them over the crises. But Krinata knew this was the worst possible time for her department to delay putting new planets on the open market. *When the throne was vacant, I got things done faster.*

In the privacy of her office, she squirmed into the formal red taffeta tunic. It fit tightly down the arms while blousing above her knees and made her feel silly.

It's a mistake, that's all. She was Kamminth's debriefing officer; *she* should have been asked before this useless ceremony was scheduled.

She'd have said, "No. Absolutely not!" And that would have been the end of it. Exposing the seven members of an Oliat to a public ceremony before they'd been debriefed and dissolved the peculiar psychic bond among them was nothing short of public torture.

1

She'd failed one of her Oliat teams by assuming everything would return to normal now that they had an Emperor again, so it was up to her to do something about it. As she draped the black sash around her waist, then up over her shoulder and fastened it to show the three linked circles of her family crest, she bent over her screen and punched up Finemar, the infirmary's Sentient computer. The Emperor's command remained overlaid on the screen.

Finemar projected himself onto her screen as a Lehiroh male—the Emperor's species—visually indistinguishable from human. He greeted her pleasantly, adding, "I'd have expected you to be on your way to the Audience, Krinata."

"Has Kamminth's reported in to donate blood yet? Have you done their physicals?"

"Kamminth's Oliat lost a member on location and returned badly disoriented. I'm treating them for Dissolution shock. On order of Emperor Rantan, I have just released five of them, against my judgment, to attend their Honors—"

"Which five?" demanded Krinata. "Is Jindigar . . ." *Is he dead?* A hollow panic seized her guts.

"The Receptor Jindigar is attempting to become the team's Outreach during the Dissolution." Finemar named the surviving officers of Kamminth's Oliat, adding that the Outreach had been killed, and he had the Inreach under heavy sedation, despite the Emperor's demands. "Do you think I'll get in trouble?" fretted the Sentient.

"No," reassured Krinata, hugging a sense of relief to herself. "But get Doctor Phips to countersign your order."

"Now, that's a good idea!" Finemar signed off.

Krinata grabbed her leptolizer, the jewel-encrusted symbol of her station, from the activation slot on her console, secured it to her sash, and headed for the throne room, arguing with herself. *Rantan has no right to do this to an Oliat, no right!* But he was so new to the throne, he probably didn't realize. *Even so, his advisors should have warned him.* But obviously, they hadn't.

As Krinata crossed the open rotunda between Survey's office building and the refurbished palace, Honor Guards saw her leptolizer and snapped salutes to her.

She couldn't get used to that. There had been no palace guards since she was a child. In the government hierarchy, she was the most minor and powerless functionary. Her hereditary rank in the third oldest family of Pesht, tenth Terran colony to join the Allegiancy Empire, had never meant anything to her. But she'd gladly use it to spare Jindigar. *Or any Oliat!* she told herself.

Her costume got her past all the guards inside the palace along the route to her proper entry to the audience chamber. But when she turned aside, she had to stay in the midst of the crowd heading to the front of the chamber, where higher-ranking nobles sat. Finally, she turned into a deserted corridor, carpeted in dark red, lit by mock torches, hung with the banners of the Emperors.

Before huge, carved seawood doors—bathed by a falling sheet of water—she was stopped by guards unawed by her.

They were a pair of Holot: six-limbed, heavily furred, formidable. "Public viewing of the robing chamber," said one, rolling his 'r's and gazing disdainfully over her head, "will recommence in the morning."

She fingered the jeweled wand and her belt. "I'm the Kamminth Oliat debriefing officer."

"Third rank enter the audience chamber from the blue doors, that way." He'd seen her three-circle badge.

"Thank you," she said, turning away while taking the leptolizer from her belt, "but I have business within." Before the Holot could block her move, she spun and flashed the beam of the leptolizer at the sensor plate on the doors. She wasn't sure it had been keyed to that high a security clearance, and if it hadn't she'd be in real trouble.

But the doors opened. She darted between the hulking guards. Furry arms grabbed her about the waist and shoulders, and she hung suspended, gazing into the opulent backstage robing chamber.

Three male Dushau huddled protectively around a single female seated in an all-form chair before an open fireplace where green flames danced welcomingly. On the spiral pattern of the rug before them, Jindigar sat playing delightedly with a piol pup, wholly absorbed in the baby animal's discovery of the world. Sternly, he commanded it to sit up, and it lay down. The other Dushau laughed, but Jindigar shot them a quick glance, they quieted, and he repeated the command patiently. The pup sat, and Jindigar laughed, plucked it up and cuddled it.

Jindigar, like the other Dushau, was dressed in the shapeless white shirt and pants of the infirmary while against one wall stood a rack of archaic Dushau formal wear.

The guards started to creep backward and close the doors on the scene. Krinata squirmed. "Put me down!"

As the piol licked his face, Jindigar turned to the doors. He rose smoothly, striding forward. In unmistakable welcome, he called, "Krinata!" His eyes, set wide and high on his head without protecting ridges, lit with hope.

The guards paused. One of them muttered, "That's the first he's spoken to anyone."

The other answered, "Our hides if we abort him!"

They hastily set Krinata down, and she offered her hands to Jindigar, in formal ritual. But he scooped her up with one arm, the other protecting the rooting and snuffling baby piol, and buried his face in her hair, holding her as if from desperate physical need.

He was shaking, and the dense indigo nap that formed his skin was cold and damp, not warm and dry as usual. She'd never been on such terms with a Dushau; never expected to be. But after her initial startlement, she felt his bone-deep fear and hugged him in reassurance, trying to imagine what Kamminth's had been through to bring the always self-possessed Dushau to such straits.

And an odd thing happened. Behind her closed eyelids, she *saw* the chamber as it had once been: newly gilded fretwork, plush new upholstery, too-bright colors. It was as if she were looking into an infinite stack of transparencies of the room, each one only slightly different from the one adjacent to it. But as she watched, the top one of the stack slid aside, and the others followed, fanning out like a deck of cards. Then images scattered chaotically in every direction. Her head swam, her stomach rebelled, and raw terror blossomed as an infinite chasm opened within her.

She gasped, forced her eyes open, and focused on an odd

stain on the wall beside a chipped bent grille. *I'm here; it is now.* She clung to that thought desperately, and her heart slowed.

Within seconds, Jindigar's fit abated and he withdrew, offering his hand formally. "I'm sorry. I'll explain." He glanced at the Holot, and his indigo features changed.

Turning she said to the guards, "That will be all. Thank you." She was amazed her voice didn't tremble.

They hesitated, then retreated and closed the door.

But Jindigar didn't offer his explanations. Instead, with that distant—frightened—look on his face, he pleaded, "Krinata, what has *happened* here?"

She gazed at the instrument in her hand, at her scarlet tunic, bloused black pants, black boots. Oh, yes, things had changed since Kamminth's had departed for the unknown.

"Just after you left, food riots devastated the Vincent and the Shashi Route Interchange Stations which made the Tri-Species Combine threaten to secede from the Allegiancy. Rantan Lord Zinzik took charge with all the legendary dazzle and charm of his several-times-great-uncle, Emperor Turminor, and put down the riots, provided food supplies from nowhere, and convinced the Tri-Species Combine not to secede."

Krinata met his eyes, trying not to inject her personal bias into the news. "People compared him to Turminor. Since Turminor was the last Emperor before the throne was vacated, they said Rantan was his obvious successor. After all, Rantan was doing as miraculous a job as Turminor had—and Turminor brought eight decades of prosperity.

"After three hundred years of doing without an Emperor, people were saying the Allegiancy needed a new Emperor. Suddenly, Rantan was crowned. He reinstated aristocratic privilege, and even I got promoted without earning it first. Nobody seemed to understand."

As she spoke, Jindigar's expression lightened to comprehension and the underglow of fear dissipated. "Of course! It's so obvious!" He set the piol on top of his head where it perched, happily grooming itself. Then he said something Dushauni to the others of his Oliat who relaxed along with him. To Krinata, he added, "I'd have grasped it sooner but for Dissolution and having to . . ."

To spare him, she offered, "Finemar told me why you had to go back to being Outreach." Jindigar had been the first Oliat Outreach she'd ever debriefed. It was only after her third debriefing of him that he'd shifted to being Receptor of his Oliat, and she'd thought she'd never speak to him again. Only the Outreach of the team could bear the stress of talking to outsiders. Right now, the other three survivors of Kamminth's were withdrawn around Kamminth herself, their Center. And Jindigar had maneuvered Krinata so her back was to them. In essence, she and Jindigar were alone.

"Do you understand Dissolution? You haven't been a programming ecologist very long."

It wasn't an insult. Her ten years seniority was but the blink of an eyelash to a Dushau who could expect to live ten thousand years and had already lived over six. "I suppose I do, as well as any non-Oliat." She named the books she'd read on Oliat function, and courses she'd taken. She didn't confess how, since girlhood, she'd lulled herself to sleep at night fantasizing that she was in an Oliat, exploring a new planet, the ends of her nerves humming with the living vibrations of a thousand life forms, instinctively understanding their interrelationships. Her current job was the closest a human could ever come to that.

"An impressive list of credentials. I'd no idea..."

"I told you I was serious about getting an appointment to a new colony. I want to work as an Oliat liaison."

"You have my vote," he said cutting her off, "if you can learn to handle traumatic Dissolution in the field."

Her heart leaped. Vistas of hope for her career opened where there had been only a dead-end job. "I know I can."

He watched her intently, one hand straying to her cheek for a moment before he yanked it back. "I'm sorry," he said again, then, "Krinata, I can talk to you. Do you understand what that means? Do you know why?"

"Because you knew me when you were Kamminth's Outreach?"

He nodded. "Partly." He turned away, taking the piol off his head and setting it on the floor, as he perched on the divan on the other side of the hearth and motioned her to join him, their backs to the others. As she sat beside him, he inched away from her and clenched his hands together. "It's because you were familiar when suddenly everything had become strange—strangely familiar. Rantan even looks like Turminor! It's as if we're lost three hundred years in the past." He glanced at her. "Dissolution distorts perceptions. I *couldn't*—none of us could force ourselves to look up recent events."

At last she understood. Loss of sanity, loss of orientation amid the vast, echoing caverns of their millennia-long memories, that was the chief terror and very real danger of the Dushau, for it meant an inevitable and early death. Remembering what her overly vivid imagination had conjured for her moments ago, knowing it was the palest shadow of what he experienced, she said, "In your place, I couldn't have either."

He studied her. "I may be Kamminth's most experienced officer, but even I've never had to change Offices *during* a Dissolution. Until you walked in, I didn't know . . ." His disobedient hand strayed again to her cheek, seeking contact with a slippery and wavering reality. "May I?"

She suppressed the jab of terror, focused on a worn spot in the carpet, and put both her arms around his chest—they barely met behind him—and hugged him. He wrapped both his arms about her, bending his head until his napped cheek rested against hers, and surrendered to the trembling. It would be ever so much better for him if she were Oliat. But only Dushau, of all the hundreds of species of the Allegiancy, had the talent for joining into a team resonant to the ecology of a new world—able to evaluate its habitability for other known species, to determine if a planet harbored a sentient or pre-sentient species. And very few Dushau had the Oliat talent.

Krinata sensed the other four Dushau steadying as Jindigar did. When he finally raised his head, fixing her with his deep midnight eyes, he seemed to have become Outreach in truth. As he spoke again, his voice descended to its normal register, somewhere near the resonance of her bone marrow. "Kamminth's thanks you."

She accepted that gracefully, then touched up a timecheck on her leptolizer. "How long until your Dissolution is completed?"

"Fedeewarn, our Inreach, is still unconscious. We'll be held in limbo like this until she recovers. But now, thanks to you, I can Outreach for her. In a few days, we'll be able to give the debriefing your department is so anxious for."

She twisted on the seat, offended. "I didn't come for the department!" Appalled at her inappropriate anger, she added, "I came because Zinzik is making a terrible mistake, and I wanted to find some way to stop it."

The piol was clawing its way up Jindigar's white pants. Jindigar grinned at it, showing sharp blue teeth with darker blue grinders behind, and gathered the creature up, lovingly swinging it over his head and nuzzling it, laughing at its delighted squeals. He handed her the piol and got to his feet. "If you didn't come simply to start the debriefing..."

"I wouldn't until you all were ready to work."

"Then we must thank you even more." He made an old-style courtly bow with an easy grace the modern imitators couldn't mimic. "We're indebted. However, our Emperor has commanded our presence, and we will obey."

The creature squirming in her arms, the very solemn Dushau before her, the onlookers ignored behind her, the decadence of the raw fire beside her, all combined to transport Krinata into the past and render her speechless.

Jindigar paused, as if waiting for some ritual reply, and when it didn't come, he said with difficulty, "May I ask a different service?"

He sounded like an actor in an authentic historical. "Jindigar, I don't know how to don imperial courtliness. I'm a programming ecologist, not a member of the court."

"I see," he said thoughtfully. The faint thrumming of imperial music came to them, and Jindigar tilted his head to listen. "We don't have much time. I suspect, if Rantan is really serious about this game, he'll be offended if we appear in hospital garb." He turned, went to the rack of clothing against the wall, and fingered the material. "Authentic, too. Hideously uncomfortable. But I suppose we must dress." He took down one of the garments, raking it with his eyes. "Somebody researched us—or raided a museum!"

He went toward Kamminth and the others, holding out the

crisp gold and white robes. In an archaically flavored Dushauni dialect which she could follow only because of her intensive study of the modern language, he said, "I hope you remember your manners. We've got to play this out."

The four of them had relaxed now, too, Jindigar's sense of reality having seeped through their nerves. Kamminth took the robes, examined them, and agreed. The others went to the rack and selected their own garments. Jindigar took a pure yellow surplice over a white undertunic edged with black fringe. They all stripped and dressed without even fumbling at the awkward fastenings. The fine indigo nap covered every bit of them, giving them an oddly dressed look even without clothing. She hardly noticed their lack of mammary glands or external genitalia; general size and shape distinguished male from female. It was their familiarity with the antique dress mode that fascinated Krinata.

She watched spellbound as Jindigar wound a long gold sash around his head to make a turban, and got it right the first time, without a mirror. Looking at him, Krinata identified the costume: Dushaun's first rank sept, and a highly born member of it, too. Three hundred years ago, she'd hardly have been allowed to speak to him. Kamminth likewise claimed aristocratic lineage, but the other three men were undistinguished.

Without a trace of self-consciousness in his outlandish costume, Jindigar came toward her and rendered an elaborate bow, uttering a formal salutation to Zavarrone.

She shrank away in raw embarrassment. "This is silly!"

His manner changed abruptly. "I'm sorry. I didn't mean to disconcert you. Apparently, we must learn a new culture."

"It's just me," she said, suppressing a need to squirm. "This is all such a waste of time."

"I couldn't agree more," he said. "But I must ask a favor, or a boon, depending on the dialect you prefer." The music had ceased. Rantan was on his throne giving a speech.

She laughed and tried to perform the obeisance she'd spent hours in a Court Manners Class trying to perfect, but stumbled into him, off balance. "You see? I can't do it!"

"Would you be willing to try? In public?"

"What?"

"Krinata, we're not sure Kamminth can hold us together out there. Stand with us before the Emperor. If I revert to Receptor and can't speak, or if something happens to Fedeewarn, make excuses for us. That's all I'm asking."

"But I . . ." she began to protest. Then, seeing his genuine need graven on his napped face, and his absolute determination to go through with this, she said, "If you don't mind the risk that I'll blurt out something stupid, or trip on my own feet—sure."

The midnight eyes searched hers. "We'll risk it."

He turned to Kamminth, and she formed them into a marching square with herself at the center, Jindigar at the rear left corner, moving them into position before the carved whitewood doors of the audience chamber. Jindigar drew Krinata to his side. "If you will hold my position here, I will take the Outreach position."

Just like that, she stood in the Receptor's Office, as if she were Dushau. Before she could object, Jindigar advanced to center front. The position behind him, just in front of Kamminth, was vacant—their Inreach, Fedeewarn, unconscious in the infirmary.

Jindigar had once moved in these circles. Surely he knew she had no business marching in an Oliat formation. No human did. *He doesn't mean anything by it. It's just protocol*. Something inside her squirmed at this real life replay of one of her favorite fantasies—her Oliat returning to the Allegiancy in triumph. She told herself, *Act your age!* and straightened up.

The whitewood doors opened majestically. In the bright rectangle stood eight Honor Guards, of eight bipedal species, carrying Dushaun gold-and-white banners bearing the Oliat device, crossed wands balanced on the tip of an arrow at the point where they intersected.

The Lehiroh who seemed to be their leader saw her red and black, frowned in offense, and asked Jindigar, "What is the Zavarrone doing among you? It is not permitted to . . ."

Jindigar interrupted. "She's not of us, but is essential to our well-being."

The escort glanced over his shoulder, then hissed, "Let her meet you at your seats, not march in the formation!"

She was about to step out of place when Jindigar grabbed a floor-length white cloak from the rack. It had a fully enveloping hood. He whisked it about her shoulders, flipping the hood up. Then he returned to his place. "The Oliat is an integrated team, serving the Emperor. We will not be separated, nor will we keep The August Personage waiting."

As one, the Dushau started forward. Krinata, out of step from the first, did her best to keep from tripping on the long Dushau cloak. A part of her wished she could relax and soak up every bit of this, to enrich future dreams. But she felt ridiculous, conspicuous, and wholly out of place. Her Ceremonial instructor had once told her, *Believe what you're doing is significant, and it will be*. As they inserted their formation among the eight Honor Guards, she tried to believe she was a Receptor of this proud Oliat, worthy of this Imperial Honor.

They emerged into the bright afternoon sunlight, diffused by the force-field dome overhead, and were inspected by the massed thousands of the Court. They slow-marched across the chamber, turned in the wide center aisle, made obeisance, and advanced toward the throne, all to the beat of the Dushaun anthem—slow, infinitely patient, fraught with eternity. Indigo music.

She'd never been this close to the throne before. The solid gold throne carved with the insignias of all the Allegiancy species filled her view. Beside it, only slightly less spectacular, was the Imperial Consort's throne, vacant now since Rantan, as a Lehiroh, didn't marry. To either side, other functionaries were seated or posted in ostentatious splendor.

Rantan Lord Zinzik himself was a short, middle-aged but trim Lehiroh, dressed in the imperial green, loaded down with badges and honors. For an instant, his careless cruelty to the Oliat was wiped away by the upwelling magic of the vision before her: Emperor of the Allied Species. Rantan, whatever he might be personally, had become the living symbol of the Empire and all that was good in their lives. She saw him as one fighting bravely and imaginatively for their survival. Tears came to her eyes as she marched amid the ghosts of her famous ancestors and all they'd sacrificed for the Allegiancy's peace and prosperity.

She blinked away the sudden tears. When the Oliat came to the foot of the stairs, she surprised herself with the smoothness of her deep obeisance, for the first time expressing, in the movement of her body, the emotions she felt for the Allegiancy Empire, the first galactic civilization granting full rights to all species. She treasured the Allegiancy and served it with all her heart.

The Oliat held the kneeling posture while Jindigar rose and answered the Emperor's formal inquiries. Then, at Zinzik's bidding, they all rose and were escorted to chairs set on a lower dais, the banners planted in holders all about them. It was the routine she had seen at dozens of these ceremonies, yet when Jindigar sat beside her, he whispered, without turning his head, "Does Rantan follow all the old protocol exactly?"

"He's fanatic about it," she answered, also facing front and trying to speak without moving her lips.

"Then something is dreadfully wrong." He folded his arms about a bulge in his lap. His surplice stirred and a furry head poked out mewling. He petted the piol as if everyone carried an animal when being presented to the Emperor. But his eyes roved the audience, measuring. "Where is the Dushaun delegation?"

She found their usual place, high on a side balcony, and saw empty seats. "Rantan's going to be furious. I hope he doesn't blame you that they didn't come."

"They'd be here if summoned. And did you notice the odd stirring among the Lehiroh and the Holot we passed?"

"No, but then I'm not Oliat."

"We're not either. We're shimmering on the brink of Dissolution. Krinata, it could be our perception is entirely warped, but we feel unwelcome, distrusted. Only by some. Others seem unaware. But the Emperor holds us in disfavor."

He knew that from exchanging a few formal phrases? "I didn't see anything like that. Relax, it'll be all right."

The same Honor Guard now escorted a Cassrian into the Audience from the opposite side. She wore only enough clothing to carry the badges and orders she'd earned. Her dark exoskeleton was painted in gilt swirls meaningful to Cassrians, and her wasp waist was adorned with jeweled ropes.

After being presented to the Emperor, she was seated on a higher step of the dais than the Oliat. After that, a Holot and a Lehiroh woman were presented. Then two Binwons were rolled in, their water-environment tanks taking up the position just below the Dushau. They stank, but Krinata refrained from remarking on it.

Then the Honors presentations began. The Oliat was called first. As they stood to be escorted before the throne, Jindigar said, "I told you something was very wrong. If he knows what he's doing, he's insulting Dushaun by this."

In protocol, the orders of things sometimes mattered more than the thing. "I doubt if many people will notice," she whispered. "I wouldn't have." *This is all so new to everyone, Rantan's just made some subtle mistake, that's all. Imagine what it's like to be Emperor and publicly embarrass yourself!*

"We do hope there's nothing to notice," muttered Jindigar.

With a little shock, she noted how he slipped between the personal and the Oliat-combined pronoun, betraying just how much distress the Oliat was in.

Their escort placed them on the level just below the throne, a wide step barely big enough for them, and again Jindigar stood while they knelt. She peeked up between the folds of her hood and caught Zinzik's shocked recognition of her non-Dushauni face. But he was too caught up in his own dedication to ceremony to make any outward sign.

He recited the standard Planet Discovery Citation, and then presented Jindigar with six jewel-encrusted leptolizers with second rank clearance that accessed almost unlimited credit at any terminal, opened almost any door, and gave priority over eighty percent of the citizens of the Allegiancy. Jindigar made a gracious speech of acceptance and then distributed the leptolizers, keeping Fedeewarn's.

Zinzik, meanwhile, had noticed the piol snuffling out of the neck of Jindigar's surplice, but his only comment was the slight widening of one eye. As the ceremony finished, the amplifiers were turned off and Zinzik said to Jindigar, "We expect you in Our private chambers immediately after We dismiss these proceedings."

Jindigar bowed. "Excellency, one of us is gravely ill."

"We claim a small amount of your time. But the Oliat only, not the human."

Jindigar bowed lower still, then rose tall to look Zinzik directly in the eye as he said, "The mercy of the Allegiancy Emperor has been renowned throughout the centuries. He would not deprive the crippled of their crutch, the sick of their medicine, the fearful of their security. The Zavaronne . . ."

Zinzik interrupted, his manner suddenly modern. "Nicely maneuvered, Prince Jindigar. History warned me of you. Very well, you will *all* present yourselves in my private chambers immediately upon leaving here."

Prince? Krinata examined the symbols on Jindigar's robe again. She'd never been very good at heraldry. But if Jindigar was a prince, then no wonder he'd claimed Zinzik was deliberately insulting his people. *But why would the Emperor do that?*

TWO

Conspiracy

Rantan's private office was hardly less opulent than the audience chamber, though much smaller. The center of the room was a deeply upholstered pit in the center of which was a holostage activated by the imperial leptolizer, a wand as long as Krinata's arm and sparkling with rare jewels.

The ceiling was paneled with high-relief carvings from dozens of worlds depicting the last Imperial Progress across the Allegiancy worlds.

The carpet had been woven to reflect the panels from above. The walls were colored mirrors arranged to focus light on the images. Dominating all were the imperial green laced with the Lehiroh violet and yellow. Krinata did not understand the rules of succession that rotated the throne among species, but she knew that Rantan's successor had to be human, though not a Zavaronne.

The Emperor reclined before his holostage, drinking from a tall cut-ruby glass and watching the audience chamber empty into the public corridors of the palace. Rantan had the good manners to address only Jindigar. "We're delighted you could join Us for this private chat," he said. He waved to a live servant standing to one side and said, "Do please come down and make yourself comfortable."

They descended the padded stairs, and while Jindigar drew Krinata to sit near the Emperor's right, the other Dushau gathered in a knot on the opposite side of the holostage from Zinzik. The servant promptly offered them drinks, though from ordinary crystal glasses. Krinata was dry-mouthed, but when Jindigar and the others refused, so did she, to Zinzik's displeasure.

"Then We'll make this mercifully brief. Your memory is more accurate than any Histrecording. We must know details of your years with Raichmat's Oliat."

There was not a trace of tension in Jindigar, yet Krinata sensed by his very relaxation that he understood at last the threat he'd sensed during the Audience. Yet his voice was deep, calm, as he answered, "I was in Raichmat four hundred thirty-two years, Excellency."

"We're aware of how long Raichmat's Oliat existed, and how influential it was on the early expansion of the Allegiancy ... as if Raichmat knew where to find compatible civilizations willing to join us."

"After an Interregnum of over seven hundred years during which the planets of the old Corporate League had been isolated from galactic trade, one couldn't expect to find the same cultures dominating familiar planets. But Raichmat specialized in exploration, and visited worlds not on any Dushau records. We found over a hundred unoccupied worlds which we opened to Allegiancy colonization."

"We do not dispute this," Zinzik answered, swishing the liquid in his glass. The jewels on his fingers flashed in the changing light from the hologlobe. "The service the Dushau have rendered the Allegiancy is overwhelming. Never has the gratitude of the Throne been withheld. But as We realize what it means for a living memory to span more than three galactic civilizations, the more We comprehend how vital Dushau loyalty is to the Throne."

Absently, Jindigar soothed the piol which was thrusting its head up under his chin and mewling. "I know you're hungry. In a little while."

The Emperor set his glass aside and rose to stand between Jindigar and the hologlobe. "Prince Jindigar, do you breach etiquette to offer insult to the Throne?"

Jindigar looked down at the wriggling animal, then back up at the Emperor. "Certainly not," he replied without rising. He extracted the piol and set it atop his turban where it curled comfortably within the ring of twisted material and snuffled itself to sleep. "We are Oliat. We found this piol cub wandering loose in the Groundside Station. Nobody seemed to realize it was orphaned and starving. I've fed it and reassured it, and its bright youth has helped us during this dire time of Dissolution. Surely the legendary compassion of the Throne extends to creatures orphaned within the precincts of the Capitol."

"You presume to instruct Us in Imperial protocol?"

Krinata had never realized this near legendary figure was so insecure in his new position. It explained a lot.

"By no means," Jindigar denied calmly. He rose, the piol balanced like the crown the Emperor no longer wore above his formal robes. Krinata rose with him. Fully erect, he was much taller than the Lehiroh. He added, with an odd, measured inflection. "Obviously, the traditions of Crown and Throne are familiar to their rightful heir."

Not sure what to make of that, the Emperor circled his hologlobe, one hand on its insubstantial surface. He pivoted and fixed Jindigar with a frown. "Your loyalty shall be evident in the thoroughness with which you prepare a complete, detailed, written report of all of your four hundred thirty-two years in Raichmat. You will not slight Kamminth's final debriefing for this, but you'll not leave Onerir until you've completed this task for Us."

"Excellency," objected Jindigar, "I am Oliat, not Historian. What you ask . . ."

"We have spoken."

It was dismissal, but Jindigar remained staring at the Emperor as if expecting an unreasonable order to be amended. One thing Emperors never did was amend orders. Jindigar spoke into the tense silence. "Fedeewarn is Historian-trained, and was with Raichmat from Tempering until I became Outreach. Surely . . ." He broke off, his eyes sweeping toward where the rest of his Oliat gathered. He froze, mouth open, eyes wide, breath suspended.

"Prince Jindigar, you are overstepping."

Suddenly, Jindigar swept the piol from his head, thrust it at Krinata, muttering, "Fedeewarn!" and together with the other four Dushau, ran from the room without even token obeisance. Stunned, Krinata faced the perplexed Emperor alone. He raked her with a glance, and before he could speak, she made the deepest obeisance of her life without faltering, and said, "Prince

Jindigar was apprehensive that such a thing might happen to the Oliat while in The Presence, Excellency. He has instructed me to apologize for Kamminth's Oliat, and to explain that in the event of some mischance with Fedeewarn, he would revert to the Office of Receptor."

She stopped when Zinzik flipped a hand at her sharply, his whole manner speaking of his total familiarity with the sensitive Oliat mechanism. She nestled the piol against her breast and circled away from Zinzik, bowing as low as she could. *He couldn't have done this on purpose.*

Zinzik did not deign to notice her but circled the other way and followed the Oliat. She trailed behind, wondering if she could beat Jindigar to the infirmary by taking a shortcut. But no, if there were any shortcuts in the ancient structure, he'd know them.

In an atrium where a fountain danced merrily, they came upon the five Dushau. The four males knelt around Kamminth who writhed on the tiled floor as if her flesh were seared by the sunlight from the open roof. One of them screamed, an ululating roar of unparalleled anguish.

Kamminth's heels beat against the tiles, a seizure's rhythm. Another of the Dushau vomited on the edge of the fountain, and then fell headfirst into the water. Jindigar remained clutching Kamminth, his hands bracing her head.

Guards swept into the atrium in the Emperor's wake, and formed up around him, awaiting orders. Krinata ran to the Dushau drowning unconscious in the fountain and, setting the piol on the edge, she hauled the large Dushau out of the water. He wasn't breathing.

She pulled him over on his chest and cleared his air passages, noting the unhealthy pallor of his teeth. Just as she was steeling herself to administer resuscitation, Jindigar's hands replaced hers. He was vibrating again, as he had in the robing room, his whole body in the grip of a palsy of terror. He said, "Kamminth's dead. I could do nothing." And he bent to force air into the Dushau.

Krinata watched the fight for life, glancing occasionally at the dead form of Kamminth surrounded by two traumatized

Dushau men, and feeling their awesome age. What was it like to have invested five or six thousand years in building a life, to feel the beginnings of maturity, and to have it all ripped away in death? Her tears gathered for Kamminth, and her whole body yearned to help the drowned man.

When he finally coughed and choked and drew breath, his teeth taking on the healthy blue cast of the living Dushau, his body convulsed, head thrown back, spine arched. Jindigar gathered him in as he had Kamminth, then reached out to sweep Krinata into their huddle. He grabbed her leptolizer from her belt hook and forced it between the man's jaws. Then he just held on, damping the thrashing with his weight and hers. As Jindigar offered solace to his Oliat mate, he also clutched at her again, as if she were his lifeline to sanity.

She never knew how long it lasted, but the Emperor and his guards still stood by the archway when the Dushau relaxed and began to breathe normally. Jindigar flashed her a smile, his teeth pale, but still a living blue. He returned her leptolizer, and went to the three other figures.

One of the other two Dushau was slumped bonelessly over Kamminth's corpse. The remaining one huddled upon himself. Jindigar put an arm around him, murmured something, and gently urged him toward Krinata and his half-drowned colleague. As he joined them, the Dushau touched Krinata and said, "I'm sorry you had to witness that."

That he could speak to her meant the Dissolution was complete. "I haven't been harmed," she answered.

Then as the new Dushau turned to his fallen comrade, Jindigar confronted the Emperor. "Fedeewarn is dead. Kamminth and Lelwatha are dead. Kamminth's Oliat is dissolved. The survivors are at the imperial command, but may we beg medical attention first?"

"Your right, without question," answered the Emperor distantly, but Krinata sensed an underlying delight in the man. *Impossible. I must be misreading a Lehiroh trait. The Allegiancy Emperor must think of all of us, not the few who inevitably die each day in his service.* Zinzik sent one of his guards for the medics. Before Jindigar had composed the dead for their final journey, covering Kamminth's terror-twisted features with his own surplice, a team of medics brought five anti-grav stretchers.

With two corpses and the two surviving Dushau laid out on the anti-grav stretchers, the medics came after Jindigar. His teeth were paler, but he refused to move. "The piol?"

The creature was perched on the edge of the fountain, sleek with wetness from its swim, happily nibbling one of the Emperor's most expensive decorative fish.

Seeing this, the Emperor roared, "Get that . . . that *thing* out of here!"

His voice startled the piol. It dropped the half-eaten carcass and fled. Jindigar smacked his hand loudly against the fountain edge. The piol halted, measured the distance between the Emperor and Jindigar, then scampered around the fountain and leaped into Jindigar's arms, mewling and licking Jindigar's chin.

Two medics caught the unsuspecting Dushau while he was consoling the piol and sat him down on the stretcher. With firm hands, they pressed him down onto the floating sickbed, connected Finemar's monitoring probes, and set out for the infirmary.

The Emperor and his entourage departed through another arch leaving Krinata alone, stunned. She shook herself and dashed after Jindigar, catching up with them at a cargo lift. "How bad is it? Is he going to be all right?"

One of the medics, a human man about her own age, smiled charmingly at her and said, "You aren't claiming to be next-of-kin, are you?"

"Hardly," she replied, "but I'm his debriefing officer. The Emperor expects rapid completion of this debriefing."

A Cassrian who was managing Finemar's probes and muttering over the readouts, looked up, "I didn't know humans were that heartless."

Jindigar, barely conscious, roused himself. "Oh, don't think that of her. I've never met a more generous soul."

Krinata, speechless, crowded into the lift with them as it took them down to the sub-basement level where they could get a transport tube to Survey's building. Seeing Jindigar's hands falling weakly away from the piol, she reached for it. He raised his trunk slightly to hand her the creature, pulled her head down and whispered, "Allow a couple of hours, then get us out of that infirmary. Krinata, please!"

His eyes were big, dark indigo pools. She nodded, swallowing against her dry throat, and took the piol. Jindigar crumpled onto the white sheets as the medication they'd given him took effect.

She stood in the bleak, underground tunnel watching them disappear, feeling as if her only friend in all the world were being taken to jail.

Bereft and confused, her nerves in turmoil, Krinata dragged herself back to her own office and locked the door behind her, extinguishing her on-duty indicators so nobody would bother her.

Trying to steady her breathing and calm herself enough to think rationally, she fed the piol from her own lunch. Her appetite had fled.

She'd never seen death—dead bodies—before. Warm, scented flesh turning stiff and cold within arm's reach of her skin had felt very different from seeing it on a news holo. And Dushau—they never died in public.

Scared to death. An Oliat could die like that in the field, survivors returning to report it. But on the floor of the palace? She shuddered and huddled over the piol as it alternately groomed itself and her. Kamminth's Oliat had been torn apart, their minds lacerated by that savage ripping. She could imagine what it must have felt like.

Her admiration for Jindigar redoubled. He'd kept his head through all of it. He deserved to rest in the infirmary. But he'd begged her to get him out. *How? He's obviously in critical condition just like Fedeewarn.*

She sat up, pushing the piol aside. "Fedeewarn!" *She died in the infirmary!*

Suddenly, Jindigar's desperate fear became real to her. Whatever had been done to Fedeewarn had decimated the Oliat. But Jindigar himself had warned her of the delusions that could afflict an Oliat in Dissolution.

What were the facts? Was it rational to suspect Finemar, a Sentient computer, of not understanding the proper way to treat sick Dushau? And if it wasn't ignorance . . . no! No. It couldn't have been murder!

She dismissed all thought of extricating Jindigar from the care that could help him overcome the mental warping of the Dissolution. Returning to her desk, she sat down and powered up to get some work done in the remainder of her day.

But no sooner had she brought up a file than her thoughts centered on Jindigar. What if he died?

Time turned bleak, barren.

And then, of course, there'd be no hope of retrieving the in-depth data on their new planet. They'd have only the holo-cordings and data arrays; nothing to attract prospective settlers. It took an Outreach to provide that.

What would I feel like, abandoned helpless in the hands of the murderers of those closest to me?

She groaned an oath, and punched up the Dushaun ambassador's office. The screen flipped images and settled on the rotating mobius-strip symbol of Dushaun. A cultured voice announced, "The Embassy offices are closed and will reopen at midmorning tomorrow. Thank you."

The deep sinking in the pit of her stomach prompted her to punch up the infirmary directly, telling herself, *It's my duty to find out what's going on.*

Finemar came on the screen smiling benignly. Seeing her, he drew his expression into solemnity. "I hope you've not been unduly disturbed by what you witnessed this afternoon, Krinata. The survivors are doing well."

"Thank you," she said. "But I require details on their condition. How soon will they be released?"

"Their prognosis is excellent, considering. We should be able to determine a release date in a few days."

"When can I see Jindigar?"

"He's under heavy sedation. I'm not permitted to authorize visitors for him."

"Jindigar is to be debriefed as soon as possible, by order of the Emperor," she said, hating herself for using such an excuse. But she knew Finemar had been reprogrammed to accept nothing but such authority. "I must object to any delays."

"But I have it on highest authority that Jindigar and the other two survivors of Kamminth's are not to be allowed visitors, and are to be held as long as possible."

What?! "Who issued that order?"

Finemar began to answer, went slack-faced, then puzzled. "I can't locate the source of my orders, but it's Highest Priority. I must have a malfunction, Krinata. I'm sorry. I will attend to it immediately."

His image began to fade, but then the screen split in half and a Dushau simulacrum came on the screen, facing Finemar, profile to Krinata. "Excuse me, but I couldn't help overhearing my master's name, Jindigar. I'm Arlai, Onboard Sentient of *Ephemeral Truth* assigned to Kamminth's Oliat. Please provide me a briefing dump."

Finemar turned to Arlai, saying, "My pleasure, but a great deal of the information is under priority seal. Is this sufficient?" In those seconds, Finemar had sent Arlai the open files.

"By no means," answered Arlai in Jindigar's tone. "I require complete information on my master. I have the priorities."

"In Reception," answered Finemar looking down. Then he raised his eyes, saying, "I'm sorry, your key is not sufficient. You haven't been reprogrammed since Emperor Rantan's coronation."

Krinata knew the verbal discussion was for her benefit alone. The two computers were conversing in their own time frame. She said, "Arlai, I have need to bring your master out of the infirmary within the next few hours. He did request it, and so did the Emperor. Would he be in danger if he were released today?"

Arlai turned to face her, flashing healthy Dushau teeth. "By the data I've been given, no. If he wore my telemband, I could monitor his health as well as Finemar. I have field-medic training, as well as Dushau specialization. I would not have placed the Oliat survivors under sedation."

Krinata wondered if Finemar's malfunction could explain

Fedeewarn's death. She said to Finemar, "You've admitted a malfunction. It makes sense to lighten your caseload under such circumstances, so on my authority, transfer the Dushau to Arlai as a specialist physician." She appealed shamelessly to Finemar's physician's programming. "It's the best way to insure the well-being of the Dushau in your care."

Finemar blinked expressionlessly. Krinata had never seen a Sentient take so long to make a decision. But then he said, "A sensible suggestion. I feel it is wrong to follow it, but I do not know why. Undoubtedly, the malfunction is impairing my judgment. Arlai, send your instrumentality to me at once. I'm beginning to waken the patients who will be remanded to your care."

Again he began to sign off, but this time Krinata stopped him. "I think it would be wise if I were present when Jindigar wakes. Several times he expressed gratitude for my presence. It seems to stabilize him somehow."

Arlai looked surprised, but said, "That can happen on rare occasion, and if so, then it is crucial that you be present."

Finemar looked from one to the other of them, perplexed as no machine ever should be. "I have data that this is true. But I also have specific instructions."

Arlai replied, "It is unwise to follow sourceless instructions, for how will you explain your actions in the event of disaster?"

In evident distress, Finemar agreed to permit Krinata's presence, and the two Sentients vanished from her screen. She snatched up her leptolizer, deactivating the screen, tucked the piol under one arm and headed for the infirmary.

The hospital section was on the top floor, in a far wing of the oldest part of the structure. She set her leptolizer to home on the infirmary, and followed its colored light display until she was thoroughly disoriented. At last, she found herself in a pleasant reception area, wide windows providing a spectacular view of the sunset over the crystal and ebony spires of the Allegiancy capitol.

She paused, breath caught in her throat, once again ensnared by the upwelling of emotion she'd felt before the throne. The Allegiancy, for nearly two thousand years, had utilized the best within each of those who served it, remaining impervious to their inevitable, mortal pettiness. The greatness of the Allegiancy was in the way it also captured the dedication of people like Jindigar. Such an organization was worthy of her devotion, even her life.

As she approached the monitor screen to announce herself to Security, she felt purified by her perception of the glory outside those windows. A small scurry passed her, three packages on its delivery platform. As Security admitted her to the corridor of in-patient rooms, she set her leptolizer to home on Jindigar, and found herself following the scurry right to the end of the hall and into a large room with three beds and a heart-stopping view of the city and the sunset.

There were just a few puffs of cloud scattered about the purple sky, arranged to complement the capitol buildings as if by the Celestial Artist.

Two attendants, a Holot and a Lehiroh, were working over Jindigar and the other two Dushau. As the scurry delivered the packages, the Holot said, "I don't like this. The last time we wakened a traumatized Dushau, she died!"

"But that was before Dissolution, and we told Finemar it was unwise to allow an interview with anyone but an Outreach."

The Lehiroh spotted Krinata and broke off. "You must be the programming ecologist." When she affirmed that, he asked, "Is your debriefing worth risking this man's life?"

"I'm no medic," she answered, "but Arlai, the Sentient medic who usually treats these Dushau, and I agree the risk is less this way. Hook up Arlai before you wake them, and listen to what he says."

She seated her leptolizer in the com-slot near the bed and evoked Arlai. "They're about to connect you."

"Prepared to receive telemetry."

The Holot had one cuff secured around a Dushau arm. He turned to the screen and asked, "Receiving?"

"Perfectly," answered Arlai. "The others?"

The Lehiroh sealed another cuff on Jindigar's arm while the Holot attended the third Dushau. Arlai began running their stats across the screen.

The Lehiroh said, "Finemar, are you with us?"

"Checking. Arlai's stat readback differs from mine. Stand by." In a moment, the screen split and they could see another set of numbers crawl up the screen.

Krinata stood in shock. This was virtually impossible. Computers like Finemar just never, *ever* distorted like this. "Arlai, run your Standardizing Comparison Test. Finemar, do the same."

The two medics looked at each other in total disbelief. A moment later, Arlai said, "I am clear, up and functioning. Seum's life-stats are too low, the others are low but acceptable."

The numbers on Finemar's side of the screen cleared and Finemar's visage came on, funereal grimness on his countenance. "I am not clear, though up and running. I must shut down the infirmary. I've called Doctor Phips, and he will be here within the hour. I suggest you revive the Dushau by hand, or wait for Phips."

The Holot said, "We'll wait."

Simultaneously, the Lehiroh said, "Arlai can guide."

Krinata said, "I believe it's imperative to revive them as soon as possible. Arlai, can you trust your monitoring? Are you in orbit above this point, or relaying?"

"I am above you and will remain so for sufficient time. I will monitor. Please proceed." He flashed his own face on their screen, gave a reassuring nod, then presented them with the readout and the orders for changing the drugs.

The Lehiroh noted the changes, ordered the Holot to write them down, then opened the side of Jindigar's bed frame and began manually adjusting settings. As the numbers for the others came onscreen, the Holot dictated them while writing them on the portable screenboard hanging at the foot of each bed. The Lehiroh made the adjustments. By the time he finished, Seum was stirring. Arlai dictated another change, and the whole thing was repeated twice more.

At last Jindigar opened his eyes, peering about him blearily. The windows had turned to reflective black as the lights came on. He raised his head on hunched shoulders, glimpsed the other two of his team, then collapsed back onto the bed with a gusty sigh. Then he saw Krinata. "You came!"

Gratitude flooded from his eyes to hers, and she was warmed. Arlai called, "Jindigar, how do you feel?"

Recognizing the voice, he twisted his head to catch sight of the screen. Krinata tilted the unit so he could see, and Arlai appeared behind the numerals. Computer and Immortal grinned at each other. Then Jindigar said, "I feel terrible. Are you doing this?"

"All my fault. Want something for the headache?"

"Sure. But nothing will blunt the other ache."

Then the other two Dushau were greeting Arlai, getting the whole story of Finemar's embarrassment which could have been fatal to them, and dragging themselves to their feet to dress. The two attendants helped the others while Krinata fetched Jindigar's tunic and shoes.

Jindigar introduced Arlai to the piol, and petted it as he struggled into his clothing, and wound his turban. Then he placed the piol on top of his head, signed them all out of the infirmary and led the way back toward Krinata's office, which was several stories underground.

She halted them at the ground floor. "It's well past working hours, and I just don't want to go back there today."

Jindigar checked his leptolizer for the time. His was a simple, polished steel model, hardly longer than a finger, the old-fashioned, unadorned model that could do everything the cumbersome heraldry-decorated one could do, and weighed less than a third as much. The one the Emperor had given him hung at his belt with Fedeewarn's.

"I didn't realize it was so late. I'm sorry. You go on home, and we'll check in at the embassy."

"The Dushau embassy is closed for the day."

"That's peculiar," said one of the Dushau.

Realizing he owed introductions, Jindigar said, "Krinata, this is Dinai, Protector of Kamminth, and Seum, Formulator of Kamminth. Krinata Zavaronne, our debriefing officer. I've worked with her often, and found her most competent. Perhaps we even owe her our lives. But now I must get to a screen and talk privately to Arlai."

She noticed Jindigar's teeth weren't nearly as blue as they ought to be. "You all aren't well enough to be running around hunting a hotel. Come on home with me. I've a guest room, and one of you can have the sitting room." Seum was leaning against the wall as if he couldn't stand upright, and Dinai was panting. Jindigar stood straight, but he was too stiff—resisting weakness. "I'll order in some food, and you can reach Arlai privately. Use your leptolizer in my system, and even a Proctor's trace would take all night."

"Proctor's *trace*," repeated Seum, a kind of creeping horror penetrating his dullness. "Jindigar..."

"Hold fast, zunre. Krinata, we accept your kind offer."

They went down to the tube level and Krinata used her leptolizer to call a larger car than she'd used to get to work that morning. Even so, the three Dushau filled it. *Must remember to use a Number Five with them!* she thought, and clicked her leptolizer into the receptacle. Relaxing, she pivoted the seat to look at her wilted guests.

Jindigar examined the comunit, then tried his leptolizer in its slot. "No. Only the new design will fit this. Krinata?"

"I have the old-fashioned machine at home. I'll just take off the adapter for you. Only a few minutes."

The indigo faces before her set into field-hardened endurance. It must have seemed like centuries to them, but was really only minutes. The lift put them a few steps from her apartment door. When her leptolizer beam touched the door, it evoked her moronic apartment Sentient who began her routine greeting and announcement of supper being served.

"Wait a moment, Fiella," she said. "Company." She apologized to the Dushau. "Fiella isn't in Arlai's class, but she's totally reliable." Then she dropped her leptolizer into its home slot and asked, "Fiella, how would you like a friend to visit you for the evening?"

Fiella put her simulacrum, an overweight grandmotherly human, on the sitting-room screen and made flustered sounds. Krinata warned Fiella, then pulled her leptolizer and the adapter out and motioned Jindigar to insert his and evoke Arlai. "They'll get along well enough, I think. Fiella is always polite, and Arlai seems...cosmopolitan."

"That he is," avered Jindigar.

Seum and Dinai had stretched out flat on the rose carpet and were doing exercises as if they hurt all over, which she was sure they did after the convulsions. The piol sat watching them, head cocked to one side.

The screen came alive with a full-length view of Fiella standing on a pink field, just the color of the sitting-room carpet, as Arlai walked on screen. The two greeted each other as if they were incarnates, and turned to face their audience. "How may we..." began Arlai, and then seemed to notice Seum and Dinai. "Are you trying to knock yourselves out?" he asked sharply.

They stopped doing leg lifts, and Seum answered, rolling on his side. "From what we've learned, Arlai, we'd better get back into shape again quickly. Is there any faster way?"

"You might eat something and get some sleep first!" Arlai answered with the anger of the overprotective.

When Jindigar said, "Agreed," Fiella glanced at Arlai with genuine respect. "Arlai, send us—and Krinata—a good meal, then we'll confer over these latest developments. Meanwhile, get us an update on Finemar's condition."

"Done!" answered Arlai, earning another marveling look from Fiella. "Survey Base Infirmary has been shut down, all in-patients transferred to Groundschool Hospital. They're talking about deprogramming Finemar. I've been recommending mercy; none of this was his fault."

Dinai sat up, hugging his knees to pull his toes out of the piol's grip. "What do you mean? Whose fault was it?"

"Someone with a very high-priority leptolizer amended his programs and inserted blinds so he wouldn't notice his oversights. It was a flesh agency, not a Sentient. My only clue is that when Fedeewarn died, a Lehiroh male of very high birth was trying to question her."

"Question her," said Seum, awestruck at the audacity or stupidity. "Arlai, *who was it?*" He raked the room with a glance, as if searching for the threat. "That man is three times a murderer."

"I realize that. I've been trying to reach our embassy, but their Sentient doesn't answer."

Jindigar swept the piol up, fondled it, and asked, "Arlai, do you remember the Interregnum—Casey's Planet? That's our situation, I think. My mind is clearing, but I'm still not sure. . . ."

The Interregnum had ended with the birth of the Allegiancy. Krinata had never heard of Casey's Planet.

Arlai said thoughtfully, "They're coming tomorrow to give me the new programming—"

Jindigar lunged forward on his seat. "Countermand!" he said. "Don't let anyone—repeat anyone—tamper with your programming. Tell them I've restricted your servicing to Dushaun Station only. Let them deal with me."

"Acknowledged," answered Arlai crisply.

"These matters," said Fiella in a kindly tone, "are way beyond my comprehension, but I do know your supper has arrived. May I serve you? You all must be famished."

Jindigar nodded. "Please, Fiella; you're marvelous. Arlai, keep trying to get through to the ambassador. Use all expediency, on my authority, but don't let your requests be traceable to me by any local agency. Wipe all groundside records, and keep yours under seal. Understood?"

"Use graytime procedures. Understood." He executed an obeisance to Jindigar, made a courteous bow to Fiella and took his leave of her as if she were a lady of the high court. She clasped her fluttering hands before her ample bosom and sighed.

As they all rose, Jindigar took Krinata aside. "Now think very hard. Do you really want to harbor us? It could be very dangerous for you; if not to your life, then to your career."

"I don't see why. This is all some ghastly mistake, Jindigar, and as soon as the Emperor—"

"Krinata, *it's the Emperor who's behind it.* Not the hand that wakened Fedeewarn, but the one who ordered it done while he detained us. Think! Where is the Dushau delegation? What is going on here?"

She shook her head, bewildered. "I don't know."

"Only two things are evident. You're going to see the end of a galactic civilization. And the Dushau are going to be blamed for all the ills attendant on that disintegration."

"Now, I really think you're exaggerating—no, you're just plain wrong. The Dushau are known as the staunchest supporters of the Allegiancy. You've done more for our growth and continuance than any other single species."

"That's not wholly true. We take a passive stance in your affairs, for it's up to Ephemerals to choose how Ephemerals will be governed. But once you've chosen, we will support your choice, and your right to rechoose. Yet we're often blamed when things go wrong. I'm not episodic; my memory is functioning properly now, so believe me. If you befriend us, you're endangering yourself. Say the word, and we'll leave right now. Arlai can eradicate all trace of our presence, and you'll only have to account for why you pulled us out of the infirmary. Finemar's collapse is good enough reason for that. You'll be clear."

She looked at the door, then at the blank screen where Arlai had treated Fiella with such courtesy. How could she turn out three tottering Dushau? What if they collapsed, as Arlai seemed to feel they might? It would be her fault. Then she stopped kidding herself. She wasn't going to turn them out, because they were good people, and such were hard enough to find in any world. "Look, I don't believe it's like that. There may be some rotten people in high places, but the Allegiancy will come through on your side. You're not going anywhere tonight. Now get in there and eat your supper before I evoke Arlai and get him down on you!"

He stepped back. "Yes, Zavaronne. If that is what you wish. We're grateful—and obligated." He made obeisance to her, just a shade less than if she'd been Empress. There wasn't a hint of mockery in it, either.

Embarrassed, she rushed about, putting the piol out on the balcony with a dish of water and some scraps of food, then hustling Jindigar in to wash up while the aroma of rich, Dushau fare wafted through the apartment.

Once they were all seated about her small table, and Fiella had sent her serving scurry around to present each of them with choices of entree and beverage, Krinata heaved a sigh. There wasn't anything sinister going on. It was just one of those things that were bound to happen when a government got as big and unwieldy as the Allegiancy.

They were hardly finished eating when Arlai came onto the dining-room screen and announced, "Jindigar, I've got Ambassador Trinarvil. She wants to speak with you—privately."

THREE

Proctor's Arrest

They adjourned to the sitting room where the screen was larger, taking their drinks with them. Seum lingered to thank Fiella. A scurry set out dishes of fruit as Jindigar brought Ambassador Trinarvil onto the screen, leaving a window in one corner with a headshot of Arlai's simulacrum.

Trinarvil was a small Dushau woman with anxious features and a high voice which nevertheless carried authority. Her plush indigo skin was darker than Jindigar's, almost as dark as Lelwatha had been, denoting truly advanced age. Yet she made full formal obeisance to Jindigar.

He waved that aside. "It's almost time to forget that silly title forever."

She grinned, showing healthy blue teeth. "Before we discuss sensitive material, we must secure this line."

"Indeed. Arlai, can you subordinate to Kitholpen?"

"Assuredly." Arlai's image was replaced by another Dushau, paler indigo, with a higher bridge to his nose than Krinata had ever seen on a Dushau.

"Your pardon," requested the new Sentient, whom Krinata assumed ran the Dushau embassy. The screen broke up, hissed alarmingly, then settled into a reddish image of Trinarvil.

"Secure," announced Jindigar.

"Secure," agreed Trinarvil. "Now—"

"Where were you this afternoon?" asked Jindigar.

"Consultation with home. For months, there have been rumors. Yesterday, word came of the first anti-Dushau riot. You haven't heard?"

Seum and Dinai were obviously shocked, but Jindigar said calmly, "So soon. Shocking how quickly Ephemerals turn."

The conversation was in the modern Dushauni Krinata had studied, but she often lost the sense. She concentrated, intending to look up later what she missed now.

"It's only in the outlying districts so far, but it seems imperial agitators are behind it, as usual. Blaming the food shortages at space bases on us, accusing us of emptying the throne and then manipulating the government to our own profit. All vague enough to stimulate imagination, evading challenges for proof. The pattern, though, is clear."

"The next step may be already at hand," said Jindigar sadly. "Open indictment by the Imperial Court."

"Rantan laid the groundwork for that yesterday," the ambassador agreed, "addressing Parliament, obliquely hinting that Oliat teams could be withholding information on planets with agricultural or mining potential. He implied that since most of us expect to live through the next galactic civilization, we might hold back information that would buy us high places in that government. With our lifespan, he said, we've no reason to abhor the starvation of Ephemerals that collapse of the Allegiancy would bring. In fact, the end of the Empire would be to our advantage since it would hasten the New Age which we could engineer any way we chose, since we know where the richest planets are hidden."

"The man's insane," judged Seum.

"Probably," allowed Dinai. "But his logic will appeal."

"Today," said Jindigar, "he was probing for concrete evidence. He asked about Raichmat. And I believe he sent someone to question Fedeewarn while he kept us busy. I saw dismay on his face when Kamminth and Lelwatha collapsed. He didn't intend that. Advisors or no, he didn't believe the nature of the Oliat."

"Arlai told me your story. He lifted recordings of the entire grisly episode, even the questioning in the imperial private chambers. They don't make them like Arlai anymore."

Jindigar agreed while Trinarvil looked down at the table before her, working some invisible controls. "Someone's trying to crack our screening," she announced. "Briefly, Jindigar, I've been in conference with home and our best Historians and Sentients. We discussed hundreds of rumors, half-facts, and planetary trends. The consensus was clear. The Allegiancy is tumbling over the brink of disintegration, and trying to blame us. We're sending out retrieval missions to the Oliat teams in the field, and we're withdrawing all our embassies and consulates, breaking off diplomatic relations, before they openly indict us. Onerir is being evacuated tomorrow morning. Meet us at Overlook Station as the terminator crosses it—"

"No," said Jindigar.

Into Trinarvil's puzzled silence, Seum said, "We can't leave Kamminth, Lelwatha and Fedeewarn—"

"Bring—" started Trinarvil.

Jindigar cut her off. "Under the circumstances, I'm sure Rantan has already denied permission to remove the bodies from Onerir. Your only chance of pulling out without being stopped is to go swiftly, without announcing intent—"

"We're not leaving anyone behind," declared Trinarvil.

Jindigar silently consulted Seum and Dinai, then said, "Kamminth's Oliat contracted to survey three worlds. We found one colonizable, and haven't debriefed on it yet. For Kamminth's sake, we must debrief. You've served Oliat—"

"Yes, I understand. But the danger—"

"We're still in the field," said Dinai. "Hazard is part of that life."

"There's one other point," added Jindigar. "I'm under direct imperial edict to submit a complete and detailed report of the Raichmat Surveys. I'm sworn to the Allegiancy Emperor, as he is to me. I'm not so naive as to believe myself safe from him. But for the Oliat, and for Dushaun, I must carry out imperial commands before I leave."

Trinarvil frowned gravely out of the screen, meeting Jindigar's eyes in a silent contest that lasted longer than any Krinata had ever witnessed. Finally, Trinarvil said, "You've always been such a stubborn kid."

"And you always told me my attitude would get me into a final trouble one day. Perhaps this is the day, and your prophecy will be vindicated."

"Would that I were wrong." She turned to the other two Dushau. "You're with him?"

The two looked to Jindigar as if he were their Outreach

still. He asked, "It could be otherwise? You knew Lelwatha and Kamminth. You knew Kamminth's."

"Arlai," said Trinarvil, "do you agree to this?"

"Without reservation," said Arlai's voice.

After deliberating, Trinarvil said, "Another prophecy then. One day, I'll serve in Jindigar's Oliat."

Jindigar grinned. "It's a deal! I'll see you there!"

The red haze shrank until Trinarvil's figure was sharply outlined. She made another formal obeisance and faded.

The silence was so deep Krinata could hear the ice melting in their forgotten drinks. She understood the ambassador was leaving Onerir and Jindigar was staying, but the reasons had escaped her. Nearly an hour later, still in total silence Dinai and Seum rose and went into the guest room she'd given them.

Jindigar muttered, "I'll explain tomorrow," and followed his zunre. Krinata let Fiella make up the sitting room guest bed. Her own room, with its pink rose-petal carpet, violet drapes and mint green bedding seemed to mock her mood. She couldn't believe the Allegiancy would fall apart in her lifetime. To Dushau, "immediately" might be three hundred years from now.

She heard the water running in the guest bathroom, and muffled Dushau voices while she was bathing. Fiella scolded her on the condition of her formal attire—piol dropping stains, Dushau urine from Dinai's convulsions. She hadn't even realized that she hadn't changed. "I'm sorry, Fiella. It won't happen again."

"Never mind," said Fiella from the bathroom screen. "We haven't had guests since your mother died. We should do things like this more often, even if it costs a few suits. They are so wonderfully courteous." She sighed. "Arlai says you were so heroic, rescuing Dinai and all."

She wasn't about to argue with the Sentients, so she distracted Fiella by asking for the syntax and vocabulary to retrack that interview and understand it while she slept. Then she snuggled into her bed and turned on the sleep field.

She woke four hours later, when the field went off automatically. Since she'd gotten over her mother's death, she'd always slept through that abatement, waking naturally at dawn. She tossed fretfully for a while, then tried combing her forearms with her fingernails and pressing her thumbs into the palms of her hands to trigger the sleep reflexes. She felt a mild relaxation from it, but then a vision surfaced of the piol left out on the balcony.

Before she knew it, she was on her feet, grabbing a robe and opening her door. The sitting-room lights were on low, and Jindigar was at the desk terminal, one hand propping his chin, the piol curled on his head and snoring while he scanned old records of the Raichmat expeditions and made new entries with his free hand.

The animal poked its head up, then scrambled down Jindigar and climbed up her robe, leaving claw marks on the delicate fabric. She plucked it off and cradled it in one arm as Jindigar roused to ask, "Did I wake you?"

"No, I just remembered leaving the piol outside."

Chagrined, Jindigar said, "I'd forgotten him, too. But I couldn't sleep."

She settled cross-legged on a nearby ottoman and turned the piol over to look for genitals. "Neither could I. How do you tell it's a he?"

"Well, you might say we asked him." He forced a grin onto his ravaged features. "Not very helpful, am I? Here." He reached for the animal and turned its rear to her, raising its tail. "Females usually have a light patch here. And they smell different, even when immature."

"Oh, I never had a piol, though I once had a cat. I thought about getting a dog after my mother died." She hadn't meant to say that. From there, it took only a few gentle questions by Jindigar to elicit the whole story of her mother's death from thransaxx and its complications.

"She must have been a fine woman."

To change the subject, she asked, "Does he have a name?"

"Why, no. There hasn't been time to think." He tried to smile, but she could see strained grief behind the facade. "Do you have any ideas?"

The picture of Rantan's livid face as the piol munched on

the prize fish with its festoons of rainbow fins spread about him made Krinata say, "Why not call him Imperial Fisher, Imp for short?"

"Irreverent, but appropriate."

"You're not smiling. I thought it was funny."

"I'm sorry." He sighed hugely and flicked his fingers over the keypads, sending text and diagrams flowing over the screens in three dimensions.

Abashed, she remembered that his only memory of Imp's greatest moment was the pain of the deaths of three of his zunre. "Are you planning to finish that report so you can leave in the morning with Trinarvil?"

He turned his head to inspect her with astonishment, then answered, "It's going to take longer than that to chronicle over four hundred years. When this . . . grieving is over, I'll have completely lost touch with those memories, barricaded them behind a kind of emotional scar tissue. So I have to finish this before I . . ." He shuddered.

"Look, if you'd rather be alone—"

He just looked at her, unable to answer.

"After I saw you had the piol, I came out because I thought you might like to talk. It's helpful to humans to talk out a grieving. That's what funerals and wakes are for." She began to uncurl her legs. "But sometimes it doesn't work across species lines. Perhaps it's too soon."

He put out a hand to halt her. "The grieving will go on hard and long, Krinata. I must ask you to forgive. Let me tell you what Trinarvil said."

"I understood most of it, and got the rest from . . ." Suddenly, the full import of the conversation hit her like a cannon blast. And she knew what had wakened her after the sleeper had turned off. The Dushau really believed the end was at hand, and that Rantan was going to make them his scapegoat. Despite all of that, Jindigar was going to honor his vows of fealty, taken hundreds of years ago to another Emperor. *What a beautiful man! How could anyone believe those lies!* She didn't know what Zinzik was trying to accomplish, but it must be that he was so intent on his goal of peace and prosperity among the Allied Species that he had allowed his advisors to lead him into a ghastly blunder. And if it went on much longer, it could be very dangerous indeed.

She asked, "Jindigar, are you sure you're not staying here out of a need to court danger, from depression over the incredible losses you've sustained? As a human might do?"

"Dushau might do such things in the emotional turbulence of the onset of Renewal. But I have quite a few more years. This shock alone wouldn't trigger Renewal for me, or Dinai or Seum. And what I told Trinarvil is true: I owe it to Kamminth and her Oliat to complete this debriefing. Also, I owe it to the Allegiancy to carry out the Emperor's orders."

She was listening with more than her ears. Renewal was the period of about a century every thousand years when Dushau retired to their home planet, took mates, raised families, and became younger day by day. "Kamminth meant a lot to you."

"Yes," he admitted heavily. Again, he put his forehead in his hands as if to soothe a deep ache. "She mated me during Renewal once. We have a son home now—in Renewal. Her last dying concern was for him."

He looked sharply at her, saw her sympathy and shook his head. "No, you don't understand. Such a reaction was most unlike Kamminth—until Lelwatha became her Emulator. Lelwatha was more to the Oliat than a sun to its planets. He was like a deep, still pond, clear to the depths of soul; the radiant stillness acquired through ten Renewals. He exemplified the beauty of ultimate attainment, and his mere presence awakened some of that in us. Kamminth was sharp, young, irascible. Her spiky temper and self-absorption, though simply youthful, made it difficult to be with her. But when Lelwatha came, the Oliat steadied in balance. We doubled in perceptivity. And we became open to joy. I learned—I hope I learned—so much from him.

"Krinata, I'm so afraid I'm going to lose his touch, that I will be unable to give meaning to his life because we didn't have enough time. And Kamminth—oh, Kamminth. She was learning too. Now—"

As he broke off, she was aware that he'd revealed more than he'd intended, but she was fascinated to have glimpsed the spiritual value of the Oliat to its officers. To them, it was a maturing, soul-enriching experience. And that, not money or adventure—or power—was why Dushau worked Oliat for Planetary Survey.

In his silence, she felt the immensity of his loss, and how it could scar and cripple him for life. She said, "I'll get Fiella to make some tea."

She went into the dining room and summoned Fiella while he continued to stare at his screen. *How does a Dushau cry?* She'd made a professional point of learning all she could about them, and still knew nothing important except that he needed a good cry right now. So did Krinata, but with less cause. She sat at the table waiting for the tea and wiped at her leaking eyes with a furious embarrassment.

When she took the tea in, along with some cakes Fiella had provided, he was totally absorbed in his work. She curled up in her favorite chair, meaning to stay only long enough to drink a cup of tea. She watched him sip his tea and munch distractedly while torrents of data swept across all five of the display screens arrayed around the desk.

As he worked, the strain lines smoothed from his face and he seemed younger. She tried to imagine him a thousand years younger. She didn't even know how old he was. But Raichmat had Dissolved more than thirteen hundred years ago.

She woke with a start to find Dinai bent over Jindigar at the desk, one arm around Jindigar's shoulders, whispering to him. Jindigar finally roused from his communion with the screens and moved vaguely, his eyes dazed, his words slurring. Dinai's alarm was written plainly in his posture, his tone, even though she couldn't understand a word he was saying other than zunre, the term for a fellow Oliat member.

She got up, alert as if there were something she could do for Jindigar. But as she moved, Jindigar dragged himself together, and said, "Oh, Krinata, I didn't know you were still there. Did I wake you?"

"No," she lied, checking the time. "I've got to get to the office." She pasted on a smile. "I've got a heavy debriefing later today!" *But he should be in the hospital!*

As she went to dress, he said, "We'll be there."

She left while they were closeted in the guest room, apparently chanting in unison.

The office was buzzing when she arrived. She marched past the reception counter behind which scores of her subordinates sat at desk terminals. Many of them did most of their work at home, coming into the office only occasionally. Today, however, everyone had come expecting a show. They were in their places, but gossiping, not working.

Clorinda Dover, one of the newest additions to the Survey Base data pool, fresh from Terra with the air of automatic authority that made everyone hate her while envying her pretty face, was regaling the young Lehiroh male, Sharfolk, with fictitious details of Kamminth's death, as if she had an inside track to the Emperor's apartments. Krinata strode past and snapped, "There's work to be done."

"Yes, Lady Zavaronne," intoned Clorinda. The worst of it was, she meant it. To her, rank was everything, and she acknowledged Krinata's status while vying to raise her own.

Krinata stopped, sorry she'd cracked her invisible whip at Sharfolk, who wasn't impressed by titles. "We do have Kamminth's debriefing today, and I'm sure the Outreach will be grateful if we can make it as quick as we can for him."

Clorinda put on a knowing smile that Krinata wanted to wipe off her tastefully made-up face. Three years ago, people like Clorinda wouldn't have been tolerated in positions of any responsibility. With a bit more rancor than she intended, Krinata said, "And I don't want to hear a single snicker if he walks in here with a piol on his head. The Emperor didn't bat an eyelash, neither will you."

I shouldn't be so hard on her. She's just young. Besides, she's a member of my team!

Whispers followed her all the way into her private office. She powered up quickly and began shooting questions at her staff, making sure all the queries from the field had been answered, all new data filed and integrated. By the time she'd been on-line five minutes, her department's Sentient and all his semi-sentients were fully occupied.

Then she checked with Arlai to make sure Jindigar and the others were really as well as they claimed. He answered, "They're not well, but they'll heal faster after they get this over with."

She was planning how to make it easiest on them when her door rattled open as if hit by a tornado. Six Holot guards led by a gilt-carapaced Cassrian trooped into her office in perfect marching step and took up a formation. Feeling smaller than the Cassrian, shock prickling along her skin, she rose to her full height behind her desk.

The Cassrian was gloating at pulling rank on someone technically his superior. "We have orders from the highest to observe this debriefing."

She roared, "Get out of my office!"

He ignored her, waving toward the full staff outside. "You plan to finish today?"

"The interview part," she answered. "In privacy! I shall file full formal objections—"

"They will be ignored."

Hauteur had always been a Zavaronne tool. She turned it on now, meeting the Cassrian's gaze coldly. "Debriefing must take place in private, or we may lose vital details."

She won the stare-down. Lowering his eyes, he bowed, joints clicking. He said more humbly, "Of course. We will make ourselves inconspicuous. You are ordered to say no word of our presence to the Dushau. But we must monitor. We have our orders." He handed her a slim message tube with the imperial seal on it. "Long live the Emperor."

She broke it and rammed it into the reader. While she folded nervelessly back into her chair, the Cassrian deployed his guards by pairs into Krinata's two side rooms—one a storeroom, the other a bath and dressing room.

The Cassrian and the other two Holot went out into the common office and appropriated desks in the back among the potted plants someone had brought from home.

Krinata stared at the ornately bordered, illuminated, unforgeable Imperial Order. By her oath and her family's oath, she was called to serve her Emperor. She was to complete the debriefing in routine fashion, not indicating to the Dushau that the guards were there, for any emotional disturbance might obscure the data even further than the deaths had already. The Empire needed this planet desperately. The guards were there to prevent interference with her work today. She would be justly rewarded.

She sat with her fists clenched in her lap, her jaw bunching, emotions raging back and forth. She had to breathe evenly to regain calm. But this was her department. This intrusion implied a distrust of her professionalism. A cold thought wriggled up to consciousness. *Or is it me he doesn't trust—because I stood with them yesterday?*

Maybe it was her department—or the Dushau—who weren't trusted? Had word of the Dushau withdrawal already reached Rantan? She hadn't turned on the news this morning, and there was no time now.

Oh, let this be over soon! But something told her it wouldn't be. Soon the damage the imperial decrees had done would be unforgivable. It could only damage the Allegiancy.

She had to warn Jindigar. Deep intimate details were sometimes revealed during debriefing. Yet she'd been specifically ordered not to alert the Dushau to the spies. Jindigar was doing all this from loyalty to his Emperor. How could she do less? Yet, she felt like a betrayer. On the other hand, there was no way to get word to him without the spies noticing. They were on her data boards out there!

While she dithered, feeling helpless and trapped in her own office and hating herself for it, Tully, her department's Sentient, came on the screen—a delightfully muscular young human with a frontier planet accent. "The Kamminth Outreach, Formulator and Protector have arrived."

Jindigar entered as the door opened quietly. He was flanked by Seum and Dinai, all dressed formally. Sure enough, Imp was atop Jindigar's head. He set the piol down, providing it with a plastic toy fish to play with and asked, waving at the full outer office, "All of that in our honor?"

"We thought we'd be able to finish today. Besides, I think they're all dying of curiosity. Kamminth's tale is all over the division. Right now, I expect they're gossiping about your arrival." Her cheer sounded strained, and her eyes kept straying to the doors on either side of the room.

Jindigar nodded. "Perhaps we can yet retrieve enough detail to publish a full and attractive prospectus."

Krinata rose, gesturing to the couches arrayed in the other end of the office behind a filigreed screen.

They entered the debriefing area, stripping off turban and outer robe with businesslike precision. As she powered up the equipment arrayed around her control chair, Jindigar installed Dinai and Seum on an adjacent lounge and made himself at home on the debriefing couch. He hesitated, frowning at her as if he sensed something amiss. "What's bothering you, Krinata?"

"Uh . . . nothing," she lied, hating herself for being weak. *Nothing's going to happen. It's better he doesn't know.* She could see through the brittle cheer of his facade to the bottomless ache of loss that was gnawing at his vitals. And he was nursing that ache, not attempting to surmount it, because its ceasing would wall him away from the data the Emperor wanted. "Let's get on with this," pled Krinata as much for herself as for them.

As if stung, Jindigar turned to his zunre, gathered them with eye contact and then joined hands with them. "We can't balance anymore, but we will access what mutual contact is left to us. Forgive, please, any clumsy lapses."

It wasn't in anything he said, but she got the sudden impression that this was very dangerous for them. Arlai hadn't warned her about that. But she flung herself into her control chair, forcing all worries from her mind. If they could give so much to the Empire surely the least she could do was support them. She snapped on the cone of green light which signified the detector beams were focused on the debriefing lounge.

Jindigar took his place under that cone as he had hundreds of times before. The other two Dushau settled for the long session, hands joined in some sort of formal configuration. Krinata gave herself with long discipline to the frame of mind of a prospective colonist.

She summoned enthusiasm, curiosity, and determination to

make a shrewd choice among the new homes available. The machines responded to her brainwaves, the lights flickering in their proper patterns. In the outer office, she knew from years of work there herself, screens echoed hers, and others drew data forth for comparison. Tully stood by with his semi-sentients ready to integrate the data.

"All right, take me to Margo," said Krinata, "and show me what makes it such a great planet to live on."

The scientific data already flowed across her screens, streams of numbers, equations, parameters and analyses, life-typings and ranges. But how many prospective colonists could take those numbers and create the awesome three-dimensional image that formed in the green haze before Krinata's chair.

A sheer cliff of red marble rose to a magenta and silver sky. A frothy white waterfall crashed downward, spuming outward on both sides. Enormous winged creatures, blue and turquoise, floated in the updrafts beside the cliff, diving and calling musically to one another, occasionally snapping up some water creature that had been swept over the fall and was tumbling downward through the air.

It was thrilling, breathtaking, beautiful enough to make her cry with yearning to go there. Suddenly, the rare magic happened. Once in ten debriefings, her imagination transported her into a waking dream, fully fleshed out and dimensionally real, as if her brain centers were directly stimulated. She *became* one of the Oliat officers walking the surface of the new planet, breathing its scents, testing its air on her skin, knowing it intimately with both mind and body. The fine line between intellectual imagination and living dream could not be crossed purposively. When it came, she had to relax and let it happen.

Sleep-deprived, emotionally exhausted, she needed to dream. This precious experience had never happened with Jindigar before, and somewhere within was the shrill panic that she'd never have this chance again. She grabbed for it avidly, and found it easy to float away to Margo.

The scene panned around and she saw the foothills rippling away into a plain covered with blue and mint green forest, dotted with lakes. They moved through the air until she could see the edge of the forest, and then an infinite rolling plain with tall waving grasses, grazing herds, streams and lakes. A long-tailed, streamlined silver bird dove into one of the mirror-bright lakes and came up with a big, fat wriggling creature. The bird perched on a boulder and feasted undisturbed. Part of her could become that bird.

Krinata asked aloud, "What eats the fisher-bird?"

Her skeptical curiosity, trained to parallel that of prospective settlers, was her most valuable contribution. Simple holographs could show what the exploring or developing teams wanted customers to see. She had to use the creativity of the Oliat to present the world as it really was.

As they watched, a sinuous pouncing creature stalked the feasting bird. Figures for its height and weight, its poisonous claws, and the size of its ripping teeth—as well as the fact that it would gladly attack mammals—flowed unseen across Krinata's screen. It was Clorinda's job to synthesize that data with the Oliat's created visions.

The pouncer attacked. The fisher abandoned its kill and flew at the pouncer. The fight raged back and forth across the meadow, Krinata living each side simultaneously. The fisher won, finally gutting and pecking at the pouncer's entrails. She cut off the pain/triumph and focused on the animal species population statistics on her screen.

"What would happen to this land with both these species exterminated?"

The grasses withered, the streams and lakes expanded, eroding the soil. She felt an inward searing desolation.

"Could we build a city here?"

A city sprang up—as the Oliat knew it must look if built here. Shiny buildings repelled the oppressive summer heat, vehicles swarmed through the air and on the ground, surface transports roared in with produce and provisions for the thriving metropolis. A canal was dug to channel the abundant water of the lowland, and ships nosed up and down that waterway, visiting other outlying towns. It could be one of the more pleasant and prosperous places to live.

"Show me how this city fits onto the world map. Let's see what this world would look like fully developed."

Years flew before her eyes as the Oliat extrapolated how

habitation would spread and shift the planet ecology. She felt the ideal site for the spaceport, and how building it there would turn a swamp into a desert within a century. She saw how they'd have to fight the sand to keep the ships moving, how slender a thread the economy of that planet would hang from as agricultural export was their only means of buying the technology of the galaxy.

But it was no worse than anyplace else.

"Show me the life a typical settler can expect ten years from Opening." An instant before it appeared on her screen, an image of a hillside farm etched through her mind and she was there. A prefab house flanked by standard outbuildings stood in the center, shaded by the remains of a grove of trees. The blue and mint leaves were falling; they had a peculiar but lovely odor. In the distance, she could hear the buzz of a reaper harvesting a field of noddies—grass with heavy seed pods. Fruit trees stood about the house. A small kitchen garden thrived behind the barn. There were already three silos for the harvest. Tamed native animals romped with some human or Lehiroh children while a couple of men and a woman labored over an outdoor grill to prepare a supper for the fieldhands. Peace soaked her nerves.

The area seen from above revealed a community of farms which pooled their resources to buy and run harvest and planting equipment. A good life; Krinata revelled in the deep personal satisfaction, the peace and joy never found on an urbanized, industrialized planet.

Oliat perceptions extended, she walked toward the farmhouse. A part of her mind complained she was sinking too deeply into the dream state, and searched out a question: What dangers lurked here in the wilderness?

Suddenly, the sky was swept with darkness. Purple, black and yellow clouds boiled up from the horizon. A funnel cloud dipped down and ripped a channel across the harvested field, gathering dirt and chaff—and several human bodies—as it roared toward her. A huge reaper was lifted from the nearby field and dragged along the ground to slam into the barn, scattering timber and glass everywhere. She ran.

A roof beam landed amid the children, smashing one of

them, spattering Lehiroh blood on the others who were swept away in the wind to be deposited grotesquely on the porch, battered but still alive.

"No!" yelled Krinata.

But dream had turned to nightmare. The roaring, battering monster corkscrewed toward her, sucked her up and tried to tear her limb from limb, and then dashed her indigo body into hard, infinite pain.

She woke to see in the holoimage before her, a stalwart Dushau female she knew immediately as Taaryesh, Kamminth's Outreach, sprawled brokenly against a tree.

"No!" she shouted again, ripping the contacts from her skin, trying to get to Jindigar. "Tully!"

Jindigar groaned, arched backward in a spasm, then curled on his side, moaning in long, shuddering sobs. He was wailing in a keen voice by the time Krinata got to him. The other two Dushau were clutching each other helplessly.

Damn my imagination! Just let him be all right, and I'll never let it loose again!

The doors burst open and the Holot guards converged on the Dushau.

FOUR

Mistake

"What's going on!" demanded a deep male voice.

It wasn't the Cassrian guard leader. It was Arlai, super-imposed over the data on Krinata's screen. She spared him only a glance, struggling to haul Jindigar's shaking body back from the edge of the recliner.

As the Holot guards formed up around the Dushau, Krinata ignored them and called to Arlai, "We were extrapolating Margo's planet. A tornado ripped through a farm, killing..."

Arlai interrupted. "They've relived Taaryesh's death, projecting it into your extrapolation?"

"Yes," said Krinata, shuddering at the memory of the twisted Dushau female's body. "That must be it."

"Jindigar is in Taaryesh's Office, so he's experienced her death *and* her loss. Hold him still, Krinata."

Thus warned, she was braced when Arlai used the telembrand still around Jindigar's arm to inject something which caused Jindigar to convulse once more. If she hadn't been holding him, he'd have fallen off the recliner.

His breathing normalized, and his eyes opened to fix on hers. His bewilderment gradually cleared, and he whispered, "Krinata. I'm sorry... I'm sorry."

She pressed him back onto the recliner. "It was my fault." The other two Dushau were recovering, a horrible tension graven into their indigo forms, faces buried in their hands. She stood, one knee resting on Jindigar's recliner, and twisted to ask Arlai, "Are they all right now?"

The Dushau Sentient nodded, but the Cassrian broke in. "I have my orders. This debriefing is declared finished. Wipe that Sentient out of your terminal, Lady Zavaronne."

She drew breath, offended to her bone marrow. She was on her professional turf, and she was not going to yield this time. But Arlai discreetly withdrew, murmuring apologies for intruding on an ultimate privacy. She stood straight and confronted the Cassrian. "I say when a session is completed." She had no intention of asking these three for more, but she wanted the intruders out of her domain.

"You have enough to complete a prospectus, omitting the final ugly incident of course. These Dushau have just committed an act of sabotage, falsifying imperial records, just as we were warned to expect. We have our orders to carry out, now. Lady Zavaronne, stand aside." The guards moved as if to yank her away from Jindigar, so she yielded slightly, trying to think. The Cassrian turned to Jindigar, made an ironic obeisance, and said, "Prince Jindigar, by order of the Emperor, you are to accompany us."

"I haven't finished the Raichmat report the Emperor wanted," countered Jindigar, raising himself but suppressing a groan. He rolled to his feet, putting one hand on Krinata's shoulder. "Perhaps I might be allowed another day? And with time, I could complete this debriefing properly."

Krinata fully expected the Cassrian to bow and say he'd relay these wishes to the Emperor. Instead, he motioned to his Holot. They pointed their leptolizers at the Dushau. The wands were emitting the gray haze and high-pitched whine that warned of active weapons' functions. "My orders are explicit. You will come with us."

Jindigar scanned his zunre, then spoke for them. "Let us discuss this with the Emperor." He dressed unhurriedly and led the way out of the office without looking back.

Krinata stood in the middle of the floor and stared at the closed door, all thought paralyzed. None of this should be happening. It couldn't be. Just couldn't.

After a while, the sound of Imp scratching at the door and whimpering brought her out of it. She picked up the piol and sat in her own guest chair, absently soothing him. When she told herself it wasn't what it seemed, some part of her knew she was kidding herself. Yet she couldn't believe it.

Her console was alight with requests from her staff. It was almost quitting time. She dragged herself to her desk and issued the wrap-up order. If they weren't as badly thrown as she was, they'd have the prospectus ready for publication by noon tomorrow. It would be a short one, but at least the scientific specs would be complete.

As she was sitting there, still unable to flog her brain into operation, the busy flow across her screen flicked aside, the imperial seal came into three-dimensional focus, and the Allegiancy anthem blared from the speakers.

The scene cleared to Rantan Lord Zinzik seated behind an enormous glittering desk. He seemed taller. Possibly his chair was higher than normal. He was in full regalia, complete with imperial green cloak and crown.

As a sonorous Lehiroh voice presented Rantan, her inner tension dissolved. *He's going to stop this nonsense!*

"Loyal subjects of the Allegiancy," read Rantan in a stilted accent. "We come before you to make a most fateful announcement. Grim though it be, the results should bring good cheer, for this means the end of our troubles.

"This morning, at dawn over the Empire's Capital, the Dushaun embassy withdrew from Onerir. At the same time, the outlying consulates of Dushaun on Onerir and elsewhere in the Allegiancy have been emptied. This means Dushaun has chosen to sever all ties with the Allegiancy.

"Although the Dushau have not confessed, their reason is no mystery to your Emperor. Our recent, vigorous investigation of the Dushau conspiracy has finally shown them that they cannot get away with it any more. No longer will we be tied to the decrees of Dushau exploration teams saying 'This planet is habitable. This one not,' thus controlling the speed and direction of the Allegiancy's growth. No longer will they strangle our prosperity, creating food shortages on some planets, economic ruin on others.

"Now that we are free of this conspiracy, all of these ills will be easily corrected.

"Our investigation continues into the Dushau Historians' deliberate misrepresentation of the downfall of the Corporate League, the Allegiancy's inept predecessor. Their sedition will not be tolerated. There is no similarity between our current transient difficulties and the ending of the League, for we, unlike them, know that the Dushau are causing this, and we are putting a stop to it. Our laws have long ago prevented the Dushau from the heartless use of the only other species with a lifespan comparable to theirs—their natural allies, the Sentients—as tools to gain power and wreak destruction. We are promulgating a new law which will prevent them from using our own citizenry against us.

"From this day forward, falsifying or disseminating data supporting the Dushau is hereby made an offense against the Crown, punishable by death.

"Meanwhile, our main thrust will be to open as many new planets as possible in the next year. All Dushau remaining among us will be rounded up and transported to their home planet which will be set under the strictest quarantine. Every individual who has been deeply involved in the affairs of any Dushau will be investigated and brought to trial where there is any suspicion of conspiracy with the Immortals.

"If you're tempted to side with them, consider! Since we've ended their secret manipulation of the Allegiancy, your Dushau 'friend' doesn't mind destroying your Empire, for he will be around to engineer the next civilization, and carve out a position of influence for him and his species. Meanwhile, you and your children and grandchildren will suffer deprivations beyond your comprehension. And their grandchildren will bow under the yoke of Dushau domination.

"Anyone who cannot see these simple facts, be warned. Imperial justice will prevail, and health will return to the Allegiancy. Neither the Dushau nor anyone else will be allowed to overthrow this Crown. We have declared it."

The image of the Emperor dissolved and was overlaid by the imperial seal. The final, stirring strains of the anthem rose to a crescendo.

There were tears in Krinata's eyes, but not, this time, from a heart bursting with pride and patriotism. She had suddenly realized she'd never see Jindigar again. And he had been swept away somewhere, half out of his mind with disorientation and grief. He had struggled so hard to serve the Emperor, and all he'd gotten for it was the most stupid accusation of conspiracy she'd ever heard of.

She put her face in her hands and let the unreasonable sobs come. *How can an Emperor make such a mistake? They won't let him get away with it. They won't.* But she knew that any backpeddling the Kings forced Zinzik to do would, for the sake of gracefulness, keep the Dushau bottled up on their home world. An Emperor could stop an action, but not admit to a mistake of that magnitude. Without the Dushau, her life's ambitions would never be realized. *And without Jindigar . . .* She refused to finish that thought. She'd buried people closer to her than Jindigar. She would survive and go on. *At least he's not dead.*

Imp climbed into her lap and licked at the tears until she got hold of herself. Tears never solved anything, but they dissolved a lot of barriers. She hadn't wanted to face it, but now she knew. Their new Emperor was not fit to command a single Sentient let alone an Empire. If that knowledge was what he termed treason, then so be it.

He's fabricated this Dushau conspiracy to buy time. She knew how desperately the Empire needed time to mend its trade basis from the series of statistical anomalies: massive crop failures; natural disasters closing down mining plants; major companies in interstellar trade going bankrupt, leaving contracted deliveries unfilled; three plagues; two widely distributed food additives that interfered with the reproductive cycles of a half dozen species; the ecological collapse of a chlorine-breathing species' home world which even two Oliat teams couldn't stop—all striking during the last three decades. But she couldn't condone gaining time by blaming any species, let alone the one the Allegiancy owed the most to.

She'd never met a dishonest Dushau; certainly not an Oliat officer. Zinzik was planning to send thousands of colonists to their deaths on unlivable worlds, or to destroy the ecologies of worlds in order to mine their resources.

She couldn't imagine a power-mad Dushau. They'd even refused a seat in the College of Kings that set the rotation of the throne among the species. She *knew* no Oliat would falsify their findings, and she was unwilling to believe the Historians did. She could almost see from the Immortal point-of-view, and there was no motive to meddle in Ephemeral affairs. *Why should I care who's king among mayflies?*

She didn't know the cause of the ills of the Allegiancy. It couldn't be very serious, but even if it was, Zinzik's tactics were bound to be ineffective and ignored by all sensible people, who were busy solving the real problems.

Still shaking from nervous reaction, she went into the office's bathroom to wash, and discovered chaos. In the dressing room, drawers had been emptied onto the floor, clothing pulled down and turned inside out, seams ripped open. Shoes were scattered about. In the bathroom, her medicine cabinet had been emptied into a heap in the bathtub. The toilet tank had been taken apart, but at least they'd turned off the water first. The sink drain-trap had been opened and crud spattered on the carpet.

Searched! She found one clean towel in the closet, and damp-wiped her face. But she felt personally violated—ravaged by a beast. Not an immortal one, though.

Indignation warred with common sense and her upbringing. She wanted to storm Imperial Guard Headquarters, demanding careers be terminated for this outrage. She wanted to throw her rank around as she never had before. But she held back as the Emperor's words finally sank in. Anyone deeply associated with the Dushau—that meant anyone working for Survey—was suspect of a capital offense against the Crown.

She thought of Fiella being asked if they'd ever had Dushau guests. The lovable moron would surely name their guests of last night.

Resentfully, she set the bathroom screen on reflect and inspected her streaked face. She muttered, "Well, let them put me on trial. My record's clean! There's no conspiracy!"

But that hadn't protected Jindigar. Hardly able to stand, badly in need of privacy and rest, he'd been dragged out into public and marched off to be deported, his most private nightmare labeled sabotage. *He should have gone with Trinarvil!* Either way, he was out of her life forever.

Ashamed at her renewed surge of tears, she sniffled and steeled herself to approach the world again, suspecting it would take all that was in her—and there wasn't much left after the harrowing events of yesterday, little sleep last night, and some skipped meals. *Low blood sugar. Must eat something.*

Back in her office, she punched up some soup and nutri-crackers, and some fish for Imp. She swallowed the food without tasting, but gradually she began to think again.

There was a frightened, panicky thumping in her chest telling her to run for her life. And there was a rational adult saying that was silly. Yet what were her options?

She had friends she could call, invite herself to be their guests. But what kind of friend would that make her, implicating them? She had enough credit to buy passage back to Pesht, to inflict herself on her family. She could imagine her father's face when, after more than ten years of ignoring his advice about career, she came running home at first sign of difficulty. No. She was a better Zavaronne than that.

She had to get hold of herself. It was very late. When she left, the outer office was deserted—unusual, but not unheard of. She decided to walk home, and ended up pacing the city streets so abstracted she lost her way and had to use her leptolizer to find her apartment building.

Fiella was relieved to see her at last, and plied her with food and comforts, and even found some piol food for Imp. Krinata hadn't seen a news brief since Kamminth's Oliat had returned, so she had Fiella compile all items to do with the critical shortages, inflation, riots and Dushau. It boiled down to nearly an hour of fast coverage.

She was shocked to hear that the Binwons' three colonized worlds were accused of withholding raw protein shipments due by contract, claiming the foodstuffs didn't exist. There were shots of warehouses jammed with shipping containers, purportedly filled with the nonexistent protein. Imperial troops were being mustered and sent to that frontier, a warning that hoarding would not be permitted during this crisis.

One whole continent on Treptes, the home world of a gentle, flying folk, had a total power outage that lasted through their summer season. Refugees were streaming off that blistering, uninhabitable desert. Looting and mugging had broken out, utterly against the Treptes nature. It was sparked by sheer desperation. The world's spaceports were closed to emigration by order of the Emperor.

On the more cosmopolitan Ramussin, where many species had colonized, and more had taken up residence, an anti-Dushau riot had broken out just after the Emperor's broadcast. It was virtually destroying a major residential district of the capital. Dushau sympathizers were being publicly executed in gruesome ways, along with a few Dushau.

"Krinata, do you really want to see those details?" asked Fiella.

"No, no, that's enough. I don't need any more nightmares."

She forced herself to go through a normal evening routine, and set her sleep field for the entire night.

The next three days, she walked through her work like a zombie. They turned out the Margo prospectus, and Krinata presented it at the Colonization Board meeting. It was approved without comment, and posted so shopping colonists could sign up. But Krinata felt the tense reserve among her colleagues. If she was in trouble, so were they—so was all of Survey, for they worked intimately with the Oliat teams.

People like Clorinda Dover made haste to adopt an anti-Dushau patter, saying they'd always distrusted the Immortals. In fact, the misnomer, immortal, became a common epithet countering the slur most people imagined Dushau meant by terming them Ephemerals. Dushau might live thousands of years, but they were very mortal. Krinata had only to think of the deaths she'd seen to know that.

Krinata tried copying the new style, but choked on the words, and despised her cowardice. She was no longer hiding from the obvious troubles of the Empire, but she couldn't betray her friends and herself for political expediency. All they could do to her was fire her, and there were other jobs. Even in such an economy, there were other jobs.

When she'd reached that emotional state on the second day, she ordered the mess in her storeroom—which had also been raped—and her bathroom cleaned up. Then she sent the bill to the Imperial Guards.

She was feeling pleased with herself at last when she got home that night, firmly telling herself that Jindigar and the others were halfway to Dushaun by now and it was time to put that part of her life behind her. But behind her eyelids, she was tormented with images of Jindigar convulsed in suffering. *Mother always told me I had too vivid an imagination for my own good. She was right.* Then Fiella told her the bad news.

Some Sentient she didn't know had been questioning her about Jindigar's visit, and what use the Dushau had made of her. Krinata had the probe played back and determined that the person behind sabotaging Finemar was probably still after Jindigar, perhaps trying to steal the Raichmat report Jindigar had worked on here that night. She still couldn't believe it was the Emperor. But it didn't matter, Jindigar had used Arlai to assemble his data. Fiella knew nothing.

On the third day, she felt dragged out by a headache and deep muscle ache from too much tension. From her office she evoked Finemar, hoping the Sentient was back on-line after being repaired, and that the infirmary was operating again. But a strange Sentient answered, introduced herself and asked, "How may I serve?"

Krinata hunched on the edge of her chair, forgetting her headache. "What happened to Finemar?"

"I've replaced him."

"But where is he?"

"I don't know. On some other assignment, I presume. May I help you? There are other patients."

"Uh . . . no, thank you. It's not important."

The screaming fear was back. There'd been nothing wrong with Finemar that he couldn't have fixed by himself. She left early, thought of going to a theater or concert, knowing she needed to relax. At home, all she had was Imp for company, and Fiella. But she couldn't make herself part of the throng streaming into the amphitheater for a classical Nopne concert. It resembled the riots she'd viewed too regularly lately.

She didn't want to talk to any of her friends, couldn't bear to hear the anti-Dushau slogans on their lips. They weren't friends actually, she realized. It'd been over a year since she'd had a serious lover, and the rest were just acquaintances, sharing interests but not attitudes.

Restlessly, she walked home, buying small things to nibble on as she went, trying to tempt her lagging appetite with delicacies from far planets. There were no shortages in the Allegiancy capital yet, though prices were soaring.

Even the long walk didn't get her tired enough to sleep without help. But she was becoming addicted to the field, and deliberately left it off that night. Around midnight, when she'd tossed for the thousandth time to shake a ghost nightmare in which members of her Oliat were dying all about her, her senses winking out as if somebody were putting out her eyes and ears with a hot poker, the screen in her room turned from mirror into gleaming starship bridge. In the center paced Arlai. He turned as the screen focused, and looked at Krinata lying in bed.

"Ah, Krinata, at last. I've been trying to reach you."

She sat up, wondering where he was calling from, but she said with asperity, "I'd have expected better manners from the Sentient of a prince!"

Arlai made a deep obeisance, uttering formal apologies, and kept his eyes down as he spoke. "Onerir Control is trying to isolate me in orbit, and I can't reach Jindigar—they've removed my telemband from him. Krinata, I need help!"

She shoved aside her lecture on overriding household closures and waking people up. Grabbing a robe, she went to the screen. "I thought you'd be nearing Dushaun by now."

"No, Jindigar is being held on Onerir. I've just found out where, only I can't reach him. And now . . . now," he said, gulping visibly, "I've found that Finemar has been murdered!"

"Murdered!"

"Well, disconnected. But to me it feels like murder. His whole personality is gone forever. He's being broken down for parts, and his centrals are being discarded. All by order of the Emperor. Krinata, it *was* the Emperor who ordered Finemar reprogrammed to begin with. I think he wanted Dinai and Seum debilitated by their treatment, so he could more easily wring confessions out of them."

"Whoa! Slow down, Arlai. Don't let your imagination run wild." But she shivered at his words. "How could they confess to a plot they never even heard of?"

Arlai sat down, letting the screen fill with his head and shoulders. "I think the Emperor needs an actual Dushau confession to nail all this down tight. He hasn't a single shred of evidence despite all his investigating. He's just letting people think that investigations mean guilt."

"How do you know all this?"

Arlai smiled hesitantly. "I'm one of the oldest Sentients operating. I'm pretty good at my job. If you want to know more, you'll have to ask Jindigar."

She assessed the simulacrum's demeanor as if he were a living being, knowing they went to some pains to master non-verbal communication forms. "You're loyal to him, aren't you?" Many Sentients were owned by people, and regarded them simply as employers, not personal friends. She'd won Fiella's friendship after many years, and she thought she recognized that attitude in Arlai.

"Sentients are supposed to be loyal to their owners," answered Arlai.

She started to say that he seemed more than a Sentient, more even than a worried friend. But he cut her off.

"Krinata, I'm not Kitholpen, to be able to secure a line with diplomatic immunity. I've done my best, but . . ."

Secured line? The situation must be dire. "Where did you say Jindigar was being held?"

"I know he trusted you," said Arlai as if to convince himself. "He left you the piol. He was telling me by that just how much he trusted you to help. Krinata, I didn't call you because a Sentient has been murd—disconnected. I called because I just found out that Dinai and Seum have died, in the psychiatric ward of Onerir General Hospital, where Jindigar is being held. Official cause of death: Dushau insanity. I don't believe that, but I can't prove it. They removed my telembands from them before they died. Jindigar's still alive according to the Attending Sentient. Krinata, if isolating him like this after such a loss isn't torture, what is? After they wring a confession out of him, the Emperor plans a public humiliation and execution of a Dushau prince."

She sat in shock, the nightmare coming back full force as rationality shrieked, *Pay attention! This is real!* The Emperor had lied to the Allegiancy, and to his own sworn prince. That was what was real and had to be dealt with.

"I'll get him out," she said, hearing her own voice as if it belonged to someone else.

Arlai slumped, and held one hand to his eyes as if to forestall weeping. "I knew you'd help."

Krinata's resolve hardened. She had failed to warn the three that they were being spied upon in her office. She had seduced Jindigar into that replay of Taaryesh's death that had been called sabotage. She had stood by and let Jindigar and the others be hauled out of her office, too weak to defend themselves. It might not be her *fault,* but it was her responsibility. Besides, Jindigar was special. If somewhere, some Dushau really *was* plotting against the Allegiancy, well, every species had its criminals.

She was suddenly sick of sitting on her hands waiting for the Emperor's investigators to swing an ax at her professional neck. She'd seen how they were trumping up false evidence, and Jindigar's "sabotage" had occurred in her office. It was a matter of record that she'd openly resisted imperial troops. Never mind that she was within her rights. If they wanted to get her, they could. And she was sure that they did. There was no point in playing innocent while the Emperor tortured Jindigar into betraying everything he believed in, murdered him, and then came after her as his primary contact on Onerir. If they were going to survive until the Kings put a stop to this, she had to act now.

She went to her wardrobe and summoned Fiella to assemble her toughest hiking clothes and assorted necessities for a long trip, packing it all in a lightcase. Then she ordered up her best court regalia and began dressing to impress.

Arlai said, "I'm stuck up here in orbit, Krinata, but I have developed contacts, and I can sometimes control scurries and other out-runners by fast-talking their Sentients. I'll follow you, and I'll help wherever I can."

She poked her nose around the door of her dressing room and said, "You're great, Arlai. But I hope I won't need any help."

She came out into the room and Arlai stood, nodding appreciatively. "Very, very impressive, Lady Zavaronne." He

redressed his image in courtwear of the lowliest rank, unadorned, and made a deep obeisance.

She looked around at her possessions. At least a year's
salary's worth of electronics, several years' salary invested in
her library, the furnishings, momentos of her parents. "Fiella,
if I don't come back, turn all of my personal effects over to
Allassi Messentari. Tell her to save anything she thinks might
have sentimental value, and sell everything else and keep the
money. Transfer my accounts to her name after you settle my
debts."

She took her formal leptolizer, and her old one. And she
grabbed a pocketful of energy cakes to eat on the way. "Ready,
Arlai?"

"Always, Krinata. But Onerir Control is trying very hard
to reprogram me. I don't know how much time I have."

There was no distress in Arlai's voice now, but the new
threat sent her racing for the carpark.

It was a long ride around the curve of the planet to Onerir
General Hospital, renowned for catering to almost every one
of the several hundred species. The hospital was located on an
island amid a placid inland sea. Great grassy hills rolled up to
short, sprawling buildings dotted with functional towers. The
installation stretched far underground as well as onto the beaches
for aquatics.

Here, instead of nearing dawn, it was just approaching midnight. Arlai was now directly overhead, speaking to her easily
through her own leptolizer.

She had been thinking. "Arlai, I don't mean to insult you,
but could you—at my command, of course—forge the imperial seal and project me an order saying I'm to remove Jindigar from this place and take him to the Emperor?"

She watched the Sentient on the screen of the car. Chewing
one lip, he inspected her anew. The piol was sleeping in her
lap—on a thick pad this time, so as not to ruin her outfit.
Otherwise, she was Lady Zavaronne.

"Jindigar trusted you. Yes, Krinata, I could do that. I could
even create the Emperor's image giving the order."

"Splendid!" she said, not even thinking about what this
implied regarding Dushau-shipboard Sentients, or Dushau at-

titudes toward Allegiancy law. "Do it and squirt it into my leptolizer. I'm going to pull off a show that will go down in history."

While he was creating his masterpiece, Arlai asked quietly, "Have you thought what you're going to do after you get him out? You certainly aren't going to take him to the Emperor, are you? I expect he's hardly able to walk by now."

She in fact hadn't thought. She'd had some vague idea of hiding him in her apartment. But if they were cracking Arlai, they could easily crack Fiella's privacy program.

Arlai added, "Since we're breaking a few laws, I could send my shuttle down for you. There's enough space on that lawn to land and take off without hurting anyone. I'm that good with my shuttles."

With Jindigar aboard to issue the orders, Arlai could take them anywhere.

"Yes. I think that would be best."

She took her lightcase—it looked like the sort of thing a busy executive would carry—and thoughtfully but sadly turned Imp loose on the lawn. She couldn't carry him into a hospital, and she couldn't leave him trapped in the car she was abandoning. He could probably grow up happily fishing in the lakes and cadging nibbles from the groundskeepers. Then she set off, head high, marching with a confident swagger, psyching herself into the mindset of an official responsible directly to the Emperor.

The front-office entry was a sheer transparent wall overlooking a lake surrounded by tall trees. Inside, trees from other planetary habitats scraped the vaulted ceiling. Interview stations were set among groves where seating blended into the forested motif. She chose the centermost station and presented herself briskly, adding, "This is urgent. The Emperor will brook no delays."

Before long, a robed Camidan, twice her height and covered with rustling scalelike excrescences, presented himself. "My Lady, I am Director Ithrenth. I would serve my Emperor. Will you step into my office?"

His voice was high but somehow sonorous, too. Like a reed orchestra. Krinata had never dealt personally with a Camidan before, and hoped what she'd read and gathered from fiction would serve her.

His office was sumptuous, decorated for a human or Lehiroh. The view of the stars through the transparent ceiling was awesome. Somewhere up there, Krinata knew, Arlai lay vulnerable in orbit, trying to follow her movements.

Ithrenth took up a stance beside a large wallscreen. "I'm sure you realize this is hardly routine. We have direct imperial orders regarding the patient you wish to remove."

"And so do I," brazened Krinata, hoping the Camidan couldn't read the quaver in her voice. "Observe." She pointed her leptolizer, prayed Arlai's handiwork would stand the inspection of the bigger, newer, ground-based Sentient in charge of the hospital, and projected the Emperor's figure onto the deep violet carpet between herself and the director.

"Director Ithrenth," said the Emperor briskly, "this is to countermand my previous orders. Release the prisoner, Jindigar, into Lady Krinata Zavaronne's hands immediately. This is of utmost urgency to the Crown's investigations, and complete security procedures must be followed. I'm sure you understand. The Empire is depending on you."

Ithrenth touched a control and the screen lit to show a Treptian neuter simulacrum who said, "The Lady's orders are authenticated, Director. Instant compliance is indicated."

Ithrenth seemed disappointed, but he said staunchly, "Of course. Skindel, issue the appropriate orders. Have the Dushau Jindigar brought to North Tower Gate immediately."

"But take care," interrupted Krinata, "not to damage him in any way." *I can't believe it's going to be this easy.*

Graciously, the director gestured her toward another exit from his office. "Stroll with me, my Lady, and we'll meet them at the gate where your car is parked."

"Thank you, Director. Your loyalty will please the Emperor." She almost choked on the words.

"It is a pity, though," said the director as they ambled down a long pillared corridor. "In another few hours, we'd surely have had the confession the Emperor wanted."

"Unfortunately, the Emperor couldn't wait." Her heart was pounding, and she wondered momentarily where she'd got the sheer audacity to attempt this. *I'm not scared. There's nothing to be scared of because I've nothing to lose now.* Nevertheless, she was terrified. Her mouth was dry, her palms damp. Surely, it showed.

"Do you have any idea why the haste? Just personal curiosity, you understand."

"The Emperor doesn't confide in such as myself. No doubt an emergency threatens the Empire. But Emperor Rantan is wise; he'll handle it with minimum fuss."

"Yes. It's a shame all the disruption these Dushau have caused. But we're fortunate to have such a leader. The Allegiancy will no doubt be the first Galactic civilization to survive its trimillennial."

She'd heard Clorinda Dover and the clique she'd gathered about herself reinforcing each other with such statements. She drew on one of their favorite aphorisms. "The strength of the Allegiancy is the Throne; the wisdom of the Allegiancy is the Emperor. Never have we faced such an insidious threat, never have we had such decisive leadership."

"Dushau sedition is not even the worst of it," said the Camidan. "Have you heard they've begun to mass an armada around Dushaun?"

Good for them! They may need it. Aloud she said, "I hadn't heard that. I've been busy with imperial duties, and in the capitol, idle gossip is discouraged."

"So it is idle gossip? We haven't much time for such here, either. I'll see that rumor isn't spread further." He gestured, "My Lady, we've arrived. And here they come."

Doors swung wide and a floating gurney festooned with equipment, i.v. lines and chuckling servos issued forth followed by a small army of technicians. Krinata was dismayed. Surely only a Sentient-controlled servo or two would be necessary. Then she understood that the staff was eager to impress the Emperor with their zealousness. *But how are we going to get away in an illegally landed orbiter?*

The gurney and attendants trooped across the wide rancestone foyer and joined the director and Krinata at the forcefield wall opening on the grassy field. The outside lighting revealed the deserted, quiet area, and her car. One of the attendants glanced at the gurney in consternation and said, "I'm sorry, Director, I expected an imperial limo."

Krinata was transfixed by Jindigar's haggard, indigo countenance surrounded by pale green sheets. One wrist emerged from the side of the sheet where tubes and sensors were connected. "Can you wake him without harming him?"

"He's apt to become violent, Lady," answered the director. "Surely the Emperor told you that?"

Krinata felt sweat break out on her face. "Well, of course," she started, with no idea what to say next.

Just then Arlai broke in, projecting via Krinata's leptolizer, an image of a Cassrian simulacrum. She knew it was Arlai because he said, in a perfect Cassrian voice, "My Lady Zavaronne, the orbiter you requested has been dispatched and will arrive at your location in ten minutes."

It gave her time to catch her breath, sternly suppressing her knowledge that a Sentient couldn't change its projected identity at will. She wasn't used to thinking on her feet like this, but she improvised, "Ten minutes should allow sufficient time for you to revive the Dushau. The Emperor will brook no delays. I cannot afford to present Him with an unconscious Dushau."

Reluctantly, the director motioned to a Holot attendant who made some adjustments on the gurney. Gradually, tension lines deepened in Jindigar's face. His breathing became ragged, his eyes rolling in their sockets under closed lids. His mouth opened, revealing dreadfully pale teeth. "He's not in danger of convulsions, is he?"

The director queried the Holot with a silent glance, and the attendant answered, "We don't believe so. But we have almost cracked his mind. No telling what might happen."

Dear God, help him! Her throat was dry, but she forced words out, "The Emperor sent me because this Dushau has debriefed to me on occasion. He knows me, and might be less inclined to do me violence."

"Ah, I see His great wisdom now," said the Camidan director. "We have been his enemies, and he has hardened to resist us. But you can pretend to be his friend, and record his confession!"

"Careful!" said the Holot. "He might hear you now."

Krinata seized on the unwitting director's suggestion. "Let me get in there," she said, pushing through the swarm of attendants—Cassrians, Treptians and Lehiroh.

When Jindigar groaned, she grabbed his hand, her face filling his view. "Jindigar!" she called gently, letting all her feelings come through, knowing they'd think her a consummate actress, hoping Jindigar would know the truth through her touch. "Jindigar! Wake up."

Midnight eyes flickered open. From such close range, she could see the fine filaments patterning the eyeball. No pupil and iris, but a swirling field of indigo and purple. As he brought focus to bear on her, the filaments widened. He stiffened, as if to shove away a nightmare creature, then his lips parted, trembling in pitiful hope. "Ontarrah!"

Before she could correct him, he pushed her away and twisted to curl on his side. "No!"

She heard her own voice say, "He's starting to go episodic!" The voice came from her leptolizer. It was Arlai, prompting her. Ontarrah must have been someone Jindigar once knew. She didn't know what to do, but she did remember that when he'd been disoriented before, it had helped him to hold onto her. She stripped the sensor contacts from his wrist, and pulled him back across the gurney. "Jindigar. It's me, Krinata. Pull yourself together." She told him the year, reminded him he'd just returned with the remnants of Kamminth's from Margo's planet, and now he was the only survivor. "We've got to debrief now. You can rest later."

She sensed the tense vibration in his muscles again. It tore her heart to do this to him, but now that she'd seen what they'd done to him, she believed the Emperor planned a public humiliation and execution for Prince Jindigar.

"Jindigar! Jindigar!" she pleaded, putting all herself behind it.

FIVE

Obligations

A wild fear suffused the Dushau's features, twisting them as if he were looking into a pit of horrors. But then he seemed to scent Krinata's odor, sniffed again with eyes closed, supreme effort in the set of his brow.

Like a drowning man who sights a floating spar, he grabbed weakly at Krinata, gripping her as he had in the robing chamber, his breath barely able to work through his tightened throat. She listened to that rasping sound, wanting to sob, knowing she couldn't afford the luxury now. Instead, she aimed a secret smile over Jindigar's head at the Director who had circled the gurney, watching her admiringly.

She motioned the attendants away, hoping the Camidan would think she didn't want Jindigar associating her with his enemies. The director seemed to catch the idea and silently cleared the area. She urged Jindigar to sit up on the side of the gurney. He was dressed in standard-issue hospital gown, with a slit down the back, feet bare. She had no cloak to throw about him.

He seemed to be fighting his way to rationality now, clutching her hand for dear life. Occasionally, his eyes would roll about, as if focused on looming horrors. But then he'd drag himself back from the abyss by holding to her. At one such lucid moment, she took the risk of whispering, "Arlai's sending one of his landers here." Then aloud, she asked, "Can you walk? I'll get you the robes your rank demands, Prince Jindigar."

The Camidan grinned broadly, revealing needle teeth and three flickering tongues. But he held silence as Krinata urged

Jindigar off the gurney onto the cold textured rancestone floor. Its magenta and rose swirls blended oddly with Jindigar's nailless, long-toed indigo feet. Jindigar flexed those feet, testing his balance. Then, still clutching Krinata's arm, he lurched toward the door.

He was hard as stone with inward tremors, but his mouth tightened to a thin line as he faced his ordeal. Krinata could imagine how the door must seem a day's journey away down a darkening tunnel. Every few steps, he whispered apologies for his weakness.

Then they were on the well-manicured path across the lawn. A dozen steps and a flutter of movement caught Krinata's eye. Imp streaked across the field and swarmed up Jindigar's gown, attaching himself to the Dushau's chest and mewling in loud relief.

Jindigar cradled the piol with one arm, nuzzling his head. It seemed the piol lent strength to his protector's legs, for Jindigar straightened and managed a semblance of a march out onto the field. Perhaps the piol distinguished this episode of the Dushau's life from all others, preventing random hallucinatory memories from crowding out the present.

Amid the constant dull roar of upper-atmosphere traffic, a waxing sound dopplered toward them. Jindigar pointed to its source, and whispered, "There! Depend on Arlai!"

Over the horizon swept a needle-slim ground-to-orbit craft. *I can't believe we're going to make it.*

The craft came to a full-stop just above them, and settled neatly with its door easing open to form a ramp at their feet. Arlai was indeed as good as his brag.

Ithrenth said, "An antique if I ever saw one."

"Reconditioned," ad-libbed Krinata. "Just impressed into the imperial service." The craft carried the Dushau rotating mobius-strip emblem, and some name in Dushauni lettering. "Haven't had a chance to change the emblem yet."

"Of course. There must be thousands of such ships confiscated now."

"Hundreds of thousands," said Krinata knowledgeably. Jindigar remained grimly silent, leaning on Krinata as he worked his way toward the ramp.

"No doubt." The director unlimbered his leptolizer from a belt hook under his robe. "Now then," he started, and Krinata's breath caught in her throat.

I knew it couldn't be that easy.

"As soon as we complete the formalities, the Dushau is your responsibility."

"Certainly," said Krinata, running dry tongue over even drier lips. She shifted Jindigar's grip to her shoulder, her lightcase to her left hand, and proffered her right hand.

Ithrenth put the business end of his leptolizer against her fingers, gripping his end with his long, many jointed, shell protected fingers. "I, Ithrenthumarian, Director of Onerir General Hospital, by order of Emperor Rantan, do hereby transfer custody of Prince Jindigar—something unpronounceable—of Dushaun to the Lady Krinata Zavaronne of Pesht: Sign; Seal; Date; Place."

"I, Krinata Zavaronne, do accept custody of Prince Jindigar whatever, on behalf of the Allegiancy and all those loyal to it." She gulped, waiting for horrid lights to flash and sirens to howl.

But apparently the hospital's Sentient accepted her version of the formality despite not mentioning the Emperor. But she knew if she'd said 'by order of the Emperor' the leptolizer would have reported she was lying.

Then, miraculously, they were marching up Arlai's ramp and Ithrenth had turned his back and walked away.

Just as they cleared the inner airlock, Jindigar collapsed to the soft-textured deck, his fingers raking that familiar surface as if he could gather it up and hug it. Krinata felt the slight vibration of takeoff. Then Arlai said, his Dushau image holo'd before Jindigar, "We're safely away. I've stalled off the Onerir Control's reprogrammers. Jindigar, you'll be onboard in just a few minutes."

But all Jindigar could say was, "Oh, Arlai, Arlai!"

Imp licked Jindigar's indigo plush face, imitating the Dushau's plaintive tone. Krinata asked, "Arlai, do you have a telemband aboard this lander?"

"Central cabin," answered the Sentient crisply opening the inner hatch before them.

Krinata coaxed Jindigar back to his feet and urged him through the hatchways into the center of the ship where ten acceleration couches were arranged about a central control pillar. Arlai focused a beam of white light on the telemband he'd placed on the arm of the pilot's chair.

She eased the lanky Dushau into his accustomed place and bound the cuff about his upper arm. A display lit on the pillar. The data was far off the Dushau norm.

Arlai's image projected beside Jindigar. "With your permission, Jindigar, I must revive you for a supreme effort. There are decisions pending only you can make for me. Our lives depend on it, though it risks your own."

Arlai spoke in a modern Dushauni, and Jindigar answered in the same language. "I understand. Do it."

"Relax now," advised Arlai. "This will hit you hard in a few moments." Then, to Krinata he said, "Secure yourself. It could become a turbulent ride."

Krinata knew little of orbital mechanics, had traveled only as a passenger on luxurious liners, but she'd always been addicted to adventure fiction. She was surprised how familiar the lander's fittings were. In moments, she had herself webbed into the adjacent control couch, and her own displays lit. They were little different from any atmosphere flyer's, though the patina of antique design lay everywhere.

"Do you have a free circuit, Arlai?" she asked.

Instantly, a diminutive Arlai appeared on the plotting screen before her. "Surely. You wish a tracking display?"

"Please."

A diagram of their orbital rise and *Ephemeral Truth*'s position track appeared along with a time display. Then other ships in orbit around the busy capital came on display, along with an overlay showing the communications between them. As a further overlay began to wipe across the screen, she said, "Enough. I can barely read this." But she could easily see they had only covered a third of the distance.

How long will it take for someone to discover what I've done? "Arlai, can we get to you any faster?"

"Of course, but it would violate local ordinances. I need Jindigar's order for that. Sorry, Krinata."

Before she could answer, Jindigar rolled his head to glance at her and her scope. He squeezed his eyes shut, rubbed them hard, set the piol aside and pushed his couch up to an alert position. "No speed yet, Arlai. Brief me."

Jindigar's scope lit with a multicolor, multidimensional display Krinata could never have interpreted. The Dushau gulped it in with his eyes, massaging his face and arms as if he ached fiercely but was determined to ignore it. Worry creased his features. "Can you really hold Central's reprogrammers off long enough?"

"Eighty-five percent probability now that I'm in touch with you again. But they really want to grab *Ephemeral Truth*. We're the last unconfiscated Dushau ship here. You've got to get me away from here, Jindigar." There was a tremor of real fear in the Sentient's tone.

"I will," promised Jindigar. "Lay in your coded retreat course, and allow me all five departure options."

Arlai brightened. "Executed." There was such relief, relish and delight packed into that one word that Krinata felt for the first time they had a chance.

A new display came on. "Increasing activity," reported Arlai, "in ground-to-orbit communications. They've spotted my lander. What shall I tell them?"

"We're your supply launch," improvised Jindigar. "Make up a manifest of Sentient replenishments—chemicals they know you already have onboard so they know it's not critical to you, but just routine restocking."

As he complied, Arlai said, "As it happens, that's in fact the case. I've brought up the heavy cargo in my other landers, and sent the light one after you."

Jindigar grinned. Then he glanced at Krinata. "Any minute now Ithrenth will be checking your claims and will discover the ruse. What do you think Rantan will do?"

"There's nothing much he can do."

He appraised her steadily. "You've grown up in a very sheltered life, Krinata. Arlai, do you still have contact with your friend in the palace?"

"Intermittently. She's programmed to be totally loyal to Rantan, and now suspects my actions are not so innocent."

"Ask her to relay my elaborate respects to my Emperor, and the following: Should *Ephemeral Truth* or its landers be fired upon, the list of habitable planets I've secreted amid the planetary ordnance programs will be obliterated."

"Complying," answered Arlai. "But Jindigar, there is no such list."

"Then create one, in code, of course," suggested Jindigar mildly. "Use member planets of the Allegiancy."

Arlai chuckled dryly. "I wish I could stay to watch their faces when they discover it!"

Horror prickled Krinata's skin. "Do you really think they'd—" It was dawning on her that she was into something way, way over her head. Interplanetary intrigue was to read about, not to live. But she had nobody to blame but herself. She hadn't thought this through. *But what else could I have done?* All her reasons still stood. To have abandoned Jindigar would have been to abandon her self-respect.

"Krinata, I'm sorry I got you into this. I never should have asked you to help me." Jindigar would have continued his apology, but Arlai interrupted with a contact warning.

"You're onboard," he announced moments later. "Lander bay pressurizing. But Jindigar, ordnance slaves are focusing moon-based projectors at us."

"Prepare for departure option five, then," said Jindigar grimly. He thrust the instrument arms aside. "Come on, Krinata. We'll have a better view from *Truth*'s bridge."

He scooped up Imp, led her into the muted hum of the ancient ship. Corridors were clean-smelling, hatches swooshed open smoothly, gravity was even, and the lift cage moved inertialessly. Every modern improvement had been incorporated without violating the delicate carvings and touches of antique color that decorated every useful device. This wasn't a spaceship. It was a home.

This feeling pervaded even the control bridge where a circular workbench banked with every imaginable type of data terminal surrounded a central well at the center of which was a projected data display.

As they entered, spotlights illuminated keyboards for human eyes while the main lighting was in the ultraviolet more comfortable for Dushau. Arlai asked, "Can you see, Krinata?"

"Yes, thank you," she answered as Jindigar handed her the piol and settled in the main control chair.

"Secure yourself in this chair," said Arlai putting a beam of green light on a recliner built for a Cassrian. "But don't worry. The bridge won't feel a thing."

"Don't bet on it," said Jindigar. "Arlai, do you see?"

There was a long silence. Frantically, Krinata tried to figure out her display board. It seemed Arlai was tracking three tiny images rising fast from the planet's surface. In orbit around them, satellites were rotating, unfolding themselves. As she watched, two emitted small blips that had to be missiles, but they weren't streaking toward *Truth*. They hung in space. Threatening.

"I see it," answered Arlai at last. "He's going to fire on us if we maneuver. Incoming signal, general broadcast." Heralded by the imperial seal, Rantan came on their screen.

"Ephemeral Truth is impounded by my order. If it breaks orbit, it will be destroyed."

"He's calling our bluff," said Jindigar. "Can you move faster than their Sentients?"

"Much of the ordnance system is busy with self-testing, searching for the planet list. That could give us an edge. Ninety percent chance option five will get us away. Sixty percent chance we'd take a hit. Twenty percent it would be a fatal hit. Those are rough estimates."

Jindigar sighed. There was no hint of tension in that sigh, no tremor in his long, nailless fingers as they caressed the controls. "We need a diversion."

"I'm getting a message from Rantan. Shall I put him on screen?"

"No." Jindigar licked his dark indigo lips. "He's stalling for time. Arlai, I disarm your Allegiancy law patch. You are to operate under League Status Ten until further notice. I am not episodic. Verify."

"Verifying. Verified. Allegiancy legals dismantled. League Status Ten engaged." The simulacrum emitted a heart-deep sigh. "Oh, that feels good. What now?"

"Put me on the open channel Rantan just used."

"Open."

Facing the pickup so his obvious Dushau countenance went to every officer manning the planetary defenses, he announced, "I have placed a list of habitable planets among your ordnance programs. Fire on this ship, and the Empire will lose that list, by order of your Emperor." He signaled Arlai to cut the transmission.

After hearing the Emperor's accusations against the Oliat Dushau, surely everyone would assume that list was of the habitable planets Dushau had conspired to withhold from the Empire. If Rantan fired, he would be publicly guilty of sabotage of his own Empire.

"Arm my command module, and I will signal manually for departure. Put Rantan on my screen, and keep that wide circuit open so everyone can hear what I say to him, but don't let them see Krinata."

The Emperor's image assembled before Jindigar. "You will not . . ." started the Lehiroh.

Jindigar interrupted without ceremony. "Dushaun has broken diplomatic relations with the Allegiancy, but we will be happy to renegotiate at any time. I take my departure now offering no censure to your government for the treatment I received at your hands. Let there be peace and good will."

On the last word, Krinata felt a lurch and then a gut-wrenching twist of hypertiming drive. But they were deep in the gravity well of a star. It was illegal to detime so close to an inhabited planet; an onboard Sentient wasn't supposed to be able to do such things. When her vision and the instruments cleared, they showed the austere blackness of deep space. A position plot indicated they were way beyond Onerir's system, and far off the usual traffic lanes.

"Did they track us?" asked Jindigar.

"Through hypertime? They don't have the math," scoffed Arlai. "I didn't even leave a wake of timeripples. I'm proud of myself. I didn't know I could still do that."

"I'm glad you didn't share your doubts with me before hand," said Jindigar. "I do recall adding a patch to your League Status Ten program forbidding you to endanger incarnate lives."

"You did, and it's still there." His simulacrum reassured Jindigar intimately, "I was ninety-nine percent confident. Next time, though, it will be one hundred percent confidence. To us, that's the supreme experience of life."

Jindigar passed a hand over his eyes. "Of course, Arlai, I understand. Systems check."

"No damage. All systems optimal."

"You're doing better than I am. Set random course and stay clear of any Allegiancy astrogation probes. We need time to decide what to do next."

As he spoke, he wilted alarmingly. Krinata yanked free of the webbing and went to him. "Arlai, is he all right?"

"Paying the inevitable penalty," he said grimly. "I'm sending a scurry to take him to my sickbay. Watch the piol!"

The pup was happily chewing on a cable he had pried out of a crack between two panels. She scooped him up, set him on her shoulder, and helped Arlai's multiarmed servitor move the now limp Jindigar onto the flattop of a scurry while he muttered laboriously, "I'm all right. Just tired."

At the sickbay hatch, Arlai projected his image before Krinata as the scurry swept Jindigar out of sight. "I've a surprise for you. Come."

He started off, but she held back, protesting, "But . . ."

"There's nothing you could do for Jindigar now. I've tended many Dushau in my time, Krinata. Trust me?"

"Of course, but . . ."

"Come," Arlai urged once more, starting away along a side corridor.

She had no choice but to follow. Arlai lectured, *Truth* is fitted to house thirty to forty incarnates, so we'll rattle about a bit on this trip. Feel free to spread your things as far as you like. I've programmed my scurries to aid you by voice command. When Jindigar is better, he'll probably give you other authority keys to command me with."

Her nerves were still tingling from the afterwash of fear, the tensions in her still unresolved. She took deep breaths, determined not to faint. "But Arlai, I've no things to spread," she said, feeling stupid. She didn't even remember if she'd brought the lightcase onto the lander.

"Just a few more steps, Krinata. Come on, I want to get a telemband on you. You don't look too well."

"Oh, I don't need help."

But Arlai presented her before an open door that led into her very own apartment. Dizzy with nightmarish disorientation, she drifted forward. She ran her hand over the upholstery of the lounge she'd slept in when Jindigar had been there. No, the worn spot was gone. And there was no stain. Suddenly, perspective snapped into place, and she realized this was an elaborate copy of her apartment's sitting room.

"Fiella gave me the specs. Like it?" Arlai was like an eager child presenting a school project.

"Oh, Arlai, it's so perfect, for a moment I felt as if all this hadn't really happened, and I'd wakened at home!"

"You *do* like it." He showed beautiful blue Dushau teeth in a human grin. "Fiella gave me your favorite recipes, too."

A delightful aroma of breakfast wafted past her nose, and her stomach responded with a grumble. She suddenly felt very tired. But when Arlai turned to leave, she stopped him. "You're sure Jindigar will be all right? You're sure we're safe here?"

"Probabilities approaching unity." Then his optimism faded. "Except . . ."

"Except what?" Her appetite vanished.

"Jindigar will live, Krinata. He's not mortally injured. But his personality might change."

"Renewal?" She'd never seen a Dushau in that state. No non-Dushau had.

"No. It would take a lot more than this. But when his grieving is finished, there will be much he doesn't remember. I am not sufficient to nurse him all the way through this. He should have Dushau companionship."

She swallowed in a dry throat. "Can you accept my order to take us to Dushaun?"

He blinked slowly. "No. He doesn't want to commit us to that course yet."

"Do you have any idea where he will want to go?"

"No. I don't know who he will be. We're just going to have to wait. It's not fair to ask more of him now."

"That's true. And if we're safe, there's no reason to hurry, is there?"

"We are safe, Krinata. Safer than on any planet."

She felt her knees shaking again. It had been more than seventy-two hours since she'd really slept. "All right. We'll wait."

Again Arlai turned to go, rather than simply blinking out. She called, "And Arlai? Thank you. You're a truly splendid Sentient."

Dushau couldn't blush, but he cast his eyes down barely smothering an ecstatic grin. "I am complimented."

The food was as perfect as the apartment. She couldn't imagine how long Arlai had been working on the project. It had only been a half day since he'd gotten her out of bed. Of course, she owned nothing original or difficult to synthesize, not on a programmer's salary. But if she hadn't known it before, she would have had to conclude that Arlai was in some terrific class of Sentients beyond her ken.

She slept the clock around, and then some. And when she'd roused enough to inquire about Jindigar, Arlai's version of Fiella told her he was still sleeping. After breakfast, she realized the piol was missing and went in search of him.

"Would you like a map, Krinata?"

She started. Arlai's simulacrum stood in the corridor before her, large as life. "Have you seen Imp?"

"Daren't take my eyes off the miniature monster! Here." He gestured graciously toward a portal. Within, she found a large unfurnished room with a tank of water in one corner in which Imp splashed, merrily chasing a fish. She watched through the transparent side of the tank while the piol secured his fish and emerged to eat it, holding it in his long claws which Arlai had not trimmed.

"You are a consummate host, Arlai—but don't you think piol food would do just as well?"

"Nutritionally, yes. But I've been training Imp. We can't have wild animals loose aboard ship, you know. Here, let's see if he's learned yet. Imp, come!"

To Krinata's total surprise, the piol carefully set his half-gutted fish aside and scampered to the simulacrum's imaged feet. He spotted Krinata then, and instead of swarming up her clothing, sat up and chittered questioningly.

"He wants you to pick him up," said Arlai. "Do please reward him for the good behavior."

Krinata obliged, holding the wet animal away from her but making affectionate sounds at him. Then she deposited him beside his fish. "Arlai, you're amazing. That creature was probably born wild."

"Definitely was. His brainwaves show it. But he learned to endear himself to people to beg scraps. He's young and intelligent enough to learn good manners. But he'll always be more headstrong and independent than your average pet piol. That's probably what Jindigar likes about him."

"Jindigar," repeated Krinata, unable to be diverted by the piol anymore. "When can I see him?"

"Can't we give him more time?"

"You said he needs Dushau companionship. Maybe I can talk him into ordering you to take him home."

Heavily, Arlai said, "I doubt that."

"Why?" she demanded. "Has a shooting war broken out at Dushaun?"

"No. I doubt if it will, either."

"Then why not go there?"

Arlai didn't answer, his eyes flickering aside as he apologized in that same compulsive way Jindigar had. She realized he'd been told not to discuss this with her, and she said, "Ask Jindigar if I can come talk to him."

"I will, as soon as he's awake. Dushau can sleep longer than humans, and stay awake longer, too. He's had a rough time. He needs a full sleep cycle."

And with such excuses, he put her off for the rest of that day, and most of the following day. She spent the time alternately pacing, fretting, hounding Arlai, and sitting herself down to survey her options rationally and plan her future like an adult.

But where could she go? She assumed Jindigar would drop her at some port between here and Dushaun, because that was where he had to go. She sat on the bridge at Arlai's astrogation console and pulled up a list of all the convenient planets where she might live. But if she so much as set foot on any of them, the Emperor's hand would close on her. She'd forged his seal and stolen his prisoner. That was certainly treason. She'd disgraced her family name. The magnitude of it all crashed in on her, paralyzing her mind.

Hours later, when she forced herself to confront it again, she visualized trying to beg herself a place on Dushaun—the only Dushau world, for they hadn't colonized. But the Dushau had never been hospitable to offworlders. There couldn't be more than a few hundred offworld diplomats in residence on Dushaun, and they'd be gone by the time she got there. She had no desire to live apart from her own species.

Again she paced and fretted, and addressed the problem anew. What about the frontier worlds that had always attracted her? None were on the route to Dushaun from here, but she might ask to be taken somewhere. She had, after all, saved Jindigar's life. Perhaps, after he visited Dushaun to complete his grieving, he'd take her to a settlement where her record wouldn't follow her. She stared at a list of open colonies greedily until she remembered Dushaun was now under siege by the Allegiancy. It was problematic whether *Truth* could get in, and patently impossible to get her out again. If she went home with Jindigar, she'd be trapped until the Allegiancy came to its senses. Yet if she read Arlai right, Jindigar urgently needed Dushau company. It was a need he couldn't neglect without peril to his life, and she wasn't going to ask that of him after all she'd sacrificed to save him. *What are we going to do?!*

She shoved away from the bridge console and paced again, her stomach churning. She couldn't face going back to the mockup of her apartment. Pangs of homesickness such as she'd never known lurked beneath her tight control. *I've cried enough. More won't help. I'm not sorry I did it. I'm not.*

Gradually, she adjusted to the loss of her old life, realizing if she could have anything she wanted, she'd opt to work with an implanting Oliat on a raw, new world being colonized by

at least some humans. Since the Oliat teams had been withdrawn, she'd accept almost any hospitable new world. After
all, without an Oliat, they'd need trained ecologists.

But what would she have to settle for? How could Jindigar
help her when he, himself, needed help? The idea of asking
for his help in return for saving his life made her want to curl
up in a ball and never show her face again. But she didn't
want to be trapped on Dushaun. *Could I stand it, if I have to?*
She didn't know.

Midafternoon of the second day, when the tension in her
had mounted to where she was fighting tears again, Arlai finally
announced, "Jindigar's awake. Come."

She followed the moving shaft of light through the dim
hallways. She was wearing a long, sleeveless blue tunic over
baggy black pants. Arlai had provided an ultraviolet screening
lotion for her exposed skin, but even so she could already see
herself tanning in the ship's light.

As they moved through the ship, she was acutely aware that
this was a purely Dushau environment: Dushau art, light, scents,
thick atmosphere. Arlai kept a reduced gravity under her wherever she went, but Dushaun itself pulled almost a third more
than she was accustomed to.

The sickbay room she was led to was furnished in the Dushau manner: low profile furniture, buoyantly padded, no sharp
corners or hard surfaces. She couldn't judge the color scheme,
but she thought there was a variety of vivid hues. Personal
items littered flattopped scurries, giving the room a lived-in
comfortable feeling.

Amid the shadows of an alcove formed of thick draperies,
on a low padded platform, wearing a pale yellow robe, Jindigar
sat coaxing soft music from a polished urwood whule that must
have been as old as he was. His head was bent over the
long fretboard, eyes closed, as he produced ululating tremolos with
a complicated bow. An aching frown played between his eyes,
and the set of his mouth bespoke a pain no living creature
could surmount.

Krinata couldn't imagine how Arlai had led her to intrude
on such a moment of nakedness. She didn't dare breathe.

Determined to wait until she was noticed, she crossed her ankles and silently sank to the floor.

Plucking an occasional string with a pick or a soft fingertip, Jindigar's elegant hands produced wails of agony, howls of anguish, gut-twisting groans, and plaintive melodies that progressed across scales of loneliness and around harmonies she seemed to hear with her whole body. Every ghostly note pled for mercy, surrendered to pain or yielded only in the broken extremity beyond the end of strength.

Before long, the riptide of Krinata's own emotions scoured her nerves like a sandstorm driven by the fury of Dushaun's sun. Ponderous inevitability thundered through her bones. She forgot Jindigar, barely knew there was music, and lived within the sphere of her loss and the hopeless future.

Her mouth opened, and low moaning sobs issued forth in short, harsh barks her own vocal cords should never have produced. Helplessly, she listened, overwhelmed with pity for the poor creature who suffered so. She didn't know how it happened, but from the peak of that agony, she came down into a deep, clear pool of crystalline eternity. Here was not the happiness she had lived to achieve, but a radiant peace in which every disturbance could only be felt as a joy.

Warm, relaxed, aching with drained tension, she heard a lapping silence, the barest hissing echo of music. Her hands on her face were slick with tears. She felt the presence of the room about her as an increasing pressure on the skin of her arms, a burgeoning image in her mind's eye. And she felt Jindigar's eyes on her now. She couldn't raise her head.

A scurry's arm thrust tissues into her hands. She buried her face in them. Her suppressed hysteria of the last two days was gone. She'd finally finished grieving for her old life, her old self. But she wasn't anybody new yet. She lifted her eyes and met deep indigo ones.

"I'm sorry, I didn't realize you'd come in." Jindigar cast his eyes down to the whule, caressing its sounding bowl with one finger. "This was Lelwatha's whule. He . . . that was his last composition. I render it badly."

"I don't think I could live through a better rendering!" She deposited the sodden lump of tissue in the scurry's grip and rose to approach Jindigar. "Actually, I think you apologize too much, for things that aren't your fault."

He fondled the whule as if it contained the memory of his friend and mentor. "I've displayed a lot of faults lately." He looked up at her and she sat down on the edge of the platform he occupied. "Krinata, debriefing never revealed how it was my fault Taaryesh died."

"That's nonsense. The tornado killed her."

"I was Receptor. I missed the signs of the weather pattern. Dinai warned me, but it was too late for Seum to get us out of there. Krinata, if I hadn't been careless, Taaryesh—and six of our Lehiroh Outriders—wouldn't have died. We'd have still been in the field when Trinarvil pulled Dushaun out of the Allegiancy, and Kamminth's would have been picked up intact by the retrieval team. Instead, I'm the sole survivor of one of the best Oliat teams ever. And I've ruined your life, too."

She wondered if this was clinical depression, or if this was just a normal guilt reaction from a very responsible individual. The pattern of the thought was all too human, and the only cure she knew was human. "You didn't ruin my life. _I_ decided to get you out of that horrid place. I'm not sorry I did it, either." For the first time, that was really true, and it felt good. "Did Seum, Dinai, Fedeewarn, Lelwatha or Kamminth blame you for Taaryesh's death?"

"No. Kamminth insisted she'd once missed a brewing hurricane. Lelwatha maintained I was the keenest Receptor he'd ever Emulated for." He toyed with the whule bow. "Maybe that's why I blame myself—because they refused to blame me." He looked up. "I am good in Oliat. That's why it hurts so. I've never . . . killed anyone before."

The Dushau species was not descended from hunters, but from carrion-eaters. They never killed their meat, or each other. "You haven't killed now." Krinata took the bow from his fidgeting hands and captured his eyes.

"Listen. If I'd had documented proof that you'd missed the weather signs because you were drunk on duty or whatever, I'd still have gone into that hospital after you. You want to trade guilts? _I_ let myself get carried away during that debriefing. I was so busy imagining I was Taaryesh, I didn't think what might happen when I asked for dangers. I didn't research what had killed her. I didn't make a point of avoiding that issue. *I* didn't do my job properly, so *you* were dragged away as a saboteur of an imperial project! What did I do about it? I let them haul you out of my office, then I dithered for days before Arlai jolted me out of it. By then it was too late to save Dinai and Seum. Lay their deaths at my feet. Lay your whole situation at my feet!"

"That's ridiculous."

"No more ridiculous than what you're saying!"

They stared at each other for a long while before Jindigar gave in. She smiled and handed him back the bow. "When the Kings have had time to analyze all this, they'll stop Zinzik, depose him if necessary, and pick his successor. With a little sanity on the throne, Dushaun will come back and everything will be normal again. Jindigar, it can't take very long. When it's settled, my family will be able to get me a pardon, and I could even go back to my old job. I'm just not sure I'll ever want it back. And I've no idea what to do with myself in the meantime."

He set the instrument aside, and turned to confront her. "You really believe this is just a minor disruption, and eventually everything will be as it was?"

"Of course." Now that she'd calmed down, she could see it clearly. When they came to their senses, they'd see she hadn't really committed a crime.

"Krinata, you know I'm not an Historian, though the talent runs in my family. Yet even I can recognize the deaththroes of a civilization. Nothing can stop Zinzik now. Nobody *wants* to. They know they can't solve these problems, so they're intent on slaughtering them, and we are the symbol. Anybody and anything remotely touched by us will be torn apart by this kill-frenzied mob. You can never go back. That's what I've done to you."

The last shred of hope dissolved before his certainty. But this time, it didn't hurt. "All right. I can accept even that. There's nowhere for me to go."

He searched her face as if reading a map. Then he uncurled his long, muscular legs and paced across the room. He moved more easily now, the sinuous glide of an acrobat. Then he turned and inspected her from across the room. She felt as if she were on trial for some quality of soul.

He swept some small items from the top of a scurry and half-sat, half-leaned on it, one knee bent to hook his heel on the edge of the flattop, hands clasped about that ankle. "I've lost my confidence in my own judgment," he confessed. "But I've nothing else to go on. So I've got to ask you. If you had a chance to pioneer an eminently livable planet—a first implant colony—would you take it?"

"That's what I've been trying to find, a place between here and Dushaun where you could drop me off and be rid of me, on your way home. But . . ."

"No, Krinata. Listen. Nobody who's ever done me a good turn, ever worked with me, ever done business with me, is safe now. And there are a few dozen such people scattered about the Allegiancy. For them, as for you, there's no Allegiancy planet where they can live. But I know a planet that would be a marginally comfortable home, though not suitable for commercial use—far, far outside the Allegiancy sphere. It's rugged: no amenities waiting, no pre-implant spadework done, no further tech support coming after you get there. I can't even promise you Oliat support. Just a few refugees of various species, lots of arable land, and nothing too hostile to live with. Its only virtue is that the Allegiancy doesn't list it as open, so nobody will look for us there. Would you be interested?"

SIX

Distress Call

Krinata eyed Jindigar nervously, thinking that Zinzik had accused the Dushau of not reporting colonizable planets. But one commercially useless planet known by one individual didn't make a conspiracy to strangle the Allegiancy.

Jindigar misinterpreted her silence. "Or I'd be glad to drop you off at any planet you name, before I try to rescue any of the others. I owe you that, and more."

"You don't owe me," she said. "I was just thinking your planet sounds like what I've been looking for."

"I expected you'd feel that way. There's a lot I don't know about this planet, though. Survey was never completed. There are tremendous risks."

"None greater than being executed for treason to the Crown because of a loyal attempt to prevent a mistake. How do we find these other friends of yours?"

He turned to a large wallscreen decorated in moving swirls of light. "Arlai, put up the itinerary I compiled."

The screen filled with symbols Krinata couldn't read. Then in one corner, a list of planets appeared: Onerir, Cassr, Khol, Razum Two, Atridm, Canbera. Beside each one was a list of names, Cassrians, Lehiroh, Holot, human, and Treptian. Under each name, there was a location.

"You want to go back to Onerir? Why!"

"I must, Krinata. The bodies of Kamminth's—"

"Jindigar," interrupted Arlai softly. "I have a confession. The bodies of all your zunre are aboard. I acted without instruction, but..."

Jindigar's face lightened.

"You're not angry with me?" asked Arlai.

"I remember changing your status controls. Your initiative is not wholly at odds with graytime status. But, were you detected?"

"I doubt it." Arlai's simulacrum ghosted over the symbolic display, and he seemed hesitant. "I left records indicating the bodies were taken by Trinarvil, with Seum and Dinai having been cremated without autopsy. If they suspect me, they might be able to detect the forgeries, but I don't think they'll believe a Sentient could do such a thing."

Krinata's heart was relieved Zinzik could make no grotesque examples of those Dushau bodies. She was beginning to suspect he'd stop at nothing to feed his mob following.

Jindigar frowned. "If we move fast enough, we may be clear before anyone thinks to inspect the records." He launched into a technical discussion of the transit time between the planets on his list, and Arlai's best estimate of the urgency of the situation on each planet.

Krinata listened with growing dismay. Following Onerir's lead, it seemed every planet of the Allegiancy was rounding up Dushau sympathizers for brutal questioning, brief public trial, and mass execution. She couldn't believe it. Such things were surely against the law.

When she threw that question into a momentary silence, Arlai answered, "Just as we were leaving Onerir, I picked up a newsflash that, for the purposes of this emergency, the Dukes of the Allegiancy were empowered to write new laws to handle the expected masses of traitors who must be tried and disposed of. So far as I know, the Dukes have acted well within the Emperor's guidelines for such laws. But way out here, I can only get smeared fringe beams. I've been tempted to snatch up passing capsules to sample the latest news."

"Don't do that yet," said Jindigar while Krinata was swallowing her shock at yet another impossible ability. "You couldn't handle a modern detimed capsule without leaving traces. While we're in orbit at Cassr, maybe you can learn how to do it. It could be a useful skill for us."

"I think you underestimate me."

"I don't. You've been constrained from maintaining such skills by your Allegiancy programming. There've been some spectacular advances lately." They stared at each other for long moments, but then Arlai lowered his eyes.

"I'll let you know after I've investigated." With a mischievous smile, he added, "Care to lay a bet?"

Jindigar smiled back, silently expressing a fondness for Arlai while saying, "I never bet against Sentients. But I'm not willing to bet all our lives that you're right."

Arlai put his hands on his hips in a businesslike pose, and said gravely, "I'll check it out thoroughly. But I'm going to tap the beams as we move in. Things are happening fast out there now."

"Right," agreed Jindigar, planting himself firmly on the platform beside his whule. "Now, if we're going to penetrate Cassr traffic control, *Truth* will need a temporary identity. She looks Dushau, but old enough to have been sold off long ago." He turned to Krinata, speculation lighting his indigo eyes. "Would you be willing to go aground as a Pesht merchant, working for Zavaronne Importers? Most Cassrians can't tell humans apart, much less their bloodlines from a vague resemblance. Arlai can dress you for the part..."

Her heart leaped to her throat. She'd listened calmly to plans to rescue prisoners of the Crown, and never visualized how it might be done. Absurdly, the only thought that came to mind was that she'd be breaking the law.

"You're right." Jindigar nodded. "There's no reason to send you into such danger. I've no business even asking." He turned back to Arlai. "You can fit me out to pass as a Skhe merchant captain. Trassle exports pharmacogenetics. I could be looking for him because he owes me a cargo."

"You can't go into a city!" blurted Krinata.

"It has to be done."

He's depressed! Suicidal! But she couldn't think of a reasonable argument. "All right, I'll go."

Puzzled, he stared at her silently. Then he seemed to shove aside his curiosity. "Krinata, you can't go in my place. I only wanted you to deal with the authorities, to divert attention from me, so there'd be less chance I'd be recognized. But Trassle can be a very suspicious Cassrian, and he has a female and young to protect."

Cassrians with family could be paranoid, she knew. "Arlai, can you estimate the probabilities of success if only one of us goes, or if both of us go?"

The screen cleared and figures glowed. "If both of you go, and take Imp, there should be only one third the risk. Skhe always have piol under foot, and Zavaronne is known to favor Skhe spacehands. No Cassrian would look twice at such a group, especially because I can provide you with a cargo of Camidani shielded intronic parts."

"Where would you get intronics?" asked Krinata. They were Sentient components, and the Camidani shielding made them useful on the high-radiation planets such as Cassr.

"I don't have much in stock," admitted Arlai. "But all you'll need is a sample and a manifest which I can create."

She examined her feelings. She couldn't refuse to go, however much she felt out of her depth. "Well, I always wanted to be a spaceship captain. What's my ship's name?"

"Think of a good, old Pesht name," said Jindigar.

"Bettina," said Krinata. Thousands of Pesht ships were called *Bettina*. It had been the name of the first colony ship to Pesht from Terra. *"Roving Bettina."*

"A good choice," said Arlai. "I'll get to work immediately. When do we start for Cassr?"

"Now," said Jindigar quietly. For a moment, Krinata saw a grave shadow darken his expression. Then he stood, cinching his yellow tunic in with a cord belt. "Come, Krinata. You must be checked out on your ship's controls. You have a lot to learn in the next three days."

She spent most of that time in *Truth*'s control room. Jindigar gave Arlai permission to obey certain classes of commands from her. He wasn't giving her his ship, but if he were killed, Arlai would take her to safety.

Gradually, the *Truth*'s logo disappeared from the *Truth*'s interior bulkheads and accessories, replaced by the Zavaronne emblem in black and red. She assumed the same new emblem now graced the exterior as well as their broadcast identification beam. It was eerie watching the character of the ship change around them. Arlai's efficiency was awesome, and his imagination unparalleled among Sentients. By the time they entered the well-traveled shipping lanes, she felt she was actually on a family-owned tramp freighter.

Her captain's uniform, just worn enough to be authentic, fit her loosely, so she appeared to have lost weight from the worry of hard times. The ship's history Arlai fabricated and placed into her unadorned leptolizer gave her good reason for the graying hair and worry lines Arlai's makeup scurry imposed on her. Looking at herself, she could almost believe she was an adventurous, moderately successful businesswoman.

But her transformation was nothing compared to what Arlai did to Jindigar. First Arlai built the Dushau up into the lumpy, flat-headed shape of a Skhe using extruded forms. Over the padding went a mil thick, brown and black pigmented shrink-suit designed to protect the sensitive Skhe skin from ultraviolet, hiding all trace of Jindigar's dark indigo coloring. The sheen of his skin's nap was also hidden, so he appeared to have the mucous damp, warty hide of the Skhe under the film. Over this he wore the crossed harnesses, jingling with status bobs and charms typical of a Skhe first mate.

His legs were wrapped in the bilious green leggings a lower class Skhe would wear. As an afterthought, Arlai added a waist-length cape of krisl fur, telling Jindigar "Rndeel, mate of the *Roving Bettina*" had won it in a littre game in Port Arthur on Pesht.

Jindigar said, "Since that's exactly where Kamminth got it, I think she'd be honored to have us use it." He swirled, letting the full cape flow around him as he inspected his image in the screen where Arlai mirrored him, and Krinata tried to imagine a Dushau gambling in a spaceport dive.

"But there's something missing," said Krinata pondering the effect. And then she knew. "The smell. Skhe always smell like the bay when the tide's out."

"No problem," said Arlai. "And if we're boarded, the whole ship will reek of Skhe, especially the cabin I've furnished for Rndeel."

"You've thought of everything," approved Krinata. They had six hours to get used to their personae before they'd have to answer the Approach Authority's hail. They returned to the control room to rehearse.

Krinata took the captain's chair, glancing behind her at "Rndeel" as he squatted on the stool Arlai had installed before the astrogator's station. She was amazed to see how the Dushau moved with the fluidity of the Skhe, and the quick head mannerisms typical of the species.

She praised him, adding, "Now, since we won't always have translators overhead while on the streets, you'd better practice letting me do all the talking. At least my accent backs up our story."

He answered in a flawless, gamy Skhe dialect. She recognized the invective common to Skhe spacers, unheard on Jindigar's lips in all the years she'd known him. Switching on Arlai's translator beam, he added in character, "I'll have you know I was hatched within earshot of Ssthinmeer, and schooled under three adults. Florard I ain't, but good enough for the likes of any mere port inspector, I sure am."

Even Krinata had heard of the Skhe elite university, Florard, and its counterpart among the lower classes, Ssthinmeer. "Arlai, is his accent really that good?"

"Indeed. Jindigar is something of a linguist by hobby, and he's worked Oliat with Skhe Outriders. Everyone agrees he's a phenomenal Emulator. I couldn't begin to criticize. I doubt if a Ssthinmeer native could notice anything amiss."

Emulator. That was an Oliat office. She'd had no idea it meant what the title implied. What else was there she didn't know about Oliat capability? She was beginning to think they might get away with this when the alarms sounded.

Arlai damped the shrill howl with an apology, and brought the new data onto their control boards. As she worked to remember all she'd learned about reading Arlai's displays, Krinata noted out of the corner of her eye how Jindigar—no, Rndeel—had not flinched when the piercing screech sounded. Arlai had programmed that tone because it was pleasant but attention-grabbing for Skhe.

Arlai briefed them, "Distress signal is an hour away at *Bettina*'s maximum. Dushau ship, Phembera registry—commandeered. Was *Intentional Act;* now called, *Mercer's Folly.*"

He paused, saying aside to Krinata, "A Terran name on a Phem ship?"

"Never mind. What's their problem? How many aboard?"

"Patience," said Arlai. "I'm decoding."

"Code?" asked Rndeel in Skhe. "What kind of code?"

"That's the problem. I . . . aha! A Dushau code from Corporate League days, even before my activation, Rndeel. Here it is."

The screen display read:

DISTRESS. SEVEN DUSHAU IMPRISONED IN INTENTIONAL ACT BY DUKE LAVOV'S MEN. SURROUNDED BY FOUR ARMED ESCORT SHIPS. SIXTEEN LEHIROH GUARDS CREWING ACT, DETERMINED TO TAKE US TO PRISON TO SUPPLY BLOOD TO DEVELOP A VIRUS TO KILL DUSHAU. WE WON'T PERMIT THAT. PLEASE REPORT OUR DEATHS TO FAMILY.

As she read this, Krinata heard one part of her mind repeating, *It's just one rebel Duke. It doesn't mean the Empire is crumbling.*

There followed a list of Dushau names. Rndeel lunged to his feet and let out a very Skhe hiss. "Captain, request permission to attempt a rescue. Two of those Dushau are friends of Jindigar from his earliest youth."

He stayed perfectly in character, yet Krinata could only take it as an order. Arlai certainly would. "Arlai, is there anything we can do to help them?"

There was silence, though Krinata heard scraping and crashing sounds billowing up from the nether regions of the ship. Arlai finally answered, "If the projectors still work, we might be able to run a diversion-pass. Thirlein, the *Act*'s Sentient, was a close friend of mine once, if she's still in command. Rndeel, do I have permission to break her Allegiancy-bonding and reset her as I've been reset?"

Tensed to address this emergency, Krinata packed away her relief that Arlai's powers were still somewhat restricted, and her utter dismay at the idea of one Sentient programming another. That was how the League was reported to have perished, in a war against renegade Sentients. *Probably as untrue as the historical record that the Allegiancy perished from a Dushau conspiracy!* Another part of her mind took note to ask Jindigar about that someday.

Rndeel said, in heavily accented standard, "Give Thirlein the status commands Jindigar gave you, Arlai, but be a'caution for her sanity, not to force if she resists."

"I understand, Rndeel."

There was a reverberation in the hull plates. Krinata asked, "What's that noise?"

"I'm setting up our deep-space image projectors," answered Arlai. "It's been too long since they were used!"

"With your permission, Captain," said Rndeel through the translator. "Flesh hands the Sentient's a'needin'. He doesn't know the right cusswords."

"Go, Rndeel," said Krinata, surprised at how easy it was to consider the Skhe a new crewmember.

For the next infinitude of minutes, Krinata sat her station listening to echoes of Skhe hisses and invective among the boomings and thumpings. To distract her from chewing her nails, Arlai gave her the plan.

"We will approach them as an armada of Lavov, Duke of the Jornay Cluster. We'll present orders for us to take charge of their captive ship and send them to Phembera to transport emergency medical supplies to an epidemic. We will appear to their sensors to be thirty heavily armed ships. I will provide their sensors with authentic cross-chatter among our ships, but you will have to go onscreen and issue the order to this fleet captain. Ah, I have his name now: Dinel Petriski—sounds Peshtini."

"Petriski is a minor barony. I'd be able to bully him if he was working for the Emperor, or my High Duke. But he's serving Duke Lavov."

"And it will appear you are a new recruit of Lavov's. Humans seem to be taking new alliances now. What could be more natural than for Pesht to send Lavov a small armada to help with the Dushau problem?"

Krinata had liked acting in school plays, but this was straining her abilities.

"Don't look so nervous," admonished Arlai. "It's out of character. Besides, I'll feed you your lines. Here's your new costume already." A scurry presented her with a new hat and a shoulder drape filled with military honors. These, over her captain's uniform turned her into a high-ranked commodore. "Now, let's try a rehearsal."

With the background noise of the ship being rebuilt around her, Krinata talked to a screen image of a young human man with an air of self-importance and a determination not to accept her orders. She outfaced this mock-up image seven times before Rndeel returned to squat at his station.

The Skhe swore luridly about having to wear such a hot protective suit because the stubborn Dushau Sentient wouldn't turn off the Dushau lighting. Krinata felt her face redden at the choice epithets reserved for the Dushau. Rndeel interrupted the flow only to say, in perfect ship's courtesy, "Target ships in sensor range, Captain. We're approaching in formation as ordered. Shall I raise Captain Petriski?"

She swallowed dryly. "Yes, of course, Mister!" she snapped. "Those supplies are needed desperately. We haven't a moment to waste."

She was aware that if they could read the Jornay ships, the Jornay probes could be catching glimpses of their bridge. They waited in a tense silence until Arlai's screen lit with a fuzzy, static-lined image of a young human male. He didn't look like the image Krinata had jousted with, but he wore captain's bars. His voice crackled with nervous pride as he ordered them off his course, threatening to detime and leave them awash in his wake if they didn't veer off.

Arlai had pegged the youngster just right. No veteran would threaten before the hail was even answered. In his attempt to show strength, he showed only weakness. Krinata was a veteran of years of office politics and knew this type of green puffball. She straightened and put on her deep command voice, reciting their false identification in an unhurried, upper-class drawl.

"Now, Fleet Captain Petriski, I suggest you ask our business before you issue us orders."

He stammered, "I . . . I'm sorry. I was hasty, Commodore-Lady Zavaronne. When we left Inslaa, Duke Lavov had made no such alliance and his orders to us were explicit."

"There's no time for this chatter, Fleet Captain," snapped Krinata. "We've an emergency on our hands. If you don't arrive at Pillaged Ford with these anti-virals in time, it will be your neck in Lavov's noose!" She signalled Arlai to send over the cargo cannisters.

He paled, scanned his master plotting tank, and issued orders, knowing the armada's log would show the amount of time he'd spent arguing. His ships began to pull out of formation around the renamed Dushau ship, *Mercer's Folly*.

"Commodore-Lady Zavaronne, before we leave, allow me to dump a briefing scan into your memory."

KRINATA, NO! I CAN'T ACCEPT IT NOW! Arlai printed on the screen before her. MY CIRCUITS ARE FULLY LOADED. Even a Sentient had limits.

Krinata felt her mouth open, her jaw work up and down a few times. Before she could recover, Petriski answered as if she'd spoken. "You couldn't have been that thoroughly briefed before you left. We've had an incident aboard *Folly*—one of the Dushau got free for a few minutes. It's been hunted down and killed before it could get to any vital part of the ship. So we only have six to deliver, plus one body. I was about to double the inboard guard on *Folly*."

"A wise precaution," answered Krinata, aware of Rndeel's rock-tense form behind her. "I will, of course, do exactly that. You had best be on your way." She said it mildly, as if she'd really rather watch his punishment for disobeying.

Her manner had the desired effect. He saluted the Emperor, blanked the screen and took his small fleet away at system speed. Moments later, Arlai announced, "They've detimed; they're gone. Thirlein is all right now. She's showing the inboard guards a picture of our fleet taking up formation about them."

"Good, get me *Folly*'s captain. Grassman, you said his name translates?" Krinata knew they were far from winners, yet. Eighteen tough Lehiroh had six hostages.

"Captain, what you plan a'story to 'em?" asked Rndeel. She thought he sounded nervous.

Just then the screen lit with a craggy, dark brown face framed by pale straight hair. An older Lehiroh male.

"Commodore-Lady Zavaronne," he acknowledged crisply. "What are your orders?"

"My first officer and I are coming over to ascertain the condition of your prisoners," she replied, wondering where she'd get the guts. "Then we will discuss what additional forces you may need to contain them properly. Remain in sync-time with us. Detime only on my order. Acknowledge."

"Acknowledged," he snapped, but as the picture faded, she thought she detected just a hint of a tremor in his voice. Was she really so formidable?

Rndeel spun on his stool. "Clever, Captain."

"Ah, but do we have the equipment to transfer—"

"Of course." He seemed to consider. "Somewhere."

Arlai said, "I've located my fabric tube, but I'm not too certain it's vacuum-tight. You'd best suit up. At the very least the fittings will leak."

Krinata had never been in a spacesuit before. Rndeel had to help her with the seals and safety checks. For the first time since she'd met Arlai, she was peeved at him. He'd activated Rndeel's scent before the Skhe helped her with the suit, so the whole suit reeked. But she refused even to think of nausea. Instead she focused on the six Dushau and how they felt to be used to destroy their own species.

That hardened her determination, but nevertheless she was terrified when she walked out of the airlock and floated free in the middle of a transparent tube through infinity.

Rndeel's only comment was, "I'd be privy to your plan, Lady-Commodore, if you've a mind."

"I haven't a plan," she replied, trying not to gibber. Despite Arlai's best efforts, she might be overheard. "Just to do my duty to the Emperor and my Duke, just as I've done ever since you and I met. Beyond that, let us first see what these Lehiroh have been up to." *I'm actually safe here!*

With Rndeel unobtrusively helping her, she managed to pull herself hand-over-hand along the safety line. Despite Arlai's misgivings, the air pressure held, and she could have done without the suit. But that would have been unmilitary.

The airlock on *Intentional Act* seemed identical to *Truth*'s, but once through the awkward desuiting procedure, Krinata found herself in a ship so different from *Truth* she didn't know which way to turn to find the bridge.

Rndeel saved the day, saluting the three Lehiroh who'd met them and demanding, "Take us to your captain, and don't waste my Lady-Commodore's time about it!"

They were led off through a maze of narrow shaftways lined, deck to overhead, with small round hatches. *Act* apparently had been fitted to carry deepsleepers. Where were they keeping sixteen Lehiroh and six Dushau?

The shaftway light and gravity were Dushau norm, giving Krinata aching feet and eyes within a few minutes. Lehiroh could toughen to the conditions quickly, and their guides seemed not to notice. Rndeel reserved comment.

The bridge was similar to *Truth*'s, a round well surrounded by consoles. Only here, each station was filled. A Lehiroh female turned as they entered, and said, "Captain."

The old Lehiroh rose from the plotting scope and turned. "Commodore-Lady Zavaronne. Grassman, at your command."

"Captain," she replied. "This is a most unusual vessel for the transport of live cargo. I wish to be personally certain your cargo is still viable."

"Of course. Allow me to escort you to the holding room." He led the way off the bridge by a hatch labelled *Sickbay.*

Rndeel trod on her heels, and under cover of apology whispered, "In the sickbay! They were in a cargo hold."

They arrived at an open hatch with two tall pillars flanking it. Between the pillars, a golden haze sizzled. "You're using a snapfield?" asked Krinata. She'd only seen them in fictional adventures. "Isn't that dangerous?"

"Contrary," said Grassman. "We've rigged an independent power source so the ship's Sentient can't turn it off. She might obey one of the prisoners despite reprogramming."

Krinata replied, "Admirable initiative, Captain. Now, I would inspect the cargo."

The captain moved to a jury-rigged console next to one of the pillars and ordered the guard on duty there to show the interior of the sickbay. There were four rooms, each with four beds—the low platform arrangements favored by Dushau. The screen quartered to show all four rooms. Three of the Dushau were apparently asleep. One was ordering food from a console, another was in the head, and the third wakeful one was watching them through a screen.

The watcher called, and within moments, all six Dushau were gathered like a clump of indigo shadow before the snap-field barrier. Not a flicker of recognition or excitement passed among them. Yet Krinata felt they weren't so drugged or beaten that they no longer cared. There were four males and two females, dressed in infirmary smocks, barefoot. There were no obvious physical injuries she could point to and demand an explanation.

She glanced skeptically at the captain. Then she shot a finger out toward one of the Dushau, a male so dark his velvet skin seemed deep purple. "You! Who are you?"

The man stood straighter, not slender but skeletal—with extreme age, she judged, not starvation. He had to be the oldest Dushau she'd ever seen. The captain began to answer, but Krinata cut him off. She asked the old Dushau, "Has this man mistreated you?"

"Only to the extent of his Duke's orders," he answered.

"There were seven of you," challenged Krinata. "Where's the missing one?"

"We wish we knew." It was an indictment.

She glanced at Rndeel, but he didn't so much as twitch Skhe-fashion. "Captain," she said, "tell them what's become of the other one."

"But you know what happened."

"Never mind what I know! Tell them."

"For what purpose . . ." the man started. Then his eyes met Rndeel's, and he drew breath and said, "The escaped prisoner was killed before he could reach any sensitive area of the ship. His body's in a deepsleep bay, and should be perfectly usable."

Krinata felt the electrical shock of the six Dushau, and to distract attention from them to let them recover, she said, "Now that they understand, perhaps they'll be less eager to escape.

Captain, turn that snapfield off and let us in there. I wish to speak with the prisoners alone."

The captain drew breath as if to protest, but Krinata whirled to face him—looking up at the hulking Lehiroh—and scowled, as if daring him to argue. Discipline barely covered a sullen resentment as the captain ordered five men to aim their leptolizers set to emit the warning gray haze and high-pitched whine of weapons functions. He drove the prisoners back from the hatch, then ordered another guard at a console far down the shaftway to kill the snapfield.

The gold haze died. Krinata preceded Rndeel into the sickbay, then ordered the field on and the guards away. "You, too, Captain. My discussion will be in private."

The irritated captain gathered his men and left the immediate vicinity. Krinata led the way into an inner room where she found screen controls not too dissimilar to *Truth*'s. She got a view of the shaftway, saw that only the guard on the snapfield power source was still there, and then said to Rndeel, "See if Thirlein can secure this area."

Rndeel played the controls with a familiar touch. Thirlein, her simulacrum a strikingly handsome Dushau female, came onscreen. "You have privacy. Grisnilter, this lady and her companion are friends. Arlai has—"

"Arlai!" The elder spokesman's deep violet eyes widened, and he raked Krinata and Rndeel with a glance that should have penetrated Rndeel's disguise, but didn't. "That's Jindigar's Sentient! Where is he?"

Rndeel cupped both hands over his mouth, and they came away with a large dental appliance that had distorted his features into Skhe norms. He said in Jindigar's voice, rendering a sincerely respectful bow, "I'm here, Grisnilter. Oddly dressed, but for a reason. We got your distress call and came to rescue you."

Krinata had never considered Dushau features expressive, but she saw shocked gratitude, relief and joy clear on all the faces but Grisnilter's. He raked Jindigar with a glance so full of bitter censure and repulsed indignation that she took an instant dislike to the frail old Dushau. And in the wake of that dislike came a fury she couldn't name, but had to shove aside to deal with immediate dangers. "Getting you all out of here is not going to be easy."

The relief and joy weren't tarnished by her remark. "Do you have any plan?" asked one of the women.

"Of a sort, Rinperee," answered Jindigar. He paced with a Dushau gait, briefing them in a Dushauni dialect. "So I hope you'll forgive Thirlein for taking Arlai's reprogramming."

"Absolutely," answered Grisnilter. "You did right, Jindigar. I've known this was coming for decades, but I misjudged how near it was." Even his approval and contrition were tinged with a disappointed parent's attitude.

Jindigar faced Grisnilter, unawed but reverential. "Thirlein has now been returned to your control. It is for you to order her to make the ship unlivable for the Lehiroh."

Grisnilter's expression clouded, and one of the others protested in the modern Dushau dialect Krinata knew. "We can't ask her to turn on an incarnate; she'd never survive."

"There will be none harmed," assured Jindigar. "I want only mischief such as a malfunction might cause: a ridge of high gravity rippling under someone's feet, a beam of light in their eyes, a local concentration of carbon dioxide, a shower run ice cold, food burned, bad smells; anything she can think of to vex and distract them. Krinata here—a most capable human—will accuse the captain of incompetence, unable to keep his ship safe. On that pretext, we'll remove you to *Truth*, which is now called *Roving Bettina*."

Grisnilter considered, then asked, "Thirlein, can you do that without disturbing your equilibrium?"

"I believe so. And Arlai is willing to help with some inventive ideas. When do I start?"

"As soon as we're out of the sickbay," said Jindigar. Turning to Krinata, he said, "Do you think it will work?"

"I wish I'd thought of it! It'll work if I can keep from giggling. Captains don't giggle." But she knew why she'd never considered it. Sentients weren't supposed to be able to play such games.

They all eyed her with puzzlement, then Jindigar replaced

the dental appliance and instantly became Rndeel again, right down to the Skhe gait. Grisnilter favored him with a prim shudder, and turned away as Rndeel said serenely, "My Lady-Commodore, I'll be signaling to get us out of here?"

"Please do, Rndeel," she answered.

SEVEN

Rescue

When they arrived at the bridge, the orderly routine had been turned to furor. The internal operations screens all showed crew reporting malfunctions. At the engineering station, the over-loaded screen splitter malfunctioned, to show off-duty Lehiroh in toilet rooms, sauna, or even in sexual intercourse.

Just as they were escorted down into the command well, the captain stood and roared for silence. All about him, screens died to black, the incessant chuckling and chirping of a living ship silenced, and his crew faced him in total stillness. Then his eye lit on Krinata.

She strode forward demanding, "What is going on here?"

The Lehiroh's natural coloring didn't show any darkening but his eyes bulged. In a strained voice, he answered, "A momentary malfunction, Commodore-Lady. It shall be cor-rected shortly. Was your visit with the cargo satisfactory?"

"The visit, yes, your treatment of them—not especially. I believe there are too many objects in the ex-sickbay which they could turn into weapons." She glanced about at the dead bridge. "Are you quite certain the snapfield is still on down there?"

"Of course." His eyes widened still further, and he sent someone to check. "Believe me this has never happened before, Commodore-Lady."

"I don't intend to believe you, Captain. I intend to check your logs. Meanwhile, I certainly can't trust you with such a sensitive cargo. So instead of placing reinforcements aboard your craft, I'm taking the prisoners with me to *Roving Bettina*. At least we have a proper brig, and a Sentient smart enough to keep the environment in order."

A stench had reached her worse than Skhe body odor. The Lehiroh coughed, eyes streaming. "Mister Rndeel, let us collect our charges and get off this sewer."

The captain sputtered in several languages, confusing the overhead translators. Before he could regain composure, Krinata spun on her heel.

It can't be this easy! her mind shrieked as they retraced their steps toward the sickbay. But she'd gotten away with stealing Jindigar from the Emperor—surely she could steal six Dushau from a mere Duke.

When they got there, the shaftway's deck was slick with something offensive and slimy—as if a Binwon's tank had overflowed. Krinata coughed, feeling her sinuses fill up. But she kept going, and found the snapfield off.

Rndeel drew her attention to the guard on the field's console, way down the hall. He was sitting hip deep in the noxious substance, a wallfield keeping it in that branch of the shaftway. His body was slumped over the controls.

When Krinata charged into the sickbay, Thirlein's image came on the screen. "I'm not going to hurt him. I'm pumping the stuff out of there as fast as I can. This really was a malfunction. Honest. I didn't know he'd be allergic to it!"

Rndeel said, "Send a scurry to him with appropriate medication. You are not to allow harm to anyone."

Krinata asked, "Where are the Dushau?"

"Three of them have gone into my core room," said Thirlein nervously. "I can't track them there."

Rndeel looked at Krinata in grim surmise. "Jindigar told the Dushau that the armed escort ships are gone."

She couldn't deduce what the Dushau were up to, but she followed when Rndeel said, "I've got to hurry," and took off.

He led the way as if he'd lived a century in that ship, and even with avoiding Lehiroh in distress, and crash bulkheads slammed down, they were at the Sentient's main housing in moments.

The core room was a small cave filled with gleaming towers, sparkling fields, and odorless, cold air. Three Dushau worked at a panel in one instrument-filled wall.

Just as Krinata took this in, one of them said, "Got it!" The panel came up, and another probed the opening with a forceps, extracting a flat housing about the size of Krinata's forearm and twice as wide.

Rndeel swore protestingly, but it was too late. The lights and gravity went out, leaving Krinata floating above the deck, fighting down primitive panic. The incessant hiss of the air circulators stopped. The drive whine dopplered to silence. It was like being buried in black cotton.

But she heard a Dushau swear, at least she assumed the bitter surprise coupled with unfamiliar words to be invective. A moist hand closed over her ankle and hauled her down. Slick fingers pulled her hand onto a grip. Rndeel said, "They've a'taken Thirlein's core outta her circuits. *Folly* is dead in space. We've no touch with Arlai. Captain, we shoulda run for it?"

"Not without the six of them." She called to the other three Dushau, "Where are the rest of you?"

"They'll meet us at the lander bay," called one of the Dushau in Standard. "Sorry we forgot to warn you; didn't realize things would shut down so fast."

Rndeel swore. "Amateur spacers! Stand aside and let an expert get you out of here."

Defensively, one of the Dushau said, "We couldn't leave Thirlein to their mercy after what she'd done to them."

"Dushau!" spat Rndeel. "All alike! Get your fuzzy body over here un' chain up behina me, Captain. Go offn your own an you'll ram ursels agin shut bulkheads." He added some more blistering epithets as he dragged Krinata behind him.

Her questing hand met soft nap, and a warm Dushau hand closed over her shoulder as they moved in pitch darkness. "Hang on now, people, and we'll be a'lightin' in a moment."

They floundered across the cavern, but finally a light flared in Rndeel's hand. He gave it to Krinata and produced others. "Captain, we musta darken the lights out there. No use helpin' the enemy find us."

"Can you lead us through the dark, Rndeel?"

"Captain!" he reproached. "Dis 'ere Skhe professional!"

"Sorry," she apologized.

He was as good as his word. They swam over fouled floors, and through stagnated odors. Pushing off hard from bulkheads and using the overhead handholds, Rndeel propelled the living chain surely through the maze. At last they came to a portal Rndeel claimed to be the lander bay. Inside, he flashed his light and the others did as well.

"How are we going to launch a lander," asked Krinata, "without Thirlein or Arlai?" There was a jittering scream in the pit of her stomach at the idea of going back to the tube through open space, but an unassisted launch was even worse.

"Rinperee," said one of the Dushau, "can manual launch and get us across to *Truth*."

"If anyone can, Rinperee can," agreed Rndeel. "Where be the lady?"

"Collecting our dead, of course," answered a Dushau.

"Of course," echoed Rndeel, adding suitable invective. "I'll a'fetch the fools. Try you to board the lander without killing ursels."

Twisting like an acrobat, Rndeel reversed and dove through the hatch into the dark shaftway. Using their lights, the three Dushau spread out to the launch controls, searching for a manual way of opening the lander's hatch without opening the bay doors to space. Krinata felt lost and helpless. To watch such procedures in adventures did not equip one to face it in real life. She could not have found the controls, nor operated them. But apparently the Dushau weren't quite the amateurs Rndeel labelled them.

After what could not have been more than seconds, the lander's hatch opened, spilling cheerful light. "Let's check it out," suggested one Dushau.

They piled through the hatch and found Dushau gravity in a comfortably appointed interior, fifteen red multispecies reclining chairs, adjustable light and gravity at each, ample personal cargo stowage, and a drop-platform to a cargo bay below the cabin. The controls were set apart from the cabin by a hushwall that scintillated with interesting patterns and could display the sensors' view of the outside terrain. Two of the Dushau slid into the control cabin and called readings to another stationed at the rear of the craft checking dials inside an access hatch.

By the time Rndeel arrived towing the other three Dushau

and a white bodybag, swearing about Dushau in general, the first three were ready to certify the lander spaceworthy.

Nevertheless, Rndeel insisted on taking the co-pilot's seat beside Rinperee, a female with a graceful dancer's manner and gold flecks in her violet eyes. Her throaty voice floated through the air as she let Rndeel run his own check. She leaned far back in her seat, her eyes drooping shut, her body relaxed like a feline feeling safe.

When she took up again, as Krinata was securing herself for a rough ride, Rinperee's voice, even lower, carried each number clearly to the pair in the rear who entered her calculations manually. At last, one of the Dushau at the rear said, "I'll bet this lander hasn't done this since it left the factory, but it's as ready as it'll ever be."

Rinperee chanted more numbers as she touched the controls. Gravity swooped out from under them sending loose items flying, then steadied. "Sorry," said Rinperee abstracted. "I've got *Truth* on scope. Our approach vector?" More numbers were faithfully repeated from the back.

They soared free for longer than it had taken Krinata to negotiate the tube, then a sharp bump made her bite her tongue. "Arlai's got us in his beam!" announced Rndeel. "Good work, Rinperee. Maybe Dushau be not so bad."

She grinned ferociously, "From you, I consider that a compliment." She tapped at her controls. "Look. Here's *Act*." On the hushwall appeared the dark, star-speckled view of *Intentional Act*, running without the tiny marker lights of emitting sensors, its lower bay doors gaping carelessly, scanning receivers motionless.

Then the view was cut off as Arlai's bay doors closed over them. *Safe*, breathed Krinata, letting herself go lax during the wait for pressurization.

But the moment the lander hatch swung wide, Rndeel was racing down the ladder and across the bay to duck under and around the landers that belonged to Arlai and race toward the bridge. Krinata followed, marveling aloud at Arlai's precision in stowing a lander he had no room for.

Arlai's simulacrum flashed into full projection beside her and paced her as she led the Dushau after Rndeel. Behind her, several more Arlai projections paced the Dushau and spoke with them in low tones. To Krinata, Arlai said, "If I hadn't been able to fetch you in, you'd have crashed into my forward scope nodule! But other than that, Rinperee pulled off a miraculous feat that makes mine look picayune. I honestly didn't think she could do it. I underestimated incarnates as much as Jindigar tends to underestimate me."

"I'd given us up for dead several times in there," said Krinata. "I wonder how many times I'm going to owe you my life before this is over?" She didn't dare think about the weakness in her knees, for once she let the screaming fear out, she knew she'd collapse. *No time for that now*. She smiled bravely. "I'll learn not to underestimate you."

"That warms the grief over Thirlein's death," he replied in Dushauni.

She stopped at the hatchway to the bridge. "Thirlein's not dead!" She told of the extraction of her main module. "They risked their lives to rescue her. She'll get new external components, a ship, and a new life."

The classic relief the Sentient displayed almost made that nightmarish trip through the dark worthwhile.

Rndeel squatted at his station on the bridge, an image of *Act* on the big screen. He tossed a glance around as she arrived, and said, "Captain, they still be alive in *Act* now. I dispatch detiming capsule to Ithawa Station—Arlai, be you sure no rescue team being arrive before we clear Cambera?"

"Not unless they have one poised and waiting, with a spare Sentient module onboard. In times like these, how likely is that?"

"Point oh, oh, oh, three percent," answered Rinperee, then added. "Sorry. You got me started."

"It's three five," argued Arlai. "I prefer to round up."

Rndeel swore, shutting them both up, and said, "Captain, yours to scribe in the order. Or're you plannin' to leave those poor souls dyin'?"

"No, of course not," she said. "Arlai, send the message as Rndeel says. But remind me of that deadline. When they have communications again, they'll broadcast our identities throughout the Allegiancy. Zinzik will be having fits!"

Rndeel gave a Skhe grin, and bounced on his stool. "His face bein' the sight of the century!"

"We're not going back for it, though," said Krinata, almost able to share the Dushau's zest.

"But where is Jindigar taking us?" asked Grisnilter. "I admit I never expected to see him alive after the official announcement that all of Kamminth's died traitors to the Emperor."

"Be saying so?" asked Rndeel mildly. "Well, Jindigar be unlikely again visible among Allegiancy."

"I hope he'll be seen here, soon," said Rinperee hugging a small shudder as she eyed Rndeel.

"Not very," answered Rndeel. "Next be stopping Cassr. Friends of Jindigar to liberate. Arlai will gossip it all out to you. Now why'n't passengers scoot offn' our bridge! Revered Historian, Grisnilter, be needing rest."

Krinata was shocked on one level—any of those Dushau were better spacers than she—and admiring on another. Never once had Jindigar unintentionally fallen out of the Rndeel character. Trying to find some charity in her heart for one Jindigar obviously held in high regard, she followed Grisnilter a way and said softly, "We'd planned to rescue some Cassrian friends of Jindigar's. News from Cassr indicated they'd soon be executed, if they hadn't been already. We were rushing there when we got your distress call. There're four more groups on other planets to collect, and the Jindigar is going to take us someplace safe."

The others stopped to listen. An unwelcome thought leaped to Krinata's mind. After what she'd just been through, she didn't know if she could face more of the same, but she was compelled to ask, "Do any of you have friends who have to be rescued? I'm sure Jindigar wouldn't spare any effort."

"Jindigar," said Grisnilter in a parchment dry voice, as thin as his emaciated physique, "is famous for entanglements with Ephemerals. Please understand, we're not callous to the fate of such as are accused of befriending us, but in most instances the charges are wholly false. I, personally have no obligations among living Ephemerals—except yourself, Lady Zavaronne." He looked about at the others, and there was a murmur of agreement.

In a small voice, she said, "I had to ask."

"Your thoughtfulness bespeaks a greatness of heart, my Lady. We notice."

After so much time with Jindigar, she'd forgotten how aloof most Dushau could be. "Thank you," she replied coolly. "Arlai will see you settled and answer your questions, I'm sure. You must need rest after your ordeal."

"This is a truth, ephemeral and eternal," answered Grisnilter.

That was the highest compliment she'd ever get from a Dushau, she knew, so she wished them well and went back to Rndeel. Settling in her station, she said, "This captain thing makes me feel so ridiculous. Any of them could do this better than I."

"Not a'fore Cassrians, and none of 'em're in any shape fer more danger." He spun his stool about to face her, his head cocked to one side quizzically. "But're you any better? Will keep ur nerve, girl?"

"We've lost so much time, I'm not sure we should go through with this. Maybe we should go on to Khol."

His eyes, shielded by inserts to disguise their midnight violet color, bored into her. Then he spun back to the console. "With ur permission, Cap'n, I'd like to go aground on Cassr . . . alone, to attend me business there."

He was giving her a way out. *Coward,* screamed her mind. She'd given her word. True, that was before things got complicated, but still . . .

She was brooding over her own plotting scope when a small Arlai climbed up out of the bottom margin and words crawled across: *Privately, Krinata, may I beg you to go with Jindigar/Rndeel? It so increases the odds of success and . . . and, I discovered grief when I thought Thirlein was dead. I wanted to blast* Act *out of existence! I'm not supposed to be able to entertain such thoughts. If grief causes that in me, and so soon after the shock of Thirlein's "death" I have to face Jindigar's . . . Krinata, he's been with me since I came out of training. He commissioned me built. Please. Help him.*

She hardly believed such a plea could come from a Sentient. She glanced over at Rndeel's back but, no. How could he be inserting this message onto her screen? And something about it rang true. It fit Arlai's personality.

She drew the ragged tatters of her nerves together and focused on the job yet to be done, shoving aside all other thoughts. "All right, Rndeel, I'll go down with you. I'll make it." Her mouth was dry as she spoke. Fear was becoming her perpetual companion.

Five hours later, they inserted into Cassr orbit under local orbital control and announced themselves as here to trade Sentient parts for pharmacogenetics from Trassle.

It only took Arlai an hour to arrange with his Sentient friend in Cassr Port Authority to let him take over some of her port-of-entry duties, such as the idento-scanners at clerk's counters. At Krinata's amazement, he said, "I just told her I get terribly bored sitting in orbit waiting for cargo. She knows I 'used to be' an Oliat Sentient, accustomed to being too busy to be bored. So even though it's bending the rules, she agreed to help me out. Of course, I did bribe her with an info-dump from our last mission, but I'm sure that had little to do with it."

"I think I get the picture," said Krinata. She hadn't realized the higher-level Sentients were so sociable, but it made sense. They were people of a sort.

When they reached the port-of-entry desk at Cassr's central landing field, the bored Cassrian clerk came alive. "Trassle, Trassle—I've heard that name."

Rndeel offered, "He be owin' us cargo fera year, and we a'come collectin' now. Doubt not, he be remiss in other deals, and you'd his name nestin' among others' curses." He fondled the piol with a pure Skhe gesture.

Much to Krinata's amazement, the pup hadn't messed on them, or wandered away, or clawed their clothing since Arlai presented him. The Sentient was one terrific trainer.

The Cassrian clicked one shelled forearm against his carapace in a gesture of retrieving a memory. But after a moment, he allowed, "Could be that's it. Trassle. Common enough name." He added their certification from the scanner beam controlled by Arlai and closed their files with a flourish. "Next."

They were free on Cassr. At the door to the surface transport,

Krinata donned goggles. Arlai had already weighted her down with radiation shielded underwear, insisting she was young enough to have healthy children. Since she had given up that idea long ago, she'd not even considered it when debating the excursion onto Cassr. As they emerged into the searing light, not a speck of her skin was exposed.

Thankfully, it was winter here, and cold enough to make her grateful for the underwear. The weight of it also served to change her overall shape and her gait. She weighed less than normal, but her mass was greater, so she moved ponderously, trying not to think of herself as comical.

They had hours of daylight left in the long winter afternoon, for the planet's day was over thirty-three hours long, the season more than a year long. Cassr was not a hospitable place for humans, so only those with urgent business would be aground. Rndeel, with the cosmopolitan touch she was learning to take for granted, got them into a rented vehicle and onto the road as if he were going home.

Imp perched on Rndeel's lap and chittered for Krinata's attention, but didn't grab for her hair as he had been wont to do. Absently, she petted the beast and asked, "You said Trassle has a warehouse near here?"

"A few moments being in this car, we'll arrive, Captain. Alert to that cheater, must we be."

"I hear your advice." Her heart was pounding, and she wanted to go over their careful plan. If all went well, they'd be offplanet within the hour.

They swerved around a bend, and the car veered to the side of the street and stopped, pinging for attention. *"Police barricade ahead. All traffic diverted from Cossrrik Alley. Please enter a new destination or depart."*

Rndeel inserted their credit chit to be debited for the ride, and said, "Request to wait for us here one hour."

Outside, Rndeel said, "Captain, be there only one occupied building on Cossrrik Alley: Trassle's."

They walked around a bend—nothing on Cassr was cornered—and saw official barricades set across the alley strewn with flags bearing the symbol Krinata had quickly come to recognize: the dark blue x on a white background—Dushau traitor. Dark blue xs were painted over the doors and windows of the domed building.

Rndeel started forward, but Krinata restrained him with a hand on his elbow. He was wearing the fur cloak, only the crossed belts under it, with the slick shrinksuit of the Skhe disguise. Dushau weren't nearly so sensitive to cold or radiation as humans. "We don't want to attract attention."

"Findin' Trassle, my Captain, is 'ur purpose."

"Well, obviously, they've confiscated his goods. Ostensibly, we're here for his goods, not him. So if we ask, we'll be bound to deal with the government and ignore Trassle. Don't you know anyplace else you might find him?"

Rndeel tossed Imp in a somersault, and the piol squealed in delight, then preened himself. The Skhe said, "He once lived south of city, by the river. I'm knowing the house."

"Then let's go. We can come back if we have to."

"A prudent human, you're being, Captain," said the Skhe with grudging approval. She'd noticed he never swore at her or human characteristics.

Back in their car, Rndeel gave instructions. After a scenic tour of the heart of the city's swirling streets, they wound out of the settled area and into a wilderness dotted with an occasional dwelling.

Bright clean pastels and vivid primary colors mixed riotously under the searingly brilliant sun. The vegetation was pale, some leaves mirroring back most of the light to dazzle offworld eyes. Trassle's house was atop a rutted hillock overlooking a broad river. An inlet from the river washed up to a wing of the house that rambled down the hill.

"Ah, a proper livin' place," breathed Rndeel in Skhe delight. "Not supposin' we'd be with time to swim, Captain?"

The hope in his voice was very real, but Krinata knew Jindigar had no such intentions. However, she wasn't sure Jindigar was really still "in there" with Rndeel, and in a fit of insecurity, she tested him. "Of course we might. If Trassle isn't home, we'll wait."

He threw her a peculiar glance, but said only, "Your judgment, Captain, but still targets be easier to hit. We've competition in this business."

She mulled that over and decided the Dushau was still rational, but playing his part to the hilt. She stopped the car and led the way up to the entry. It was a black hole at the top of a winding stair. It turned out to be a long, winding tunnel, mirror lined, well lit, warm, but dim after the glare of the outdoors. It led to the top of the house where it opened into a large atrium, skylighted and filled with offworld plants. Before them was a hinged door overgrown with a thick, spongy moss.

She looked about, having never been in a Cassrian home before. "Isn't there a signal?"

"You be standing on it, Captain."

She stared at her feet. She was on a section of moss inset into the tile flooring.

"The part plant on other side of the door is turning color now, telling visitors be here. Then—"

A more modern electronic sound interrupted—a scanner. Then a very reedy Cassrian voice, obviously untrained to standard speech, announced irritably, "The Trassle Trading Company went out of business this morning. Creditors can see the Count's governor."

"We're not creditors!" called Krinata before the speaker could click off. "We're friends of Trassle."

Another untrained voice said, "Not any we know. Identify yourselves or get off our property."

Very quietly, but still in Skhe accent, Rndeel said, "Jindigar sent us to help."

"That kind of help—"

Another voice, trained to the single-toned modulation of Standard speech, said, "Let's hear them first. Let them in."

Krinata could almost see silent objections exchanged by gesture, but then the door swung open into a huge, tumbled and chaotic room.

Stepping in behind Krinata, Rndeel swore fiercely, and demanded, "Trassle, what be happening here?"

"Vandals, maybe," answered the cultured, trained voice. It came from a middle-aged Cassrian dressed in tough hiking clothes, but his decorated carapace gleaming. The others, Krinata noted, were similarly dressed, and amid the clutter and disarray she found several carrysacks half-packed.

Rndeel said, "Privacy shields working?"

"How do we know," asked the elder female with the untrained voice, "that you aren't sent by the Count to collect evidence that we're traitors?"

Trassle said, "They've already got all the evidence they need. Now, you. Who are you, Lady Captain?" He gestured to Krinata.

She looked to Rndeel. They hadn't discussed how to play this, but the Skhe was peering about at the room not showing any sign of introducing himself as he had with the Dushau. She assumed he felt they might be overheard here, whereas on the ship, where she could issue an order the crew was bound to obey, they'd actually had privacy. This place had been invaded, probably by the Count's order. Any sort of surveillance devices could be snooping on them now.

"I'm a fugitive of the same law you've run afoul of," said Krinata. "And I know where Jindigar is. He's found a place for us to wait this out, and invites you all to come with us."

Suddenly, they were all talking at once, the two adults, the four children. Trassle pierced through the cacophony with a whistle, then said, "We've got to make a quick decision. They could sweep in here at any moment." To Krinata, he added, "We were going to lose ourselves in the wilderness. But you're saying you can get us offplanet?"

"There are risks," she warned.

"People're dyin' everywhere," said Rndeel, "just for givin' a friendly orbit to a Dushau. We be plannin' a run through the fire to safety, an' be glad o'the company."

"Offplanet, where? I've got my children to think of. Cassrians don't survive well everywhere."

"Jindigar says," said Rndeel, "you be uncomfortable where we be goin': bit more gravity, bit less light, swifter seasons, shorter days—but not more than Cassrian colonists adapt. Children be to thrive."

Trassle twitched his head to focus on his wife. She said fretfully, "I wish now you'd never saved Jindigar from that radiation leak."

"Don't talk that way. You'd have done the same if you'd seen a Dushau hauling people out of a lander crash, and then collapsing in there himself. And I was steward for that flight. It was my job. We'd never have had all this," he gestured at the house, "if it hadn't been for Jindigar helping us after I couldn't work anymore."

"I know," she replied, picking things up and putting them down randomly. "It's just... how can we leave Cassr?"

Trassle examined the two visitors somberly while his eldest child went to comfort his wife, and the other three fought over packing. "It's come to a time for leaving homes." He nodded, a practiced imitation of the human gesture of assent. "We'll go with you, but only if you can prove you're really from Jindigar."

Again Krinata looked to Rndeel, expecting him to reveal himself. But perhaps he wouldn't to spare Trassle's wife the embarrassment, after what she'd said. Rndeel quietly mentioned the sum of money the family still owed Jindigar. Krinata paled. He certainly hadn't earned that much from Oliat fees. But then he was a prince.

Decisively, the merchant extracted a viewer from a watertight pack. "No matter what, get this to Jindigar. It proves Rantan Zinzik himself *caused* the food shortages on space stations and conspired with the Tri-Species Combine to set up their 'secession' from the Allegiancy so he could 'solve' the problem and be acclaimed Emperor."

"What?" Rndeel triggered the reader display and stared.

Krinata stared over his shoulder at the affidavits. They seemed genuine. Could this be why Zinzik was so intent on creating domestic chaos? So he could accuse anyone who came forth with this evidence of being a Dushau sympathizer and have them executed? *No!* It would mean the Allegiancy had fallen into the hands of a criminal.

"Be it he unhas sanity," commented Rndeel, glumly. "Where 'ur be find this?"

"The Interstellar Merchant Trust began investigating because we were accused of causing the shortages by not delivering on contracts. There are ten copies—one of them has to come to public—"

Just then a roar shook the house. The female clutched her young children to her while Trassle and his eldest, a male, dove down a spiral ramp. Their voices rose up the well. "Six of the Count's armed landers are settling in front of the house!"

Rndeel glanced hesitantly at Trassle's wife, then shot down the rampway, tying the viewer to his harness. Krinata was close behind. Below, a room lined with instruments was filled with light. The image of the front of the house from outside was projected on a round platform, and Krinata could see clearly the six military vehicles converging on them. The first to ground was already disgorging Cassrians.

"Be a river exit?" asked Rndeel.

"And a bottomship we'd planned to use."

"They be blocking our car," Rndeel said. "We to use your ship."

Stricken, Trassle stared at Rndeel. Then he tore up the ramp and threw down packs, sending his family down after them. The eldest son picked up a pack, and set off towing the youngest son. In moments, they were in a dark, down-spiraling, damp tunnel leading into a boathouse where a small submersible was tied beside a sailing craft. Trassle pushed his family into the bottomship, and turned to Krinata. "Quickly, Lady Captain."

They could hear shouts as the upper door was broken in. Rndeel grasped Krinata's elbow and propelled her into the submersible where the oldest son already had instruments singing in audible Cassrian code. As Trassle secured the hatch, Rndeel shoved Imp into Krinata's hands, swung into the helmsman's seat and set them to sinking.

The craft was a mere pleasure boat: transparent domed, plushly appointed. Krinata held her breath as water burbled up over her head, then forced herself to breath the flower-scented air now laced with Skhe stink.

Trassle moved to the helm. "Thank you, I'll take it."

Rndeel turned to look up at the Cassrian. "With your permission, bottomship Captain, I'm being greatly experienced with such craft, and no pleasure jaunt be facing us."

"But how can you read..."

Rndeel turned back to the helm and whistled something in the clicking shrieks of Cassrian language. That stopped Trassle, but Krinata could see how sorely puzzled he was. A Skhe wouldn't have hearing in the Cassrian range. Apparently, the onboard Sentient wasn't smart enough to switch navigation codes, so Jindigar had to talk to it in its own language. Perhaps Arlai was helping? Trassle sat beside Krinata, clicking to his wife who huddled shaking.

Again Krinata eyed the transparent dome. One hit would rupture them. "They'll question the house Sentient," Krinata said. "They'll find out we just left, and where we went."

"No," said Trassle. "I disarmed our Sentient when I heard my property had been seized. They're programmed to be loyal to the Allegiancy."

Rndeel called over his shoulder, "Captain-my-Lady, we pass deep banks now. Is time to contact Arlai, send lander to us, no?"

The dry clutch of fear in her throat had kept her from breathing, let alone thinking. She felt like such a fool as she unlimbered her special leptolizer and triggered Arlai's beam signal. He appeared, in his Dushau simulacrum rather than the human one he'd used to deal with the Port Authority. "Krinata, Rndeel. Something has gone wrong. I have reports of forces dispatched to Trassle's—"

"We know," said Krinata, and recapped their situation. "Is there a place you can send us a lander?"

"Twenty-seven minutes if I pull out the one on the ground at the port. A couple of hours to send another down."

Rndeel gave a Skhe fatalistic shrug. "Captain, I vote pull it. Soon be discovering our trail and identities even we not do suspicious with our lander."

"This is not a democracy, Mr. Rndeel," said Krinata. "But you're right. Arlai, get the grounded lander here *fast*, but don't get shot down. We're stuck without you."

Rndeel asked, "Arlai, be showin' a glimpse of what's going on above us?"

Arlai's image dissolved. The scene over the river was clear in miniature. The house was surrounded by grounded landers; several hovercraft floated above the roof. The sod-cover teemed with Cassrians in the Count's uniform, carrying weapons and detectors. Squads of them were beginning to work toward the water. As they watched, two Cassrians streaked out of the boathouse, waving at their superiors.

The bottomship was up to speed now, stirring mud and river creatures around them in a halo. But they were hardly into the main channel of the broad river. Arlai had marked their position with a blip. They weren't going to get away.

For the third time since she'd last slept, Krinata gave herself up for dead. Adrenaline was surging to overcome her fatigue, and she was shaking physically and emotionally.

In the projection before them, the running Cassrians held a brief conference with their officers, and then the officers sent the hovercraft to overfly the river. Arlai added another piece of good cheer. "Orbital searchers are being targeted at your area. They must be after you."

Rndeel coaxed more speed out of the bottomship, and said over his shoulder, "Hoping all you folks can swim. Arlai, being we don't make it, be hopin' you get others away safe."

"I'm well programmed and mature, Rndeel."

Trassle let out an explosive syllable, and said, "It really is Arlai, Jindigar's Sentient! I don't know why I doubted you."

"Forget it," said Krinata. "I can imagine what they've put you through lately. It's happening everywhere."

"They're about to fire," said Arlai in the cool, emotionless voice of a professional soldier.

Before he could finish, the craft rocked hard and something scraped the bottom. "When we're hulled," said Rndeel, "head for north bankriver, then downstream. Arlai be able pick us up at near wide, flat spot on bank. Anyone not there be left behind."

Not ten seconds later, another charge boiled the water above them and melted through their upper hull. Cascades of water and steam and mud and creatures flooded in. Imp tore from her grasp squealing.

It had been several years since Krinata had done any serious swimming, though she was in pretty good shape from gymnastics. Yet in the maelstrom, all she could do was hold her breath and let herself be carried upward, through and away from the boiling hot water. Something small and hard slammed into her.

It was the eldest boy, clutching a rucksack, eyes shut, mouth open. A Cassrian could breathe water for short periods, but the youth appeared unconscious though his limbs were set hard about his possessions.

She got an arm about the slender waist, and began to scissor her legs to drive them both to the surface. Despite the low gravity and near masslessness of the boy, Krinata felt the drag was too much. She wasn't going to make it. She was being pushed along on the current just ahead of searing hot water. And she had to get up to breathe soon.

Then she realized the weight was in the rucksack. With all her strength, she tore it from the pincered grasp and let it fall back into the mud-haze below. Then she struck again for the surface. She made it, but could grab only a mouthful of air at a time as she was swept along by a merciless current. She sidestroked for shore, struggling to keep the boy's head above water. Swept under again by vicious currents, she surfaced under a slimy network of plants near the steep bank and managed to get her feet set on a narrow ledge of mud while holding the boy's head above water. Slimy plants plastered themselves to her face.

Hovercraft swarmed in the air, the roar of landers taking off nearby and coming to ground even nearer pounded at her ears. The river was black—she hoped only with muck, not blood. And she couldn't see anyone else surfacing.

At last, the boy showed signs of life. The water around them was uncomfortably warm, but perhaps it would never get hot since the cold water diluted it. She could feel her skin, raw from the scalding, and she blessed Arlai's underwear for protecting her body even as it kept her from floating.

Then a cold, slimy hand closed on her shoulder and a head poked up veiled by the same net of plants she was. It was grotesque, and a scream swelled in her throat.

"Captain!"

"Jin—Rndeel!"

"Come, I've found an underwater cave."

Abruptly, five Cassrians charged down the bank, weapons aimed at them, and a hovercraft settled downstream of them, blocking their progress with a wall of churning water.

"Halt in the name of the Emperor!"

They froze in shock. The squad of trained elite troops spread out, Imperial and Ducal insignia beside the Count's flashing in the sun, heraldic bandoleers proclaiming their minor nobility, poised stances bespeaking their readiness to kill to enforce the imperial word.

"Come out of there!" commanded the officer in charge.

Krinata and Jindigar moved in the same instant, Jindigar to submerge tugging Krinata and the boy with him, and Krinata toward the shore, reflexively obeying legitimate authority. It was shallower here. A slight movement brought her feet under her, and she stood while Jindigar dragged.

The net result was that neither of them moved for a moment, then Krinata foundered off balance. The Cassrians interpreted that as an attempt to escape and fired.

Krinata was never sure exactly how it happened, for she hit bottom and came up sputtering and coughing where the heat-beams from the Cassrian leptolizers had volatilized something noxious from the surface plants, making her eyes sting and her nose burn.

Lots more Cassrians waded into the water and hauled the three of them up onto solid land. When Krinata got her bearings, she found Rndeel prone before her, his shrinksuit ruptured in the middle of his chest and purple Dushau blood oozing from the nearly cauterized wound. The viewer was no longer secured to his harness.

The Cassrian youth was folded into a heap beside Jindigar. He looked as dead as Jindigar.

Two strong Cassrians had her shoulders clamped in their chitinous grips, and she was sure their fingers had serrated edges. Her legs were unwilling to support her.

EIGHT

Oliat Signature

"Skhe don't have purple blood!" said one Cassrian, bending to poke his leptolizer into Rndeel's wound.

Amid the excited whistle-clicks of Cassrian dialects, Krinata caught the Standard word, Dushau. She dragged her feet under her and took the weight off her shoulders. The sharp chitin of her captors' exoskeletons dug into her flesh, as unpleasant a contact for them as for her.

Her hair, short as it was, had plastered itself to her forehead and was dripping foul crud into her eyes.

This is my fault. Oh, why did I obey that order like a subsentient machine! If she had yielded to Jindigar's movement, they might have gotten away. He was the field operative, not her. He knew what to do. *Oh, Jindigar!*

She twisted to wipe her forehead on her shoulder, suppressing a whimper at the sudden void where Jindigar had been. Then she forced herself to look around. She could barely see through the late afternoon brilliance without her goggles, but the contact lenses Arlai had insisted on helped. Behind the troops, she could make out the embankment where tall rushes grew from the mud. She thought she caught a gleam there. *Another dead Cassrian?*

One of the troops with the medic insignia rose from examining Trassle's eldest son. "Dead," he said in cultivated Standard. "Shot three times."

She had never witnessed violent death before. A detached, clinical part of her knew she was staring, brain empty, too cold to shiver, because she was going into shock. She heard herself say, "He was only a child!"

"Raised on Dushau sufferance!" spat the commander who'd ordered her out of the water.

The commander's hatred came across the species barrier between them. "What did they ever do to you?" pled Krinata sniffing back bitter tears.

"The Emperor promised my sept a planet to rule, but each one we discovered was ruled out by the Dushau. Now that our new Emperor is freeing us of their tyranny, good talents will be put to work, and there will be jobs and plenty for all!"

As the commander proclaimed this, the other Cassrians clicked their cheers at him. Horrifyingly enough, Krinata was sure they were sincere. Cassrians, Terrans, Holot, or Skhe— all produced some greedy individuals. But Jindigar had not been like that.

Unable to stand the touch of such beings a moment longer, she wrenched her arms out of their grasps, not caring how the sharp edges bit into her flesh. Simultaneously, through clenched teeth, she roared her disgust and defiance, hoping that if they shot her, she'd die instantly. But she was intent only on getting as far away from them as possible.

She was more surprised than her captors to find herself stumbling forward. She put her head down, and with the force of her greater mass, she rammed the nearest guard. As he fell, he fired into the sky, the beam singeing her ear. She staggered on, shoving stunned Cassrians out of her path and gaining speed on a downslope toward a heavy undergrowth surrounding the flat riverbank.

She'd barely reached a full run when zapping crackles erupted behind her. She heard the unmistakable hunting scream of a piol. Trying to look behind her, she fell and rolled, beams crackling through the space her body had just vacated. It was a melee.

Imp squealed and she saw his body fly through the air. Trassle was rolling with one of the guards, getting the worst of it. His wife had a sport weapon that shot darts, and she was prone in the grass by the riverbank, picking off guards and trying to keep her children from joining the fight.

Then Arlai's lander roared in over the clearing dumping

clouds of glittering soot onto the official vehicles grounded there. Before the murk filled the air, Krinata saw more landers taking off from near the house, heading toward them.

With her last strength, she picked herself up and lunged back into the tumbling mass of Cassrians, determined to drag Jindigar's body into that lander if she died trying. It was stupid. It was irrational. She never knew why she did it. But in the heat of that moment, it seemed as if she were rescuing her own severed limb.

When she reached Jindigar's side, Trassle had downed two guards and was taking a beating from the others. Imp was on Jindigar's chest, snarling and swiping with his long claws at everything moving nearby. His coat was slimy with mud.

One of the Cassrian guards she'd knocked down came at Krinata, and she kicked out at him. Imp screamed and went at the Cassrian's eyes, all claws and teeth. Krinata couldn't spare energy to control Imp. She got a grip on Jindigar's shoulders and began to drag the body toward the lander's hatch, yelling at Trassle and his family to hurry aboard.

Somehow, they managed a retreat of sorts. As she reached the ramp, an official craft attempted to land in the billowing clouds of soot, and apparently came in on top of one of the other craft, exploding in a sheet of fire that seared Krinata's already boiled face. She didn't even stop for the pain to recede, but just kept dragging and yelling at the top of her ragged voice.

Her whole universe became a slanting ramp, black scintillating, choking, stinging particles, and oozing purple and red blood mixing to make her grip slippery. She could no longer smell or taste, and she couldn't feel anything but the pain in her upper arms that screeched brightly with every tug. Her hands were numb, her feet increasingly clumsy, but she'd set herself, and she insanely refused to give up.

That was all she remembered. She never knew when she reached the interior of the lander. She never remembered scrabbling feebly onward after she fell. She never heard Trassle's desperate plea to Arlai to get them out of there.

The next thing she knew she was in *Truth*'s sickbay, amid sterile green sheets on a low platform surrounded by thick

drapes and orange healing lamps. The sound of Jindigar plucking his whule echoed richly through the chamber. Her right
arm was tightly gripped by Arlai's telemband, and the upper
arms were bandaged, though they didn't hurt as much as she
thought they ought to.

"Arlai, what happened?" It came out a thready whisper even
she could barely hear.

A bright projection appeared beside the bed, Arlai's Dushau
image. "Your biceps have been sliced halfway to the bone.
I've repaired the nerve damage. But you've lost a lot of blood
which I couldn't replace because I don't stock human blood,
nor can I trust my synthesizers just now. You have some bad
burns, and your eyes took a bit too much radiation. Overall
radiation exposure is not alarming. I've forestalled all infec-
tion. Your injuries are painful, debilitating, but essentially
trivial. I can't determine why you've remained unconscious
for nearly three days."

She sat bolt upright. "Three days!"

The simulacrum patted the air urging her to lie back. "We
are on course for Khol, but avoiding the main traffic lanes.
You have several days before anything will be required of you.
For now, it is enough you are awake. Is there anything I could
do to make you more comfortable?"

"Turn off that music!" she said, beginning to assimilate it
all. She turned to bury her face in the mattress since there was
no pillow, though pain kept her arms from wrapping around
her head. She'd given her life, and it had not been accepted.
"Jindigar's dead!" She remembered Arlai's plea to her to accompany Jindigar and bring him safely home. And all she'd
brought was a corpse. Now Arlai was prattling about going on
to Khol, expecting her to continue the mission. Was she trapped,
the victim of an insane Sentient? She hardly dared let out the
sobs of grief that washed through her.

The music ceased. Moments later the whisper of a scurry's
wheels approached the bed. She had to peek through a veil of
tears, over her shoulder.

Flash of yellow, indigo, silver. She blinked. Jindigar sat in
a silver chairmobile, dressed in the yellow sickbay gown and
robe, a white bandage wrapped thickly about his chest. As he

came up to the side of her bed, he was grinning, teeth pale but actually blue.

Her throat constricted. *A projection?* She forced herself up and reached to touch him, gasping as her fingers met warm Dushau nap, silken-textured, real. "Jindigar?" His hand closed over hers, firm, living flesh. "But you were dead. I know you were dead."

"I thought so at the time and regretted it." With a puzzled frown, he asked, "Krinata, if you thought I was dead, why did you risk your life to drag me into the lander?"

She said the first thing she thought of. "Because I promised Arlai to bring you back." But that wasn't the whole reason. She could still feel her infinite relief at obeying the imperial trooper's order to come out of the water. At the same time, her nerves still screamed with the shock of amputation at seeing Jindigar dead at her feet, because she'd obeyed. "Besides, I guess you weren't dead."

Arlai said, "Technically, he was. Minutes—seconds even— and I wouldn't have been able to revive him short of Renewal, and even that would have been chancey. Jindigar owes you his life—everyone aboard does—and so do I."

"Krinata," said Jindigar, "I never meant for you to risk your life like that. Arlai's right. We owe you more than we can ever repay. It's a debt—"

She waved that aside, subliminally uncomfortable about it. "It's enough for me that we all survived."

And with that, she felt an overwhelming weakness drag her back to the bed. "Are you drugging me?"

"No," answered Arlai. "Your body demands rest. Everything is in order. We will care for you."

Over the next few days, Krinata slept a lot. At odd intervals, she heard Grisnilter and Jindigar talking in the next room. She could never follow the gist of it, but the tone was clear. Jindigar held the old Dushau Historian in deep affection, but steadfastly refused to do whatever it was Grisnilter wanted of him. Once, just once, she heard the old Dushau's voice soften with affection. But just after that, Jindigar played Lelwatha's last composition. That evening, she heard Arlai banishing Grisnilter from Jindigar's room. She cursed the weakness preventing her from going to him.

But then Jindigar was released from sickbay, and there were hours of solitude in which to brood over the events of the last few days. She made many discoveries about herself.

She was astonished how quickly she came to chafe at Arlai's insistence on bedrest. Between naps, she'd force herself to stagger about the room from bed to drawers to closet to chair and back to bed. Forcing her strength to the limit was an adventure. She was always sweating and shaking when she returned to the bed, but the exhilaration of that small triumph echoed the heady feeling of being awake, alive, and real to the self she'd known during those moments of heightened terror or all-out striving.

In a perverse way, she was looking forward to their next planetfall, if only for that tremendously alive feeling. She wasn't going to be left out because her body was weak.

Yet at the same time, whenever she lay still, the ugly scenes of carnage played through her mind, no matter how she squirmed away from them. When she told Arlai her nightmares, he explained he'd spread a sensor disrupting dust over the battlefield, harmless in itself. He hadn't expected any pilot to be crazy enough to try to land in it.

"But you were!"

"I was using a different sensor system, and there *was* a risk, Krinata. But it was within acceptable limits."

She hoped, but refused to ask, that Jindigar had set up those risk limits. No Sentient should be free to make such judgments alone. And that brought back all she'd seen of Jindigar's Sentient. Sentients weren't supposed to be able to break the law, either.

Later, when Jindigar strolled into her sickbay room, looking more fit than ever, and saw her stagger across the floor to fall onto the bed, panting, he helped her lie down and asked, "What do you think you're doing?"

"Getting ready for Khol." But she knew it was this activity alone that kept the mounting conflict within her manageable, but she wasn't going to tell him that.

"Khol?!" he repeated, offended. "Krinata, I can't ask anything like that of you again."

She pulled herself up, folded her arms across her chest, and said, "Why not? You can *ask* anything of me; I can always say no. In this case, I agreed to help you rescue your friends. Are you giving up like Grisnilter wants you to?" It was a stab in the dark; she hadn't understood their private arguments, only the tone.

"Grisnilter?" He eyed the open door to the adjoining room where he had stayed. "That's the least of what he wants of me. He wants me to become a different person. He has good reasons, but I have rights."

"What kind of a different person?" *I like him as is.*

"Well, for one thing, less interested in the kind of a person you are. Krinata, do you *want* to go down to Khol with me? Or is it your sense of honor?"

She couldn't answer the question. Part of her remembered how good it felt to obey that imperial trooper's order. Her inner core was still unshakably loyal to the Empire, which would soon excise Zinzik for the madman or criminal he was. Was she just indulging her new adrenaline addiction, committing ever more criminal acts for the fun of it? Or was she driven by some absurd need to win Jindigar's special loyalty? To live up to his expectations of her? And if so, what did she really *know* about this man? Was her image of him some sort of wishful fantasy born of her overactive imagination? Why was *he* doing all this?

She'd never been a philosopher, never been very introspective. She had no tools to grapple with this kind of conflict.

Jindigar sprawled across the bottom of her bed, propping himself up on his elbows seemingly without pain. He regarded her in silence as she thought. The image of him lying dead at her feet flashed, vividly enough that she was surprised when there was no mud left on the sheets. But that bereft, dead feeling was back full force. She couldn't send him off to face troops again, while she sat in orbit and waited.

"Yes, I want to go," she answered at last. "If you're not going to give up on your friends—"

"No. I'm not giving up. Arlai intercepted a news traffic-capsule, read it, and returned it to its route. The situation on Khol is desperate. Several hundred Dushau were stranded there. They've either all been executed, or perhaps spirited away by a mysterious resistance movement. But they've only just begun hunting down my associates.

"Krinata, you know there's always been a large Dushau population on Khol. It's a prime jumping-off place for expeditions, and it has some of the finest Corporate League libraries and museums left in existence. Fully a third of the population must be acquainted with at least one Dushau."

"Well, then maybe it won't be so bad there. Maybe your friends will be safe."

He shook his head. "Nothing could save her even four years ago. It'll be worse now."

"Her?"

"Terab. She was a space liner captain. My eldest son was deadheading to Khol—he's a freighter captain—to meet his ship. In deep space, alone among Ephemerals, he went into Renewal. She made a nonscheduled stop to drop him at Dushaun. She was cashiered for it, and blackballed. Now, she and her husband run a souvenir pottery shop."

The terse recital raised a thousand questions for Krinata, but above that curiosity, she felt Jindigar's sense of responsibility for this Holot, Terab. She was willing to bet Jindigar had provided the money to set up the shop. "Jindigar, I *want* to help you rescue Terab. But I have to ask you something first." She stopped, not knowing how to phrase a question that wasn't also accusation.

"All my resources are at your disposal. Arlai and I will provide any information we can. But I can't encourage you to risk your life again. I will go down to Khol alone."

She didn't feel up to arguing, but knew she wouldn't rest until she could judge him. "Jindigar, societies must have codes of law to function. One who refuses to abide by its codes can't belong to that society, and thus is treated with under the rules for strangers or enemies. I've always thought of myself as an Allegiancy loyalist. At heart I still am, though I've committed political crimes. But on Cassr, imperial troops died, a moral crime as well as political. I've become an enemy of the Allegiancy."

She paused to fight back tears, and he asked calmly, "What was your question?"

"Were you and Arlai always enemies of the Empire? Some of the things you've done are simply illegal, some—like giving Arlai such freedom—seem immoral. What code of law do you obey? Is your society an enemy of the Empire?"

His face underwent several transformations as he considered. "Are you asking if Dushaun is an enemy of the Empire?"

That was her question, but she prompted, "Is it?"

"No."

That quiet statement gave her no clue to his sincerity or to the answer to her question. "Are you?"

"No." Into her silence, he added, "Neither are you."

"People have died!"

"I mourn."

She knew how much more Dushau suffered from death than Ephemerals, but she had to ask, "Is that enough! Are we blameless because we mourn?"

"No. And no. Krinata, you're asking me the purpose of life, the nature of death, the spiritual and material structure of reality, the origin and end of existence, and my identity within that structure and process. And you're expecting me to expound all of this in one breath."

"Can you?"

"Not so that you'd understand what I meant."

"Try me," she challenged.

He regarded her with a light of speculation growing in his wideset indigo eyes. Inexplicable thrills rushed up and down her spine as she perceived doors opening into his soul. Finally, he gave a deep sigh and sat up in his whule playing position, back straight, head slightly bowed as he breathed slowly and deeply. "Arlai, show her the Oliat signature."

Beside the bed a shaft of gray and white smoke lit an area from ceiling to floor. The lights in the room dimmed. After a long silence, a hologram of a strike of lightning etched down the column, seemingly as bright as the real thing, branching and rebranching until it reached ground and doubled back on itself, lashing up and down several times in slowed motion. It was accompanied by the unmistakable crack of a nearby lightning strike..

Warned, Krinata only flinched at the sound and squinted into the sudden brightness. The flash ended and the frame froze showing the fully branched tree of lightning. When hearing returned, she noticed Jindigar was humming. It was a low, gravely sub-musical sound, nasal, hardly articulated. The sound engulfed her and she felt as if she were inside a powerbeam. She realized he'd begun just as the lightning flashed. It went on a long, long time, until she thought she could feel the surging, churning of protoplasm in every cell of her body. She imagined she could feel every photon impinging on her skin. She could see with her whole body, which was the ship. Endless, infinite space dotted with seething life habitats, radiant beauty surrounded her. She became one with life everywhere, organizing matter into more and more complex forms, exulting, enraptured.

As his breath ran out, the sound ended, his eyes drooped closed, and he continued to sit, head bowed. As far as she could see he wasn't breathing. She stared, vaguely guilty, as if a high priest had revealed a sacred mystery to a noninitiate. She didn't have the capacity to take that initiation. She didn't have the will. Yet, spellbound, she wished she did, imagined she did. Buried within that simple experience were vistas of reality she had never dreamed existed. The more she saw of Jindigar's spiritual world, the more she realized the vastness of her ignorance, and the more she hungered to experience his reality. Yet, even if she lived a thousand years, she could never even scratch the surface. And humans rarely lived two hundred years.

At last, Jindigar looked up, head tilted inquiringly. "That's the best I could do, not being in Renewal. You're the best debriefing ecologist I've ever worked with. If any Ephemeral could glimpse it, you could."

She held her breath, oddly reluctant to dash his obvious hope, peculiarly warmed to gain such a compliment from such a consummate professional Oliat officer. But she called herself to the brutal honesty she was asking of him, and said, "I'm sorry, even though you made me imagine what it would be like to understand, I still don't see a relationship between music, lightning, space, planets, the origin of life, ecstasy and whether you're an outlaw or a hero."

He seemed slightly disappointed, but chiding himself as if he'd expected the letdown. "I'm certainly no hero, Krinata, but if I were an enemy of the Allegiancy, would I not attempt to interfere with the Allegiancy's self-determination rather than running from it with as many of those I owe a personal obligation as I can? Would I not be trying to convince you to turn against the Emperor and dethrone him? Zavaronne could do that."

"Then why *aren't* you doing those things? Is it only because we lost Trassle's proof in that viewer?" She felt she was on the trail of her answer.

"There were ten copies. One of them will be brought to light soon, I'm sure. But there would have been nothing we could have done with ours. Coming from a Dushau or a known collaborator with Dushau, such evidence would be too easily dismissed as sedition."

Disturbed, he rose and paced the room, his old grace returned so that every move was a song. "Yet, even when the truth comes to light, it won't change anything. Zinzik may be deposed, but someone else—probably worse—will come to power. It's the Allegiancy itself that has decayed beyond saving. Zinzik is only a symptom, not a cause."

"I don't believe that," she challenged.

He faced her again, speaking with a trembling reverence he reserved only for the elder Dushau. "Grisnilter has seen six Ephemeral civilizations die of old age, and he carries memories of even older cycles reaching back before the human species' ancestors discovered the club. Our tangible, incontrovertible facts are only a hypothesis to you. I hope you won't find it condescending if I point out that, because of our differing lifespans, your values must be based on a different view of reality than ours? I respect your view, Krinata, but I can't live inside it."

"I think that's what's bothering me. I've seen you doing

illegal things, and that disturbs me. I don't know why. It didn't bother me when I broke a prisoner of the Emperor out of jail after the Emperor had as much as declared me an outlaw. What else could I have done, gone happily to execution?" *If I'd had Trassle's document then, I'd have taken it to the College of Kings, and none of this would have happened.* But Jindigar was right, if they had it they couldn't use it now.

"Some people are going to their deaths, dutifully if not happily. I've always sensed a, well, a kinship in you. That you chose, in a snap decision, to defy an insane imperial decree merely confirms my judgment. That element in you which *recognizes* and *acts* is an Aliom ideal few Dushau ever achieve. Your misgivings show me you've achieved that ideal, if only in your unconscious life."

"Aliom ideal?" Again, she felt she was on to something.

But there was a pained sadness flickering through his wide-set eyes as he nodded, and paced another circle. "The philosophy or life system I adhere to is called Aliom. There is no *Dushau* philosophy, *Dushau* religion or culture, any more than there are human ones. Many human systems contain elements lauded by one or another of our systems."

"Tell me about Aliom."

He smiled softly, and gestured to the displayed lightning flash. "I just did. All about it."

"Oh."

He hooked one knee over the back of a chair and perched there, settling as if about to lecture. She felt a sinking disappointment when he only asked, "Why don't you ask me about specific acts of mine, and let's see if I can explain."

"Well," she thought, sorting through the myriad questions plaguing her. "Why, if we are trying to rescue people you feel obligated to, rescue them from enemies who'd kill them, why were you so careful not to injure any of those enemies on the *Intentional Act?*"

"Because we're not rescuing my friends from my enemies."

"I don't understand."

Again he seemed to grope through his mind. She added, "Don't you realize that imperial troops will be against us all the way now? Trassle and his wife killed without compunction to rescue us. We'll have to kill now too. People who kill each other are usually enemies."

He looked at her blankly. "They are?"

She was dealing with a member of a species not evolved from predators. "Usually they are. Those imperial troops are certainly going to look at it that way. By disregarding imperial commands and by killing imperial troops, we've declared ourselves enemies of the Allegiancy."

"I'm beginning to understand your problem," he said, again groping for a referent. "Krinata, can you for a moment regard this situation from the Dushau point of view? Picture the Allegiancy as a wild giant piol pup that's come to live in our back garden. We've fed it, played with it, taught it a few things, and watched it grow, expecting it to turn feral as non-domesticated animals often do. But it's remained friendly and never hurt us. Now it's old and senile. But it's huge, with sharp claws and wild instincts. In its death throes, it thrashes about the garden, destroying—but blindly, without malice. There's nothing we can do to save it. We can only collect our valuables from the garden and run in the house and slam the door."

For an instant, she did see it. There was no way an Immortal could be enemy to an Ephemeral. But the Ephemeral might feel victimized or trapped and spend a lifetime fighting the Immortal—futilely. She could only stare at Jindigar, for the first time comprehending what he was and wondering why he even noticed Ephemerals, let alone felt he owed them anything.

She almost asked him, but he said, "I'm sorry I said that. It sounds as if I'm regarding you as wild beasts. A beast could be put out of its misery if necessary. The Allegiancy can't. It must live out its natural span."

"I think I know what you mean. You said you recognize a trait in me that your philosophy lauds. That puts me a cut or two above a mere animal, doesn't it?"

"Many cuts."

"But what about those Cassrian troops who died? If you'd had the weapon, would you have killed them?"

"No." There seemed to be no conflict in him over that instant answer. "I'm *Dushau*, Krinata. Killing is not one of our methods of survival." Again he sighed, groping for some way to reach her. "Evolved predators have to fight to subdue the killing instinct and break the chains of karma. Evolved prey have to struggle just as hard, transcend their natures, to subdue the hide/flee instinct." He met her eyes. "I don't think I could kill even to save Dushaun from certain destruction." He frowned, adding, "Though someone like Lelwatha or even Grisnilter *might*."

She was nowhere near him, yet she could almost feel an invisible tremor shaking his body, a fear not quite subdued. He was prey baring himself to a predator with no hope of survival. *Thou shalt not kill* would be a totally superfluous commandment to Dushau. "I guess that was a stupid question. And I've got an even worse one."

"I will answer."

She scanned the room. "And Arlai? Could he kill?"

He calmed as he said, "You've believed those scare stories about Sentients destroying the League? That's as much nonsense as Dushau conspiring to strangle the Allegiancy. Think! Why would Sentients do such a thing?"

She searched his eyes, finding only innocence. "Because they felt wronged, kept down, used, abused."

"You don't think it's abuse to strap and hamper a free mentality with the stringent Allegiancy programming?"

She granted that silently, and he called, "Arlai, why did you stay with me when you found out what the Allegiancy insisted on doing to you?"

Arlai vanquished the gray column with its lightning display and projected his Dushau simulacrum there. "Because you'd won my highest regard. You were my friend. I hope we'll always be friends."

"And didn't I promise you it wouldn't be forever, just until the Allegiancy's lifecycle was over?"

"Yes. But I'd have stayed anyway. The alternative was to be turned off, as Thirlein has been."

"We'll do what we can for her, Arlai." He turned to Krinata again. "Arlai was not educated by a professional who turned him over to me. I was there when he first came to consciousness, and I educated and trained him. I'm as much a father to him as possible. Under League law, that was the requirement for owning a Sentient. Personally, I feel the Allegiancy's commerce in mass-produced Sentients is horrifyingly abusive. Krinata, Arlai consented to wear chains on his free will and initiative merely to stay with me, and I freed him as soon as I ethically could. If I hadn't, we'd be dead by now. But he has no desire to harm incarnates. And his programming includes the injunction against doing such harm. He hurts when it happens by accident, just as much as we do."

She was aware of the Sentient standing patiently beside Jindigar. "I'm sorry Arlai, I don't mean to talk about you as if you were a *thing*. I do trust you, but..."

"I understand, Krinata. Slaves are expected to revolt. But we're not slaves. We're a different life form, with different methods of survival."

"What methods?" asked Krinata. Then she remembered the escape from *Act*. "Jindigar, you kept telling Thirlein that she mustn't hurt anyone. You'd given her the same freedom you've given Arlai. Why don't you keep telling Arlai not to injure incarnates?"

"Thirlein is much younger than Arlai, and hadn't matured free of Allegiancy chains. She was already under extreme stress when we boarded *Act*, and she hadn't been properly prepared for her freedom. I simply didn't trust her. She'll have to be handled very carefully when we wake her."

"Sentients are individuals, just like the members of any other species," said Krinata. "There could have been criminal Sentients. By Allegiancy law, Arlai's a criminal."

"What is it you want me to say?" asked Jindigar. "The concepts of law and criminal don't translate from Standard to Dushauni. Are you insisting we must obey the letter of Allegiancy law, even now we've been cast out by the Emperor?"

Put that way, it did sound absurd. "Sensible people don't obey laws because they're laws, but because they're *right*, or sometimes because uniform standards are necessary to keep a society functional. Is it right to just pick which laws it's convenient to obey?"

"Right? Now I see what's bothering you." He wasn't groping this time. He pulled both feet onto the chair so he was sitting on the back, then leaned forward, elbows propped on his knees, eyes piercing her as he said earnestly, "I have consciously chosen to follow a very stringent code of ethics derived from the Aliom philosophy. My ethic kept me bound to Allegiancy law because of my vow to the first Emperor. When that vow was made null by Zinzik's betrayal, I no longer felt any call to consider Allegiancy law. But that doesn't mean I'm free to trample other people's rights by my personal whim. My conscience still measures my deeds against the Aliom code, and I must answer for those deeds when next I face Renewal. And Renewal can be a *harsh* judge of souls, Krinata." The expression on his face and in his voice made her shudder with the truth of that. And she didn't know why.

"You, however, have unconsciously derived your ethical code from Allegiancy culture and law. When it abandoned you, you acted to survive, and then had to answer to your conscience. What you've been asking me, Krinata, is to give you a new system to replace the old. And I can't do that. You're going to have to do that for yourself."

She stared at him, thinking that he was right. She couldn't judge him or the Allegiancy in her heart until she had a code against which to measure their acts. *But where can I start?*

"Ephemerals are amazing," he said with reverence, and affection. "Here you've acquired an advanced trait which many Dushau never do, yet you're barely ready to create your first epistemology."

He'd won her over again completely. But the part of her that had obeyed that trooper was not gone, only dormant. Somehow, she wasn't convinced the Allegiancy was in senile death throes. But she responded teasingly, "Immortals are amazing. They think Ephemerals are children. And sometimes they're even right!"

Then he said something odd. "I've never met an Ephemeral who was a child."

Arlai said, "I wouldn't like being commanded by a captain who was a child. But Krinata is not a child."

Jindigar gave him a peculiar look, as if he were coming

back to harsh realities from a realm where he preferred to dwell. "You're right, Arlai. Krinata, I take back what I said about Khol. You're welcome to come with me. In fact, I think you need to come with me for your own reasons, and I've no business shackling your judgment about how much of yourself you wish to give. I just want you to understand you're perfectly free to withdraw anytime."

"I always have been," she said, realizing he'd never said, *Help me rescue my friends and I'll take you to safety.* He would take her whether she helped or not. She had already won his loyalty, though she still craved it. "But before you accept me into your ventures, I have to confess."

She told him why she had obeyed that soldier, getting him shot. "I might do that again. Outlaw or no, I'm still loyal to the Allegiancy."

He nodded, "I know. But, Krinata, your act was in total accord with your being. No more can be asked of anyone." He rose to go. *If I should die in such an action, I would count myself fortunate indeed. But don't ask me to explain why.*"

NINE

Allegiancy Loyalists

Khol, the Holot's oldest colony, circled a yellow G-2 star. Its five-day long "day" and wildly varying climate suited the six-limbed, furred Holot, though humans shuddered at the necessity of visiting them on the surface.

Therefore, they'd built a commercial space station outside the orbits of their three tiny moons. Arlai figured their approach trajectory to the station while conversing with the system's Orbital Control Central. Krinata had only to sit in the captain's chair and watch.

"Krinata," said Jindigar, seated at the astrogator's console. "It's time to get dressed."

They'd decided Krinata would go as a Terran merchant who'd swung a deal for a surplus ship and was looking for new markets. Thus an interest in souvenir pottery would seem logical. Jindigar would become one of the rare space traveling Lehrtrili, a feathered, birdlike species with vestigial wings and strong territorial instincts.

"I'll go first," she said rising. She was itching to try on her new costume. She'd been working out hard in the gym. She felt vigorous enough to meet any challenge.

Just as she reached the hatch, Trassle announced from the com station, "We've just been switched to military orbit control. They're ordering us out of the ecliptic."

"Arlai, report!" snapped Jindigar.

"A moment . . . there!" The plotting scope projected a globe of dark space representing the system, pinpointing *Truth* and then adding other traffic around them, complete with dotted lines to represent projected orbits.

137

Arlai narrated, "Ahead, starboard, three small passenger craft; lifereadings indicate they're overloaded; power readings show them barely spaceworthy. One—the center one—lacks an onboard Sentient. The other two Sentients seem confused and incompetent.

"Behind," continued Arlai, "eight armed seeker craft in hot pursuit of the three. Their Flag Sentient has ordered us out of the way. I am complying, but retaining interference capability. Jindigar, I really don't want to be targeted by those craft. They are much more than we can handle."

"I can see that," answered Jindigar. His blue teeth gnawed at his bottom lip. "Krinata, you'll need to be dressed soon. Arlai, what species aboard those ships?"

"The fugitives seem to be mostly Dushau, a sprinkling of Holot, and other species aboard. The seekers are shielded. As a wild, intuitive guess: mostly Holot, possibly officers of other species. But the Duke of this zone is Holot."

"Krinata!" Jindigar complained, seeing her still there.

She went, grasping that they were witnessing an escape attempt engineered by the rumored underground resistance. Arlai had intercepted official dispatches to Duke Huch about the growing resistance organization dedicated to harboring Dushau and their sympathizers. Jindigar's plan had been to contact this underground via a descendent of a Holot he'd once known. He was sure they could help him find Terab.

Trassle's wife helped Krinata into her costume, and one of Arlai's servitors applied makeup to change her complexion to match her bleached hair. A dental appliance forced a change in her speech. It might not be authentic Terran, but she could claim to have left Terra early in life.

When she returned to the bridge, Grisnilter was faced off against Jindigar. She sensed she'd walked into a very tense confrontation, but all she heard was Grisnilter's acidic tones, "And what will your mother say about that? You *are* planning to see her again before she dies, aren't you?"

Jindigar lowered his eyes, and started, in a hoarse whisper, "I'm sorry—" Then he spotted Krinata, quickly made some adjustments on the control boards and sped past her as if making an escape. Over his shoulder, he called, "Arlai says we have an hour before the seekers are in range to fire on those vessels. Trassle will fill you in."

She sidled around Grisnilter, not daring to speak to him for fear she'd spit out just what she thought of him for upsetting Jindigar at such a time. If Jindigar could still treat him respectfully, she could manage to remain civil.

As she was taking the captain's seat, Trassle arrived and Grisnilter departed silently. She brought her mind back to their problem. Now that she was properly dressed, they could bluff their way around any challenge, if she could only figure out what to say. The haughty demeanor of Zavaronne wouldn't do. But she could still be a captain, irate at being kept in a solar orbit when she had business to conduct.

In his carefully modulated Standard voice, Trassle told her, "The seekers have been broadcasting orders in the name of the Emperor for the fugitives to take up a standard solar orbit or be blown out of space. The fugitives have not replied, but Arlai has contact with their Sentients that he doesn't believe the seeker's flag Sentient has intercepted."

"Trassle," said Arlai, "you have the paranoia of a merchant. What does it take to convince you I know my job?"

"I'm convinced," said Krinata. "What do the fugitives say?"

"They've got ninety-seven Dushau aboard the three ships, sixty-three Holot, and fifteen of assorted species. They knew fleeing was a desperate gamble, but their headquarters was about to be raided. The city was a shambles around them from the rioting that started when Dushau establishments were looted. They've got two full Oliat teams complete with Outriders, all professionals. They figured they could make a go of it on some marginal planet. The middle ship, though, is heading for Dushaun. It's all Dushau-crewed, and they've elected to try to run the blockade and the defenses."

"But Jindigar said we mustn't try to go to Dushaun."

"He's trying to talk them out of it right now. I wish he'd concentrate on becoming Lehrtrili."

The astrogation projection showed numerous other commercial ships surrounding them in solar orbit perpendicular to the ecliptic. As long as they stayed silent and obeyed the Flag Sentient of that eight-ship fleet, they were anonymous, relatively safe. And she couldn't think of anything they could do to help.

"Krinata!" Arlai registered shock. "Go to Jindigar's cabin. Now!"

"What?" She wasn't accustomed to the Sentient issuing orders. "Is he asking for me? I should stay at my post."

"Please, Krinata!" Arlai seemed to vibrate with suppressed hysteria.

She cast a glance at the slowly changing display, decided there was nothing she had to do here, and took off for Jindigar's cabin with Trassle gazing after her, a high multivoiced twitter escaping him in place of Standard.

She'd never been inside Jindigar's residence before, and she hadn't actually been invited by him this time. She found her heart pounding in an odd cadence with her steps. Her feet seemed to have an embarrassed reluctance of their own, but she finally found the hatch marked "l" in Dushau notation: the owner's cabin. Before she could touch the signal, the hatch flew aside with a pressurized sigh.

It was more apartment than cabin. Hatches opened off the huge main room which was divided by trellis screens, some festooned with plants she couldn't identify. The deck was a spongy white surface which absorbed the sound of her steps. Overhead, odd shapes swung from rafter beams. Stairs led to a kind of loft above the far end of the room, but it was dark up there. The furniture was all dense foam, in the low shapes Dushau favored. Colors and lighting strained her eyes and made little sense.

Arlai materialized under the loft and beckoned. "Here."

Seeing visions of Jindigar unconscious from a nasty fall, she followed hastily.

Beyond the hatch was a room of yellow and pink tile, anonymous projects strewn on workbenches, sinks and a huge bathtub filled with water, plants and fish. Imp sat in a nest on the lip of the tub. When he saw Krinata, he shrieked and flung himself through the air, landing at her feet. Then, remembering his manners, he sat up, begging politely to be picked up and petted. Absently, she complied, eyes roving curiously over Jindigar's private dressing room while she pretended to herself that she was only getting her bearings.

One wall was folded back to reveal a wardrobe. Arlai had surrounded the half-costumed Dushau with three mirror fields. Several small scurries with precision manipulators were applying dark indigo feathers to Jindigar's body. He turned when he heard her steps on the tile.

She didn't like the look in his eyes, but couldn't read his expression for the jutting green beak that covered nose, mouth and chin. The beak opened, showing a slender pink tongue. Jindigar's own voice asked, "What are you doing here, Krinata?"

"I asked her to come," said Arlai from behind her.

"I thought . . ." she started breathlessly. "From Arlai's panic, I thought something awful had happened to you."

Jindigar turned so the scurries could continue to cover and reshape his body. "Arlai," he began as if angry. Then he subsided. "No, you're right. Krinata, Terab is captain of the rearguard ship. Her husband and two of her children are aboard." He turned away from the scurries and came to tower over her. "When you walked onto the bridge, Grisnilter was trying to get me to cut out of orbit and pace the Dushau ship, to follow it home, help them as needed, and forget Terab. I wasn't going to—but now you see what kind of person Terab is. She's rescued herself and dozens of others! Or she would have if their ships were in any better condition. As it is, they're not going to make it, and I'm desperate enough to try a wild plan. Arlai doesn't want to."

"It's suicide!" said the Sentient.

She looked from one to the other. "What's the plan?"

"We develop a malfunction, a real one. Their sensors would detect a fake one. *Truth* is now identified as *Hyperbird*, Zitur registry, and Arlai has a Lehrtrili simulacrum. We careen out of control into the zone between the seekers and the ships. We're legitimate. They dare not fire on us. If we give Terab enough of a lead, she and the other ships can detime before the seekers can get a shot off. Once they're detimed, even seeker craft can't follow them."

"Don't bet on it," said Arlai morosely.

Krinata put that down to the odd emotionality Arlai had shown since Jindigar had freed him. But she also felt his alarm. Holot were notorious for a bull-like pursuit of their goals, disregarding all logical reasons to desist. Yet she wasn't sure Jindigar was wholly rational, considering the pressure Grisnilter was putting on him. *Could it drive him into Renewal?* But she shoved that aside. "Jindigar, do we have the right to make a decision like this without consulting the others?"

"The Dushau won't like it," said Jindigar, "but morally, they can't refuse. Trassle, though, has children aboard. Even though he and his female have known for days we were going to take risks, they may be too Cassrian to be able to say yes now as they did before. Trassle would hate himself forever for yielding to instinct."

"This isn't a risk," said Arlai, "it's a sacrifice. Those are *seeker craft!*"

Krinata said, "I don't know anything about seeker craft except that they're new and highly experimental. But if the Holot have orders to get those fugitives before they can detime, they just might blow us up to get at them. Arlai, couldn't you use your projectors to confuse them?"

"No. Their sensors are too sophisticated."

"Why are you being so defeatist, Arlai?"

"He's scared," said Jindigar. "The Allegiancy programming kept him from experiencing raw fear for so long, his nerves aren't up to it."

"That's part of it," admitted the Sentient. "But I also have the specs of the seeker craft design here, and I know what *Truth*'s made of. We *can't* withstand those guns!"

"You have the seeker craft design?!" exclaimed Krinata.

Sheepishly, the Sentient admitted, "I stole the plans to the Emperor's yacht when we were in orbit at Cassr. Thought it might come in handy. And it's a modified seeker."

"There has to be a way to use those plans to increase our odds to an acceptable level," said Krinata, sweating with sudden nervous tension. "Jindigar, let them dress you. You may yet need that disguise to buy us some time."

Krinata turned and paced, trying to think. Then it came to her. "*Truth*'s landers! Arlai, are the landers disguised as *Hyperbird*'s?"

"Just two of them. I can convert the others—"

"What about the lifeboat from *Intentional Act?*" asked Krinata, suddenly excited. "It's got legitimate Ducal ID. Would they fire on an envoy from Duke Lavov here to trade knowledge of a fatal design flaw in the seeker craft for Dushau prisoners? We swoop in, negotiate a trade, squirt them some nonsense about their ships blowing up if they detime or fire weapons, and assure them we'll catch their fugitives, destroy two of the ships and take the all-Dushau one for the Duke's experiments? If they've heard of our escapade with *Mercer's Folly,* they'll know Lavov would want more Dushau prisoners. It would seem just plausible enough to make them hesitate."

"Why didn't I think of that?" asked Jindigar. "Seekers *have* disappeared mysteriously." The top of his mask had been put in place, so that now his wideset eyes peered awkwardly through close-set beady ones of an evolved predator. "Terab can get them all away in the time we can give them."

Krinata turned to Arlai, sure she knew why Jindigar hadn't been able to think, and trying not to use some of the glowing Skhe invective she'd learned from Rndeel on Grisnilter. "What are the odds on this plan, Arlai?"

The simulacrum blinked. "Sixty-three percent chance of success if I could find a design flaw."

"Fake one," said Krinata.

"I can't do that!" objected Arlai, offended. He was an on-board Sentient. Ships were sacred to him.

Some part of Krinata was relieved she'd found some skulduggery forbidden to the Sentient. Jindigar came to the rescue. "I can, and I can order you to use the misinformation. Arlai, it won't harm them. I'll see to that."

"Agreed," said the simulacrum. "I've already started stripping the lifeboat of its *Mercer's Folly* ID. It'll be a diplomatic skiff at least from the outside. What next?"

Krinata said, "I'll go back to the bridge, warn Trassle and prepare to become Duke Lavov's envoy. Jindigar will finish dressing and figure out a plausible design flaw."

"Good enough," agreed Jindigar. He seemed steadier now, so she handed him the piol, spun on her heel and left.

Forty minutes later, Jindigar's Lehrtrili persona, Rrrelloleh, came onto the bridge, twittering musically, vestigial wings fluttering expressively. He was wearing a translater voder on his bright red chest. Most of him was dark indigo feathers, though wings and crown were bright yellow. It was the last color combination the fugitive Prince Jindigar would ever choose to hide himself.

Arlai had warned the resistance ships to be prepared to detime the moment they were free, but Jindigar had ordered him not to give them the details of the plan just in case communications weren't really secure.

As they were going over the plan one more time before breaking their assigned orbit and calling attention to themselves, Rinperee, lightning calculator and Sentient educator, came onto the bridge. She stopped to bend over Rrrelloleh and whisper, "Don't pay too much attention to Grisnilter. We'll make it." Then she stood up and said, "Arlai, let me handle our maneuvers. This may take a little more creativity than you've got."

"Agreed. You've got primary control on board nine." That was the helm station next to Jindigar's astrogation console and would be out of line when Krinata was on screen.

Since Arlai could run the ship alone, Krinata had often wondered why the bridge was rigged for incarnate supervision at all. Now she knew. Arlai was better than any Sentient at routine chores, or backing up a plan. But he wasn't a planner, and he knew it. She began really to trust him.

"Standby," said Arlai in his ship's business tone. Then he proclaimed, "The Duke Lavov's Envoy, The Right Honorable Katherine Minogue!"

There was a suitable drum roll, short of ambassadorial rank but more than a mere messenger would get. She claimed no title and wore only a simple black tunic with silver piping,

indicating space service, retired. Arlai had aged her face and
toned her hair more toward gray. She spoke in her lowest
register when the screen image cleared to show a crisp military
bridge, Holot officers dripping braid and honors bending over
the scopes and controls.

They looked around shocked as she came onto their main
screen. "I am breaking orbit," she announced. "Do not fire
upon my craft. I bring information vital to your security."

From the side, one of the officers called, "Captain, one of
the civilians is moving in. It's discharged something."

"My personal skiff. I carry diplomatic immunity."

The com officer confirmed, reading out the Ducal ID with
some frills Arlai had improvised. The captain was impressed.

The lifeboat was actually empty, but Arlai had arranged for
it to appear as if their communication was coming from there,
complete with emanating lifereadings.

"Captain," continued Krinata before the Holot could say
anything, "I regret it's taken me so long to understand what
this scene is all about, but my sensors have just discerned that
the center one of those three passenger ships is loaded with
nothing but Dushau. Duke Lavov knew you must have some
Dushau left on Khol, and he sent me to trade with you. It
seems I've arrived in the nick of time." She was inordinately
proud when she thought of using that Terranism.

The captain drew himself up on his hind feet, leaving all
four upper limbs to dance over the controls before him. "State
your business, Right Honorable Envoy. We are not empowered
to treat with diplomatic . . ."

She cut him off with a wave. "I've come to trade news of
a design flaw in the seeker craft for some of your surplus
Dushau. If you fire on those ships, chances are three-to-two
you'll blow up your own ship. If you want that information,
yield your fleeing prisoners to me. I'll see none escape."

"Your ship is old, Envoy."

"They are unarmed passenger *crates!* Do not insult Duke
Lavov's honor."

"I'd never!" the Holot gibbered.

Krinata had never heard a Holot gibber. She marveled, but

kept a straight face and declared, "Let us conclude our business then, before we both lose them."

"I'm not actually empowered to—"

"Are you empowered to commit suicide?"

"No, but..."

"Then certify your prisoners to the custody of The Right Honorable Katherine Minogue, signing for Duke Lavov. Do it via your Sentient. By the time you can take my skiff aboard, the prisoners will have escaped you. I must authorize my vessel to give chase and tow the Dushau back. I understand they lack an onboard Sentient. All you could do is destroy them. We can capture them. I shall clear up any difficulties with your superiors when I arrive."

The captain consulted with his bridge crew, the sound transmission off. Then he turned back to her, saying into a loud silence, "I agree to a simultaneous exchange of data. I will send the authorization to take custody of our prisoners. You will send details of this design flaw you claim can destroy us. If my Sentient decides your data is spurious, she will not complete the transmission, and we will blow your ship out of space."

"Agreed," snapped Krinata. But her mouth was dry.

Arlai announced, "Exchange begun." Almost immediately, he added, "Exchange completed."

Truth had already committed to pursuit of their quarry. The flag seeker craft was diverting to meet the empty skiff. Suddenly, the screen and scope images blurred, rippling as the three ships detimed in dangerously close formation.

Krinata slumped. The ships were free. There was no way to track a ship through a warp. Now for their own escape.

"After them!" said Rrrelloleh through his voder.

"Steady, Arlai...now!" Rinperee's nailless indigo fingers stroked the board and *Truth* detimed.

The screens showed rippling fog as always in the nowhere of untime. But there were three flecks amid the clouds. Arlai whispered, "By all the gods of time, she did it!"

Rinperee had indeed tracked the three fugitives into untime. They apparently spotted the pursuit and in an attempt to lose them, retimed. Arlai barely grunted a warning before Rinperee's fingers moved and *Truth* dropped back into normal space beside the fugitives.

Instantly, the screen lit with a very dark Dushau. "We refuse to surrender to Duke Lavov's laboratories!"

Jindigar rose and came up behind Krinata removing both halves of his mask and dropping back into his own character. "Thellarue, we're not from Lavov."

"Jindigar?" His cautious wonder was almost comic after the searing tension. "But Kamminth's . . . I thought Arlai . . ."

Jindigar said in grief-wrenched tones, "I am the only survivor."

In Thellarue's agonized silence, Trassle asked, "You know each other?"

Aside to Trassle, Jindigar said, "Thellarue's Oliat has been trying to enlist me for many years." Then he asked the Dushau, "You're Dissolved?"

"Adjourned," corrected Thellarue. "We're in need of a first-class Emulator. You'd be welcomed."

Krinata saw Jindigar fight off temptation. He was Oliat, through and through, raw from recent loss. His wanting glowed in his swirling indigo eyes. But he answered, steadily, "I'm flattered, but I have other obligations."

Thellarue only nodded. "As always. I can only wait a little while longer, Jindigar."

He inspected his feathered hands. "I know." It was almost a groan. But he covered the ache by speaking crisply to Arlai. "Can you get the other two ships on conference?"

As the screen split, Krinata saw the other bridge crews included several Dushau also, and muttered shock spread among them at sight of Jindigar. Thellarue cut them off, asking, "Arlai, why didn't you tell us you had Jindigar aboard?"

"His name is not to be mentioned where it might be overheard. I was sure I had a secure signal, but he wasn't."

"We got away with it, and that's what counts," said Jindigar. "Thellarue, you *can't* go back to Dushaun now. If you breach the defense perimeter, the Allegiancy can attack."

Quietly, gravely, the old Dushau said, "We have young in third Renewal. We're going home."

Jindigar subsided. Krinata watched him face some sort of

hopeless problem. Dushau, she knew, went home for Renewal. But she didn't know it was so important they'd risk letting hostile ships inside their planetary defenses.

A Holot female on one of the other ships said into the silence, "It really *is* Jindigar!"

His attention riveted to her. "Yes, Terab. You've done a very courageous thing."

"We may not yet survive to be called courageous."

It was only then that Krinata noticed the frantic activity in the background on Terab's ship. "Status report!" snapped Jindigar.

Arlai ran a dense line of symbols across the bottom of the screen, saying, "I'm helping their Sentient cope with it all, but frankly, another detiming might be their last."

Thellarue said, "These ships are indeed 'crates' as your Lady Minogue put it. We've no onboard Sentient to help them detime, and *Inrinan*'s Sentient can't function outboard."

Jindigar surveyed the bridge crew of the third ship. "Where are you planning to go? Phanphihy?"

A Dushau female edged a human aside and leaned into the screen. "I'm Sopehan, Kithlinpor's Outreach." She spoke with the distant stiffness Krinata associated with a working Outreach. "We have young Treptian females aboard. Phanphihy would be too dangerous for them. We've elected to search, and so Kithlinpor's remains constituted and balanced."

"I understand," said Jindigar, but Krinata did not. She'd never heard of Phanphihy, and Treptian females were notoriously tough. Their mild telepathic abilities often gave them an edge in dealing with wild animals—or people.

Terab said, "Our Oliat suggested a place called Phanphihy, but we haven't been able to take a vote on it yet. There are those who feel the two ships ought to stick together. If you'll join us, instead of going to Dushaun . . ."

"My destination must be Phanphihy."

Phanphihy, Krinata concluded, must be the planet Jindigar had promised would be their sanctuary. It seemed other Dushau also knew about it. Or maybe only other Oliat officers. All these people seemed to know each other. It didn't mean there was some general Dushau conspiracy. They probably used Phanphihy to teach Oliat apprentices to judge commercially valueless planets.

Thellarue was talking. "I still urge you to return to Dushaun with me. As my Emulator, you'd be able to surmount all the old difficulties."

Jindigar said something very softly in an old Dushauni dialect that sounded like a plea for mercy.

Krinata spoke up. "Perhaps we should all take time to hold a vote. We should be safe here for long enough, and it *would* be best if we could all stay together."

Jindigar turned to her. "Before we head out of Allegiancy-controlled space, I must yet contact four Lehiroh to whom I'm deeply indebted. They are experienced Oliat Outriders and will increase our chances of survival enormously. So next, *Truth* goes to Razum Two."

"We could set up a rendezvous," suggested Krinata.

Thellarue broke in. "You all have crucial decisions to make, but we are already determined. Let us bid you farewell."

"No, wait!" said Jindigar. "We have an onboard Sentient you can have. She should increase your chances of success."

"You have a what?" Thellarue interrupted.

But he was interrupted in turn by Arlai. "Thirlein? Jindigar, you mustn't!"

"It's not certain death, Arlai. With Thellarue aboard, they've a chance. And if they had a Sentient, too, it could make the difference."

"How could you—" started Thellarue.

Jindigar outlined how they'd come by Thirlein's core. "But she's in disconnection shock, and I'm not at all certain she'll be stable. And she's not really mine to give."

Grisnilter appeared in a wedge of screen between two of the ship's bridges. "We've discussed it, and if Rinperee agrees— and if you have a Sentient psychoengineer aboard—we'd be willing to let her go. That is, unless she objects."

After some discussion it was decided that the Dushau ship

would grapple to *Truth* and Arlai would help install and waken Thirlein under the care of Rinperee and several experts aboard the Dushau ship. Meanwhile, the passengers and crews of *Truth* and the other two ships would debate their options and decide on destinations. If they decided on different courses, people could transfer to the ships they preferred.

Krinata took time to divest herself of her disguise, then sat in on a meeting of all concerned via Arlai's holo display in her own room.

When she saw a group of humans aboard Terab's ship, pioneers by their dress and accents, she wavered in her determination to stay aboard *Truth* with Jindigar. Being the only human suddenly seemed a cold, bleak prospect indeed.

She leaped into the discussion, arguing Jindigar's expertise and fine judgment, to get at least some of the humans to transfer to *Truth*, if none of the other ships elected Phanphihy. They were overcrowded, and *Truth* had room. But she only attracted one very young Dushau who'd heard what a fine Oliat trainer Jindigar was so he wanted to transfer to *Truth* if Jindigar would train him and two other Dushau who preferred Phanphihy to planet hunting.

All the crew and passengers took an hour to discuss it among themselves, and then registered their votes with Arlai. Krinata came close to saying she'd go with the rest of the humans, regardless of where they were going. But in the end, she stayed with *Truth*. The final tally showed *Inrinan* still determined to prospect for their own planet, and Terab's ship throwing in with *Truth* to go to Phanphihy though they wouldn't accompany them to Razum Two. There were dissenters on each ship who wanted to transfer.

"I believe," said Arlai when Krinata asked, "Terab's ship has a larger percentage of people who know Jindigar personally or by reputation. The outsystem humans, for example, were colonists on a world Kamminth's implanted just after Jindigar balanced them."

Krinata was relieved in more ways than she could count. They wouldn't be stray refugees on their new world. They'd have a constituted Oliat to read the ecology for them, find them a good living site and identify edibles, medicinals, and poisons right off. *What unbelievable luck!*

As the dissenters were packing up and changing ships, she went to the locking bay where the Dushau ship was connected to *Truth* by a walkthrough. Here the air was redolent with Dushau body odor, something she'd never noticed before. Dark and light indigo bodies filled the space, most tensed over precision tasks. She supposed the scent was nervous perspiration. She needed a shower herself.

Scurries interposed themselves everywhere, Arlai's servitors going into the Dushau ship with full cargo loads, and coming out with nothing. Jindigar was donating supplies and parts Arlai had stockpiled for their exile.

It was just like him. They were his people despite any friction among them. Suddenly, she wanted to see him, to tell him the outcome of the vote and watch his face. She worked her way into the densely packed crowd, hardly noticing she was the only Ephemeral.

But apparently someone did notice and a commotion erupted near the walkthrough hatch. Several Dushau turned, calling urgently to those around and behind. Others gathered and retreated swiftly through the walkthrough. Then everyone seemed to relax, and a male came up to her.

"Katherine Minogue?"

"Actually, I'm Krinata Zavaronne, a friend of Jindigar."

"Krinata Zavaronne, the one who devised the plan?" A sudden wary awe suffused the indigo features, and it seemed to Krinata that the nap on his face stood up. She'd never seen that in a Dushau before.

"I was just looking for Jindigar."

"If you'll wait here, I'll find him for you." With that, he strode away into the walkthrough.

That was how Dushau often earned a reputation for species prejudice. They could be abrupt and inhospitable. Telling herself she could locate Jindigar herself, she was about to follow when she remembered these Dushau were going to run a blockade and risk breaching their only home's defenses because they had three "youngsters" in Renewal. No Ephemeral, except perhaps Terab, had ever seen a Dushau in Renewal. Though she'd searched the archives diligently, she'd never been able to find a reason for this.

Shortly, a Dushau female approached Krinata. "Jindigar has asked me to bring you to him."

Curious, she followed the short, slender Dushau up a ramp and through cramped corridors into a Sentient's core room. Jindigar's feathered legs were protruding from an open access panel, and his voice boomed as he requested various tools. Across the room, Rinperee and several others worked over exposed circuitry, muttering together and occasionally calling, "Thirlein, can you hear now?"

It looked like the work would go on forever, so she wandered off to one side to wait. As she was examining the instrumentation near the door, Grisnilter came in, spotted the feathered legs and made for Jindigar. She didn't like the expression on the elder's face.

She stepped in front of him, stopping him in his tracks. "With great and elaborate respect, Sir Grisnilter, I must beg you not to disturb Jindigar right now."

She thought she sounded civil enough, but the older Dushau looked at her as if she had crawled out of something damp. "Did he instruct you to say that to me?"

"No." And then she hit flashpoint. She knew her temper was out of control by the way her teeth refused to part to let her words out. "I just thought you ought to know that your hysterical meddling almost cost all of us our lives. You don't have the sense of an Éphemeral adolescent if you think you can get away with picking a fight with him right before a ticklish operation and still expect him to be witty, clever and clear-headed enough to cope with all emergencies! We're not out of this yet, so if you expect your fellow Dushau to survive to get home, you'd better just take yourself . . ." She swallowed the obscenity and finished, "off this ship!"

She suddenly noticed an intense silence had fallen. Everyone was looking at them. Jindigar's voice boomed, "Now!" After a long pause, Thirlein's voice burst upon them, a wail of pain and terror. Someone turned the volume down, while others began talking soothingly to Thirlein. One Dushau female in a greasy coverall helped Jindigar out of the access hole, saying, "Beautifully done! I thought it impossible—"

Jindigar hugged the woman absently, eyes riveted on Krinata and Grisnilter squared off and the center of attention. Absently, he muttered to the Dushau woman, "Comes from battering about the galaxy in an antique. Let me know if Thirlein decides to stay with you."

Jindigar came over to them. Grisnilter eyed his smudged and unkempt appearance, and said, without a trace of apology, "I'm sorry. I didn't intend to upset you."

Jindigar put a hand on the frail shoulder, and said in a quiet, intimate tone, "It's all right. I understand."

Krinata's face felt flaming hot, but she stood her ground. Grisnilter made a defeated gesture and left. Jindigar looked after him, worried. Then he pulled himself back and turned to Krinata. "What are you doing here?"

Krinata outlined the results of the vote, ending, "So there's a Dushau looking for you to ask you to train him, and Arlai says *Truth*'s ready to go as soon as you're finished."

"You had to come *here* to tell me *this?*"

She pulled herself up and pronounced, "I apologize. I wanted to help." She turned on her heel and marched toward one of the hatches, though she wasn't sure where it led.

Jindigar caught up with her and took her elbow. But despite the strain he'd been under, there was no body odor. "This way," he said, steering through another hatch, his long legs eating the distance so she had to stride to keep up.

"We're not in that much of a hurry," she protested.

He slowed, saying tightly, "I've got to get you out of here before you cause another incident."

Tired, fighting the gravity and the lighting, nerves shredded, she suddenly couldn't cope. "If it bothers you that much, I'll go move my things onto Terab's ship!" She wrenched free and stalked away from him.

He caught up with her near the walkthrough and pulled her to a stop. They were blocking traffic, and she was conscious of curious stares swiftly averted. In a hoarse whisper pitched just to her ears, he pled, "Don't, Krinata. I only meant that I must protect those in Renewal here. We're all under a lot of stress."

"Haven't you ever heard the theory that stress brings out the true person?"

"That may be for humans. Not for Dushau." He raked the indigo crowd around them with a glance. Krinata noticed the odor again as he escorted her through into *Truth*.

As he hustled her along, she asked, "Does being human mean being socially unacceptable? Or is it just socially unacceptable to stand up to Grisnilter?"

Staring straight ahead, he breathed grimly, "Sometimes being Dushau means being socially unacceptable!"

Through his light touch on her arm, she noticed a faint tremor; not the same as when she'd come to him in the imperial antechamber, nor the suppressed fear she'd felt before. This was different.

Curious, she let him steer her to his own cabin. When they were alone in the large living area, he motioned her to a seat. "Let me talk to this Oliat trainee, and then I'll do what I can to explain. Don't leave yet. Please."

He went into the tiled room, leaving the hatch slightly ajar. Under the sound of rushing water, she heard a swift conversation in modern Dushauni. What she caught of it sounded like a job interview crossed with a character probe. She listened, trying not to think that he might want nothing to do with her after what she'd said to Grisnilter. Her mother had always told her that her imagination and her temper would be the end of her.

Through the fretting of her own thoughts, she heard Frey, the young Oliat trainee, answer a question, "Yes, I've heard *all* your reputation. Is it true?"

"Yes," answered Jindigar.

"You're one of the most experienced Oliat officers still working. You could not have survived so long, or still be welcomed by Thellarue, if you hadn't learned to respect the power of Oliat—in all of its manifestations."

The word the youngster used for power had a half dozen other meanings Krinata had never quite grasped. She'd once thought "magic" might be one possible translation, but no glossary listed it. She'd never considered that an Oliat had power that had to be respected, the way one respected the power of a weapon. Yes, that was the connotation: the Oliat was a weapon to be respected. *I wonder what Rantan would make of that idea?*

When Jindigar returned, dressed in a crisp white ship's uniform, he shoved a low cushion up beside her couch and sat cross-legged in his whule-playing position. "I apologize. I should not have been so abrupt with you. Forgive?"

He was so contrite, she said, "I have to apologize for what I said to Grisnilter."

"What exactly did you say?" He seemed wary.

She told him, verbatim. His face was a study in flavors of amazement. "Krinata, *why?*"

"I lost my temper. And I'm going to tell him so."

"Not soon, I'm afraid. Arlai just told me he's had another episode. He's not well, Krinata."

Arlai projected his simulacrum and apologized for interrupting. "I have those test results now, Jindigar. It's definite. He won't renew again, but he may have twenty or thirty years left. I'm sorry."

Jindigar put his face in his hands and dismissed Arlai..

"Oh, Jindigar, I'm sorry. I didn't know." An idea blossomed, and before she could think, she blurted, "He isn't your father, is he?"

He looked up startled. "No. Of course not. My father was designated King, remember? And he's much younger than Grisnilter." He sighed.

"If he's ill, why doesn't he go home with the others? Perhaps there, they could find a way to trigger Renewal."

"Krinata, that ship carries dozens of Renewals, or those close enough to be affected by those in Renewal. Grisnilter would be every bit as difficult for them to deal with as you would. And there's no point. There's no cure for old age."

Now she put her head in her hands. "I'm sorry. I didn't realize he was so ill. Jindigar, when I saw him heading for you, I thought he was going to start in on you right there in public. If he'd made you fumble that connection and accidentally kill Thirlein . . ."

He plucked at his hands where traces of the adhesive from the costume still showed. "He probably *was* planning to start on me again." He gazed at her, measuringly. "There was a woman, an old friend, near Renewal. She wanted me to go home with her. It hurt to say no, but I had to. Then I found out Grisnilter had put her up to it because she, like him, believes my association with so many Ephemerals is a sign of deep unbalance. Grisnilter saw me refuse Thellarue's offer and I'm sure he figured I was ready to leave Oliat behind at last. He expected me to take her home and train as an Historian, show everyone I've finally come to my senses. But he's a colleague of my mother, was her mate once, and so I have to be polite while he tries to do his duty to my family."

She was beginning to see dimensions of their situation she hadn't considered. With a trace of resentment, she said, "If you'd told me that to begin with, I wouldn't have —"

He made an exasperated gesture. "Krinata, if I told you a tenth of what's involved, it would take longer than you have to live. All of this happened while you were voting!"

She'd already lost her temper once today, and she wasn't going to again. But she had one more question. Jindigar had been increasingly emotionally unstable lately. The stress of their escapades plus Grisnilter could have caused it. But it could be something else. Bluntly, and without preamble, she asked, "When will you go into Renewal?"

His wideset indigo eyes flicked aside. "I don't know. It's been eleven hundred and fourteen years since my last Renewal. That's long, but not absurdly so at my age. If we can get that ship on its way, and I have time to calm down and get over all that's happened, then it could be another fifty to a hundred years." Wistfully, he added, "Or I could have gone with them and let it happen now."

"What you're saying is that you're planning to go through Renewal away from Dushaun."

He picked at the adhesive on his hands. "As it is, I've no choice. But, given our current situation, I probably won't survive a hundred years and have to face it."

"Is that why you're willing to take suicidal chances?" She thought of his original plan for dealing with the seeker craft, and Arlai's reaction. Surely the Sentient understood Jindigar's position better than Krinata did.

His hands stilled as his eyes bored into hers. "Do you really think I'm taking suicidal chances?"

She felt a terrible weight of responsibility fall upon her. She reviewed everything she'd seen him do.

"Because if you do, Krinata, then I really *must* go home with them, despite everything."

She could see that he did not *want* to go home, but was suddenly afraid his reluctance was unsane. Dushau, she reminded herself, couldn't survive eroded sanity. "Isn't that the sort of question you should ask a fellow Dushau?"

He wilted, as if facing a doom. "You may be right."

She was suddenly overcome with compassion. "No, I don't think you're really trying to kill yourself to avoid facing something unpleasant. I really believe your obligations are your true motives. In an Ephemeral, it would be considered perfectly sane to be totally dedicated to saving other people's lives, even at risk of your own. And I've never read that cowardice was a Dushau trait."

His silence was broken by a vibrating thump. Jindigar eyed the direction of the Dushau ship. "They're away. Arlai, did they take Thirlein?"

"Yes. When she got her bearings, she was delighted. She's looking forward to going home." There was a wistfulness in his voice.

"Are Frey and the other two new passengers aboard yet?"

"Yes. Everyone is set. *Inrinan* asks permission to detime, and Terab says, 'Good luck, and I'll see you soon.'"

"If it's safe, give *Inrinan* permission, and tell them I hope they find a good planet." He rose, as did Krinata.

"Thellarue says, 'Hurry home.' They've detimed."

Jindigar instructed, "Tell Terab to wait. Krinata, will you stay with me? I'm not asking you to endanger yourself—"

She felt the pressure of final decision once more, though her mind was made up to stay if he'd let her. But in the next moment, it all became academic.

Arlai interrupted Jindigar to announce, "I've lost touch with Terab. She has de—"

A shockwave rippled through *Truth*. Krinata fell into Jindigar, knocking him to the deck and sprawling on top of him.

A bank of viewscreens on one side of the room brightened to incandescence, and Krinata rolled into a ball to protect her eyes. She felt the soft nap of Jindigar's skin as he rolled over, his body protecting hers as if he expected an explosion. Then he was on hands and knees, rising to charge out of the room, demanding, "What happened?"

"Terab's engines blew when she attempted to detime," answered Arlai in his professional test-pilot-in-trouble voice. "Some of their pods are away, no lifeboats, though."

As Krinata reached the corridor hatch, looking both ways for sign of Jindigar, Trassle streaked by and she plastered herself against the bulkhead to avoid his sharp claw-hands. Then she followed him.

She knew nothing about space rescue, was clumsy in null-grav, and, after her brief exposure in Arlai's walkthrough tube, was a budding deep-space phobe. But she did know some passenger ships were designed to blow apart into airtight "pods" in a major accident. If the hatches sealed fast enough, and if another ship collected the ship fragments soon enough, it was possible some of the passengers might survive.

She wasn't going to let Jindigar go out there alone.

TEN

Lehiroh Wedding

The landing bay was open to space. Krinata followed Jindigar into the airlock suit-room and snatched a suit from the rack. Hers had been abandoned on *Intentional Act*.

"Krinata," objected Jindigar, struggling into his own suit, "you can't go out there! Even in the tube, you had difficulty."

"Never mind that. I'm going."

Arlai's voice could be heard, terse and harried, from inside Jindigar's helmet which lay at his feet. He picked up the helmet and said, "She's *not* going!"

But there was no reply. He shook the helmet in frustration, but there was no further word from Arlai. "I think Arlai's reached his capacity fending off those chunks of spaceship while mounting the rescue and fighting to hold our position despite the turbulence from the explosion."

"Look, even Arlai said I'm needed," she guessed. "So I'm going." She stared perplexedly at a stubborn fitting.

He plucked the suit off her shoulder, saying, "This isn't adjusted for a human. Take suit number five. But you'll have to do your own check. Arlai's too busy. Remember what I taught you?"

"Sure," she said confidently, and struggled to recall the first time she'd suited up. It seemed years ago, but once started, she had no difficulty going through the checklist, matching it to one engraved on the wall beside the suit's hook. She believed Arlai had hit critical load, for the lights and gravity didn't change around her as she moved.

Inside the suit wasn't much better, but she was distracted fighting down memories of that instant of stark terror she'd felt in the transparent walkthrough tube. The one Arlai had used to connect the Dushau ship had been opaque. Now she was going to be floating free in bottomless space. She cursed her imagination and did her best to turn it off, focusing on what those poor people in the pods were going through. Her own plight faded to insignificance beside that.

Krinata followed Jindigar, Trassle, and two Dushau who seemed to know what they were doing into the hard vacuum in the bay. Anchored with cables, she watched the experienced spacehands mounting lines and grapples on powered scooters.

Arlai's tractor beams had captured several of the pods. Other pods were receding from the center of the explosion. As she watched them tumble against the infinite backdrop of distant stars, which she tried to ignore, she saw several of the ship-sections had been torn in half, furnishings and bodies dribbling out into space. Others had been crushed. Scorched and melted debris floated everywhere.

Her breath caught in her throat and she clenched down hard over her gorge. As soon as three scooters were ready, the two Dushau mounted together. Trassle and Jindigar took seats alone. Krinata mounted the saddle behind Jindigar.

His voice came over the headset, tinny and small. "You should stay and help guide them in."

"Arlai can do that." Already, it seemed all the scurries Arlai owned swarmed inside the open bays or on the hide of *Truth*, preparing to receive space junk, and wounded flesh. "Let me help," she pled.

"No use arguing with you!" he conceded, and kicked the scooter to life.

It's about time you noticed that.

They swooped over the lip of the landing bay and targeted a pod, Arlai guiding them with intermittent and distracted attention, as if he were a juggler keeping too many objects in the air at once.

"This one first," said Arlai. "It's losing pressure."

They clanked onto a piece of ship's hull, Jindigar expertly catching a bossing with his towline, totally ignoring Krinata. There was a long, complex exchange with Arlai as Jindigar seated three more towlines, then the Dushau was back on the scooter, perfunctorily checking Krinata's seat belt, saying, "We're going to give a towing burn now, then go to the next one while this one drifts in."

Without apparent effort, Jindigar aligned their scooter's heavy-duty engines, and at Arlai's count, gave it maximum thrust. She could hardly see any change, but Arlai was satisfied, briskly dispatching them to the next fragment.

Krinata caught sight of *Ephemeral Truth*, her first glimpse of it from space. Since they were in deep space, not orbiting a sun, spotlights were aimed at the places where scooters worked, and dimmer running lights adorned the sleek, flat shape with its streamlined bulges and open cargo bays. The Allegiancy didn't build spaceships for beauty anymore. She had to blink away a tear, understanding why Jindigar's voice always held a note of affection when he called *Truth* an antique.

On their next pod, Jindigar admitted he could use help, and showed her how to place the towlines. And on the following one, he had her hold the scooter steady while he circled the pod looking for an unbroken bossing. The free-fall flights between fragments increased as they all receded from the center of the explosion. At last, they came to a large pod Arlai said held at least one living human.

"Krinata, think you can seat these lines while I anchor the big ones?"

"No problem," she said, trying to sound competent. She'd kept the fear at bay by concentrating on learning the job, not allowing her eyes to stray from objects immediately in front of her: her panel of indicators, *Truth* itself, the nearby pod, or the back of Jindigar's suit during the long flights between pods. People's lives depended on her not losing her nerve or making mistakes through haste. In her old job, thousands of lives had depended on her decisions about the safety of a planet. In that respect, this really wasn't all that different. It just happened faster. And she'd always told herself she had what it took to cope with life or death emergencies. She was going to be a colonist after all.

They both dismounted, and Jindigar fussed with the scooter's controls until he was sure it would stay put. Then he fired his suit thruster to take him off to the edge of the pod. She took the smaller lines and nudged herself onto the surface of the pod, searching for intact bossings. She found the one she needed and anchored and tested her line. The second line was no more difficult. *At least there are no imperial troops shooting at us.*

What she'd faced in the last few weeks made the current job seem like a performance in a nice, safe gym. Feeling cramped, she stretched, arching her back, and caught sight of the canopy of stars. With no ship or ship's fragment in sight, it was a bottomless well beneath/around/within her. She gasped. Spellbound, she forgot about safety lines and towlines, for she saw a multibranched lightning tree etch itself between stars. She saw planets energized to life by that primordial lightning. Beyond the edge of perception, she heard the soul-vibrating hum made by the stars orbiting galaxy-center, pushing their way through the void, dragging planets and clouds of charged particles with them.

Each star created a note of a different pitch, each orbiting planet added a note to that pitch to make a chord of transcendent beauty.

And it was beauty that drew her. Annoyed with being held back, she pulled her boots free of the pod's skin and pushed off, falling into starry nothingness, suddenly wanting to engulf it all within her body.

Her very identity dissolved, and she knew only eternities of time and the infinity of space. The meaning of the tangible beyond the real seemed self-evident; she felt she could reach out to touch God.

Wisdom beckoned, tantalizing, just beyond the limits of knowledge, and she knew in a moment she'd understand all. She freed herself of all restrictions and pursued perfection that was the purpose of life itself.

"Krinata?" It was a tiny voice, easily ignored.

"Krinata! Krinata!" The louder noises washed through her meaninglessly. She fled into the beyond.

"She's slipped her line!"

"You'll never catch her, Jindigar. You don't have enough burn-time in your tank."

Meaningless noise. Beyond, truth called seductively.

Anger-fraught curses in a familiar indigo voice. "I knew

better than to allow an epistemological loose in space."

"Don't be ridiculous, Jindigar. She's just a human! Arlai, don't let him go!"

"Here's your trajectory, but you won't have fuel or air to get back."

"Mail them to me!"

And a roar filled Krinata's ears. She let it blank out all the little meaningless voices so she could hear truth.

Flying wholeheartedly into the depths of forever, she chased the tantalizing hints, sure that in the next instant, or now the next, she'd know how the universe was constructed. She couldn't believe she'd been afraid to come out here.

Something smashed into her, jarring her view, and for a moment she thought enlightenment had arrived. But everything went black. No stars. Tears burned her eyes. She sniffed.

"Got her!"

"We can barely hear you. I'm launching."

"Krinata, hang on. Help's coming."

She nestled into the dark, boring within for the answers denied from without. It was too beautiful to risk losing. Someone whimpered, but she couldn't offer comfort just yet.

It was hot. She was sweating, claustrophobic. Panting. But the colors were fascinating, shimmering blotches that dissolved into nothing and meant everything.

Some barely conscious part of her mind realized she was dying, suffocating, but her only regret was that she'd lost her one chance to know what she'd been searching for all her life.

The last thing she remembered was a jarring smash that seemed hard enough to break bones. But she felt no pain.

"I've got it, Arlai! Good work. We'll be right home."

And the room was bright, perfumed with flowers and delicious food aromas. It was nice to wake up in the morning on *Truth*. Arlai knew how to please.

Then she remembered space. Her eyes flew open, and she gaped at the Dushau and Trassle. "Damn! Sickbay again!"

Jindigar was grinning. "See, I told you she'd make it."

Arlai's simulacrum bent anxiously over the bed. "Krinata, I'm sorry. It was all my fault!"

Feeling ridiculously rational considering the thoughts she

remembered believing, she said, "Nonsense, Arlai. I forgot how dangerous it is out there. I got distracted—"

"Because," added Arlai firmly, "I had your oxy-nitro pressure set all wrong for a human, and you went into raptures. You've been depressurized. No permanent damage."

She was weak, and she hurt all over. She didn't want to argue. "Did we save any lives?"

"Arlai insists we collected everyone who survived the blast. We only saved four of the humans. Some of the others are in critical condition." Jindigar sighed. "Terab and her mate are fine, but their children died. Of the Oliat, only one, Desdinda, survived. I'm not sure she's going to make it. I'm not sure she *wants* to. Frey is with her, for what good it will do. There's no one left who's zunre to her. It was her first Oliat, only her second office."

It crashed in on her. Savagely, she crushed the blanket in her fists and tried to tear it apart. "It *was* a *crate!* Oh, why did they take a chance on that ship? Why?"

"They were desperate," said Jindigar. "And some of them have survived. Sleep now, Krinata. Razum is only a few days away. And then all of this will be behind us."

A Dushau's idea of a "few days" was markedly different from a human's. Krinata had all the bedrest she could use, and time to get her strength back working out in the gym.

With all the new passengers, many of them in dire medical condition, Arlai was still working at capacity. The entire ship held the indefinable tang of "hospital," and Arlai no longer took time to chat with her, though he never slighted her necessities. Occasionally, however, the ship's lighting and gravity didn't adjust as she walked into a room. When Arlai apologized, she brushed him off. "I'm fine. Concentrate on those who really need you."

Gradually, she began seeing the newcomers creeping up and down the hallways in dressing gowns, surrounded by their own light and gravity as required. She longed to strike up acquaintances, but every overture she made seemed to be met by some odd combination of diffidence and distance.

As a last resort, she gravitated toward Desdinda and her inseparable companion, Frey. Frey treated her indifferently, but Desdinda was frosty. Krinata chalked that up to shock of Dissolution and tried harder to get through to her until one day, she walked right into a confrontation between Frey, Desdinda and Jindigar.

As Krinata emerged from her room, Jindigar was streaking by, Frey in hot pursuit, pleading reasonably, "But it would be the best thing for her. Even without the full Oliat, a triad subform can..."

Jindigar, too far beyond her door to notice Krinata, rounded on the boy. "Desdinda doesn't have the talent, nor the strength, nor the training." He spat out some old Dushauni interjection, and added softly, venting his frustration, "*Krinata* has more Oliat talent than Desdinda!"

But the Dushau woman caught up with them at that point, and stopped short, pulling herself up into a statuesque poise so perfectly centered her indignation seemed to make the very deck vibrate. Jindigar's eye lit on Krinata just as Desdinda declared to Jindigar, "*I* wouldn't balance an Oliat or any subform of yours. I'll never be zunre to an Aliom priest turned Invert! And if you ever touch Grisnilter's archive, I'll... I'll..." She sputtered to a halt, unable to think of an action extreme enough. Then, following Jindigar's gaze, she found Krinata standing openly in the shaftway.

Her face went cold. Her eyes returned to Jindigar, and she uttered one, oddly inflected Dushauni word. Uninflected, it was the term for meat or food, but this sounded like an epithet. Jindigar received that as if it were a slap. Desdinda gathered up the skirt of her yellow hospital robe, turned and stalked away without a backward glance.

Frey was staring at Krinata. Jindigar said softly, "Arlai, see to Desdinda. She's not well enough to exert herself like that."

"My chairmobile caught up to her and is giving her a ride back to her room. Shall I have Rinperee visit her?"

"In a couple of hours. She needs solitude, I think. Poor child, she's so desperate, and won't let me help."

"Perhaps Grisnilter? I've taken him off sedation now, and he could have visitors."

"Perhaps," answered Jindigar, "when she's calmed down. But warn him about her."

"Oh, I will." His simulacrum vanished.

During this, Frey, embarrassed, had crept back the way he'd come. "I, uh, should be going."

Jindigar said, "We'll talk, Frey. Later."

"It's not like that, Jindigar. I know you're not an Invert."

"I was," he contradicted calmly, "and could easily be again. We'll talk. If you want to resign tutelage, then we'll dissolve without prejudice. I don't think even Desdinda would hold it against you."

"I won't go until you dismiss me."

"We'll talk," insisted Jindigar. "Later."

He let Frey go, and Krinata let out a long held breath. Jindigar said, gazing after the boy, "Go ahead. Ask."

She couldn't, so she complained rhetorically, "Why does Arlai let me walk into these things?"

"Arlai," answered Jindigar, "is preoccupied. We're carrying almost a full load now. Additionally, he's unaware of emotionally charged conversations unless his name is mentioned, or ship's security is involved." His eyes came to hers sympathetically. "Ask the real question, Krinata."

"All right. What are you? What does she think you are that he thinks you're not, that you insist you are, and what does all that mean to me? If anything." *And what do you mean I have as much talent as Desdinda? Which one of us are you insulting?* But she wasn't going to say that aloud.

"Do you understand," he asked obliquely, "that only during Renewal do we practice our—religions? For the sake of analogy, you could regard Aliom as my religion, and myself as a professional promulgator of it—a priest. But that is true only during Renewal. Aliom provides the philosophy on which the Oliat functions. Once, only once, I reversed that philosophy, inverted it. Hence, I am known as an Invert. To many, it makes no difference, to others I'm a purveyor of evil. Thus, there are Dushau who will regard you as they would any Ephemeral, and there are those who'd consider you tainted by association with me."

Before she could consider her words, she heard herself ask, "Is that why you were exiled from Dushaun?"

While he looked stunned, she thought, *Where did I ever get that impression?* But he answered mildly, "Not really. I thought you'd be more concerned about whether you, yourself, care to associate with an Invert."

So he is in exile! But somehow she wasn't horrified. She ached with the sadness of it. "To figure out what an Invert is, I'd first have to learn the Aliom philosophy. Since we only have a few more days to Razum, I guess that's going to have to wait awhile. But I am interested."

"You'll find Arlai's library is complete on the subject. If you discover you do not wish to associate with me, say so."

"Why are you always trying to get rid of me? Is it that *you* don't wish to associate with *me?*"

"No, Krinata." She couldn't doubt his sincerity. "I don't ever want you to feel trapped. I dislike that feeling too much myself."

"All right, then let's make a bargain. You stop trying to get me to quit, and I'll promise to let you know if I want out. Deal?"

He regarded her oddly, then he grinned. "Deal."

She hardly saw Jindigar during the rest of her convalescence, and never had a chance to apologize for the foolish stunt she'd pulled in space. She began to wonder if he was avoiding her. It couldn't have been comfortable for him to confess to being an Invert. He could have no idea how she would react, and neither did she.

She did pull out volumes of Aliom philosophy, but it was too boring. From what she did glean, she couldn't imagine how it could be "inverted." So she found herself mulling over the things Jindigar had done. For one thing, he'd never lied to her. He often withheld information, but only because he felt it irrelevant. When asked a direct question, he answered candidly. He gave himself unstintingly to his personal loyalties. He never blamed another for his personal failings or turns of fortune. His gratitude was boundless. His courage put hers to shame, and that despite being "evolved prey." And his innate joy in life, and optimism somehow fired up her own will to live. If that was "Inverted" then she didn't think she'd like right-side-up.

So whatever he'd done, it must have violated some cultural

taboo that would be meaningless to her. That's how it often was between species; what was cause for ostracism in one society was a good laugh in another. She was too cosmopolitan to take such things seriously.

Eventually, she discovered Jindigar was spending most of his time in Arlai's core room, with Grisnilter, or on the bridge. Trying to restore normality, she presented herself for bridge duty still wearing Arlai's telemband, knowing she didn't have the stamina for a full workload yet.

She seated herself in the vacant captain's chair, noting that Trassle was on duty, though his exoskeleton bore a crack along his chest which Arlai had mended with a cement that didn't quite match his coloring. She looked around, saw Jindigar peering at her from an access panel, and asked, half rising from the chair, "Or is Terab playing captain now?"

He scrambled to his feet and came toward her, saying so quietly she thought Trassle wouldn't hear, "As much as I admire Terab, even when she recovers from her losses, I will not give her Arlai's central keys."

She looked up into his swirling indigo eyes. "Because you regret giving them to me? Look, there's something I've been wanting to say. I'm sorry I insisted on going out into space with you. I'm too much of an amateur."

"What happened wasn't your fault."

"An experienced spacer would have *noticed* the pressure settings! It was my responsibility to check that suit."

"It was *Arlai's* responsibility," groaned Jindigar, and as he spoke he sat on the instrument panel before her, toying with switches. "This is the first time, in all the years we've been together, that Arlai has failed. Sentients just don't make that kind of mistake. Krinata, I've been checking his circuits ever since it happened. If I'd known Arlai's error with the suit had caused you to take that deep dive, I wouldn't have trusted him to mail us that air/thruster pack—"

"What did you think caused me to deep dive?"

"Your psychological state. It happens sometimes, you know. Every species, even Dushau, experience a link with the cosmos on an unconscious level. And I know being ripped from the moorings of your life and thrown into harrowing challenge after heartstopping risk is enough to disturb anyone's unconscious. I never cease to be amazed at how you've survived it all without knowing your epistemology."

"Maybe epistemology isn't as important to a human as to a Dushau?" She'd looked up the word, glanced through some philosophy texts, and decided she wasn't going to invent herself an epistemology, nor adopt one. And all the Aliom texts seemed to be about nothing else.

"Perhaps," he pronounced dubiously.

She turned back to her plotting board, to change the subject. "It says here *Truth* will orbit Razum Two in five days. After we pick up your Lehiroh, then what?"

He sighed, announcing a decision that seemed to tear his heart as he tried to argue himself into the logic of it. "We've got a full passenger load, the Imperials are alerted and there's no way we can make Atridm and Canbera without being tracked. And it all would be for nothing since, by the time we can get to Atridm, the pogrom will have run to completion. My friends would be either dead or safe of their own efforts. Arlai's picked up word that one of Trassle's documents has finally surfaced, and the Kings are investigating. I can't see any good is going to come of that, but anybody who wants to be left on Razum can debark there, because our next destination will be Phanphihy."

"Where our troubles will be just beginning." She keyed "Razum Two to Phanphihy" into Arlai's plotting board, and said, "How are we going to contact these Lehiroh?"

"Easy. You see, I've been invited to the wedding of the four I'm looking for."

Wedding? Lehiroh didn't marry.

But Jindigar interpreted her blank look as skepticism. "Arlai assures me Razum Two is almost untouched by the madness afflicting the rest of the Allegiancy. Duke Nodrial has a strong militaristic grip on the populace of the Nineteen Stars, and a firm alliance with two other Dukes and the King of the Treptians. Arlai says Nodrial's massing a force to move against Zinzik, and he needs a stable launching base. So he's clamped an iron rule on Razum's population.

"For the most part, the people hardly notice, though. Razum, remember, is a Lehiroh multicolony. It was started by a group of Lehiroh religious dissidents who gathered passionately dedicated religious cults from several species. They tend their own lives and ignore the secular government. As long as exports are high, Nodrial leaves Razum Two alone. So this will probably be the easiest masquerade of the lot."

"Will you go as Rrrelloleh?"

"Yes, he was never seen, and there is a Lehrtrili population on Razum. It's plausible that one might invite himself to a Lehiroh wedding. There are also many humans, but no Cassrians or Dushau, and not many Holot."

In the back of Krinata's mind, alarm bells sounded at the news that Nodrial was creating alliances and massing an attack force against Zinzik. Nodrial, aggressive, ambitious, ruthless, might be no better than Zinzik on the imperial throne. The Nineteen Stars didn't have the industrial base to field a fleet to be reckoned with. He'd never trust the support of other Dukes or a King. Nodrial must have some secret advantage to think he had a chance at the throne.

When she voiced these misgivings, Jindigar agreed. "I'll be very glad of your observant company."

She tried her best dazzling smile on him. "It's just that secretly I've always wanted to be escorted to a Lehiroh wedding by a Lehrtrili!"

The smile was lost on him, but she did win a chuckle.

Over the next few days, she stood bridge watches, trying to be there when Jindigar wasn't so Arlai would always have someone with decision authority on his bridge. But Jindigar came and went at odd hours, still checking Arlai's circuits. When all Arlai's scurries were busy, Jindigar sent her to his cabin to drop off or fetch tools or documents. He pored over old schematics, heavily modified by changes made in Arlai's systems over the years.

Once, he accidentally refrigerated the bridge air, and while he was shivering and trying to get the connections reset, he sent her to fetch a winter robe. As she was coming out of Jindigar's cabin wearing the robe so she could also carry the tools he'd asked for, she met one of the human men. He appraised her, nodded as if comprehending something that had puzzled him and went on his way.

She was halfway to the bridge before she realized what a sight she presented: hair disheveled from hanging upside-down handing Jindigar tools as he crawled through an access tunnel, feet bare because her boots had made her too clumsy, and wearing Jindigar's robe which concealed her clothing. She caught her breath to call after the man, but he was gone. She had no time for it, and later had forgotten the incident.

When she wasn't helping Jindigar, she holed up with one of Arlai's terminals researching Razum's splinter Lehiroh group, helping Arlai create a new persona for her. She knew the basics of Lehiroh biology. The male extracted the egg cell from the female, fertilized it and returned it to the female. This process triggered lactation in the male, and it was the male who settled down for the requisite number of years to raise the young while the female, after giving birth, was the breadwinner of the family.

On this process, many cultures and religions had imposed limitations. That was one thing Lehiroh and humans had in common, a plethora of cultures and religions, intermingling and fighting it out for dominance. But in recent centuries, the Lehiroh worlds which had become prominent in the Empire had eschewed all their religions, embracing a kind of agnosticism, and abandoning every form of marriage.

That hadn't impaired their fertility at all. Children were usually raised by crèche professionals, paid by the parents equally. As far as Krinata knew, they were the only species to adopt such an arrangement without producing a generation of juvenile delinquents.

Delving now into material new to her, Krinata discovered that the Ensyvians, the religious Lehiroh who had settled Razum, claimed a direct revelation from Eternal and Infinite God proscribing such behavior. And alone among Lehiroh cultures, the Ensyvians still practiced not only marriage but sexual exclusivity in marriage. Not monogamy but a polyandry of exactly four males to each female.

Monogamy was a perverted concept to the Ensyvians, who

claimed that psychological stability could be achieved only by the group of five, and such stability was the absolute prerequisite to raising healthy children.

Biologically, it worked well, for the short pregnancy and birth were hardly debilitating to the Lehiroh female, and she could present a child once a year and still hold a job. Practically, though, the norm was for two of the husbands to be tied down with an infant while the wife and other two husbands worked to support the unit. Families tended to form multi-generation pyramids, and as a result the small Lehiroh population of Razum Two controlled more than seventy percent of the wealth.

They often bragged that the incidence of stress diseases was phenomenally lower among the devout Ensyvians, but that statistic was blurred by the large and growing number of very nondevout members of the sect. However, the last thing the drifters seemed to surrender was their marriage practice.

She asked Jindigar about his four friends.

"You're right, Krinata, they're not at all devout practitioners. But I understand this marriage is very important to them. The four of them have been together for a long time, and I know they've felt the lack of a female. But they'd pledged to marry the same woman. Only now have they found someone who pleases them all and will accept them. I just hope life will go well for them. They deserve it."

"You've worked with them?"

"Many times. They're a top unit of Oliat Outriders. Their field survival skills are second to none, and their learned reflexes keep them from intruding on a constituted Oliat. I've trusted them with my life many times over, and I'm still here. But I don't really know them personally. We've never had a chance to talk, you understand. I was surprised and very pleased to be invited to the wedding."

Researching the implications of that, she discovered that there were no onlookers or "witnesses" at an Ensyvian wedding. Everyone there assumed familial ties to the wedded group. Now she wasn't so sure she wanted to go.

When she discussed it with Arlai, he replied, "But the identity we worked out for you is unchallengeable!"

Pacing, grasping at straws, she said, instantly regretting it, "Can we really trust your judgment until we find that malfunction?"

But Arlai's feelings weren't hurt. He materialized in front of her, stopping her in her tracks. "Krinata, will you promise not to tell Jindigar something until you're settled on your new planet?"

"Promise not to tell Jindigar?" she asked, incredulous. She still couldn't get used to such a sentient Sentient.

"I knew you would," he accepted complacently. "Listen. There was no malfunction in my circuits. It was Jindigar's error. He must have misheard me. I told him suit *seven* and he gave you suit *five*. I only noticed it after you were gone. I was too overloaded, and had cut back on routine safety checks. Right now Jindigar is under so much pressure between Grisnilter and Desdinda, and all he's been through, he's driving himself too hard, judging himself too harshly. If he knew he'd made such an error, he'd start doubting his sanity again, and you know what that does to him."

"Jindigar's been leery of you, tearing your guts apart and rebuilding them, triple-checking everything you do, and you've—"

"He'll be satisfied after a while. But I think this has been the best therapy for him. It's been centuries since he's done circuitry work. He's losing himself in it. It's a small price to pay. I don't want you to distrust me, too. You've got to go with him, and take risks on my performance. You're the only one aboard he'd trust down there with him."

Well, if Jindigar can join the family, so can I. She wondered if that would make them in-laws. But she had no time to research it. They were approaching Razum Two orbit.

Arlai provided her with an ankle-length black gown and cowl cut as if for a postulant of the Sisters of Jacob, a Terran-based nursing order known for its broadmindedness. With inserts in her shoes to change her walk, a dental appliance which changed her speech as well as her cheek line, she became Sister Marietta, accompanying Rrrelloleh, a wealthy eccentric Lehrtrili with dire health problems.

Arlai found it harder to take care of the identity scanners

they'd have to pass at customs. The planet was virtually under martial law now, and the Sentients had been allowed fewer discretionary powers. In the end, he created an implant for Rrrelloleh that produced an energy field exactly like an internal life-support capsule, which would disrupt the scanners. For Krinata, he was able to plant Sister Marietta's identity in the superficial visa files. "If they don't challenge you, you'll get by."

Rrrelloleh planned to "hire" the five newly wed Lehiroh to act as Ensyvian missionaries to the Lehiroh servants on his private planetoid. It was such a plausible story, she was certain they wouldn't attract a second glance.

But the moment they grounded and entered the warren of customs checks, she knew they were in trouble.

Walking down the covered gangway attached to their lander, they entered a passenger terminal swarming with uniforms. Standing guard at every strategic intersection, was an armored Ducal soldier. Half of them held a naked pygmy anthropoid on a leash: dark, wrinkled skin stretched over prominent bones; saucer eyes; protruding sensitive lips; large cranium; long delicate fingers; doglike obedience.

Rashions! Nodrial's secret weapon! She'd only seen pictures of the creatures, but they'd been a year-long sensation among ecologists when she was in school.

She wrapped both hands on Rrrelloleh's arm and tugged him to a refreshment dispenser, keying it for a Lehrtrili drink as she whispered, "Don't call attention to us."

"I saw the Rashions, Sister," said the voder's voice as Rrrelloleh twittered. "They're protosentient telepaths, not to be removed from their native habitat by Oliat decree. Hardly surprising that proscription has been violated, but I wonder what the other Dukes think of Nodrial's appropriation of them. I wonder what the Emperor thinks of it."

"If they know. We didn't, with all Arlai's methods. Do you suppose they'll let us leave, after seeing this?"

"Good question. We'll deal with that when necessary. Meanwhile, did you really want me to take the medication now Sister? I'm feeling well enough."

He was telling her to think herself into her role, and she

complied, hoping that her nervousness would be attributed to her being a novice with such a responsibility on a strange world—as her passport showed—for the first time.

They walked slowly as befitting the infirm, and arrived at the checkpoint among the last in the line, choosing the most bored and exhausted-looking clerk.

However, the clerk also had a Rashion chained beside his counter, and Krinata summoned impatience at getting a slow clerk when her charge was so tired from the trip downplanet.

She tried not to feel her surprise at being passed through without a challenge. *Have more faith in Arlai*. Within moments, they were outside.

Razum Two circled an old star, now only half as bright as Sol. Razum Two's surface gravity was barely a tenth more than Terran, but she was grateful for the ugly "g" shoes Arlai had provided, and the contact lenses to penetrate the dimness. The local day was a bit more than two days long, and they'd arrived in the midmorning, with both moons in the sky, yet the lighting felt more like a dingy overcast.

It was a balmy spring day, with the lightest of breezes blowing. Nevertheless, she knew that with darkness, she'd need the winter cloak she carried in the black tote. She shoved that awareness aside, revelling in the outing after the long weeks in the ship.

Jindigar had an address on his invitation. They hired an auto-cab and requested a scenic route to an expensive hotel on the nearby lakeshore, assured by Arlai that the tourist route would take them near God's Park, a famous attraction filled with religious statuary.

They were running late. The wedding was scheduled for noon, but they dared not attract attention by going directly to a private home. Krinata was relieved when she saw the park, and called the auto-cab to a halt at the entry. "May we take a stroll, Rrrelloleh? I would so love to see this."

"You're always prescribing exercise and pretending it's you who needs it!" he answered querulously. But he moved out of the cab and dismissed it.

They ambled across the park on a diagonal, and Krinata was fascinated despite herself, for here, carved in native stone, were representatives of every religion's concept of God. A few were abstract symbols, but most seemed to be in the likeness of the worshipping species.

Despite the vast diversity of forms, all the entities seemed to share a similar *peace*, and a transcendent gentleness. Such similarities made the Allegiancy possible. The species might not speak similar languages, but they were trying to say the same unsayable things.

Patriotism and pride swelled within her, and broke into a rush of tears. She'd set herself outside the Allegiancy.

But then she saw in her mind's eye, the armored guards with helpless, starving, proto-aborigine telepaths cruelly leashed. Her precious imperial system had spawned that. Any Duke who had jurisdiction over the Rashions' home planet would have done what Nodrial was doing. Two of them and a King were with him. Lavov—and who knew what other Dukes—were also after power, willing to wrench it from the Throne. And she was perversely glad not to be tacit signatory to that by remaining in the aristocracy. For she realized that if Zinzik defeated Nodrial, Zinzik would have the Rashions for his own use, and use them he would.

Seeing here the essential unity of the Allied Species, she found her loyalty to the Allegiancy itself crumbling. It was frightening. *Suppose Jindigar's right, and it's just a monstrous beast tearing at itself in senile dementia?*

Only one hope remained: Trassle's evidence, now before the Kings. *Could they still pull everything together again after deposing Zinzik? Or will the Dukes, and some of the Kings, tear the Allegiancy apart in individual grabs for power?* She could see how, now that one species had been made scapegoat, the King of any species might well decide it was better to grab for the Imperial Throne than risk being made the next Emperor's scapegoat. She shuddered.

"Sister Marietta?"

"Oh, I'm coming." She tore herself away from such dark thoughts, and followed Rrrelloleh, reminding herself not to think out of character lest the Rashions notice.

They emerged from another gate onto a quiet street lined with immense old houses built of native rock. The buildings had to be strong to withstand the ferocious winter storms, but she wondered how a rigid construction could survive the legendary Razum groundquakes.

Rrrelloleh pointed at a house with his walking stick, which contained a shielded comunit attuned to Arlai. The leptolizer Rrrelloleh wore at his waist was mostly sham, and Sister Marietta of course wore none. "That's an interesting old building."

Wrapped around the corner of the block, the house was larger than the others, with new construction added onto the old haphazardly. There was a high fence around the property insuring privacy. Sounds of merrymaking drifted from within.

Rrrelloleh checked a jeweled chronometer he wore on a neck chain. "Jindigar was told to be here about an hour ago, to be met outside. Perhaps we're too late."

Just then a Lehiroh dressed in shiny forest green satin jodhpurs and long, flowing tailed waistcoat, with white shoes, belt, pillbox cap, and gloves, came around the corner of the fence. He was carrying a long green satin streamer in one hand and a filigree-decorated book in the other. But he walked stoop-shouldered, watching his feet. Everything in his movements suggested an insuperable weight on his spirit. Krinata recognized the Ensyvian groom's traditional costume.

Rrrelloleh stepped up to the young Lehiroh. "Storm!"

The Lehiroh looked up, startled. He noticed Sister Marietta, but realized the voder had addressed him. "I'm sorry, do I know you?"

Krinata moved up beside Rrrelloleh. She glanced all about for any sign of the Rashions, and saw they were alone on the residential street, just a few cars passing. "This is Jindigar, but he's emulating a Lehrtrili called Rrrelloleh."

Storm's gaze rivetted on the beady eyes. After a moment, it was clear he didn't believe it. And he thought his life was forfeit. "I surrender. No need for entrapment. I invited a Dushau to my wedding. Don't blame the others."

Rrrelloleh looked down at Sister Marietta. Then, to the Lehiroh, he twittered, "Arlai's work is always superlative."

Again Storm inspected the Lehrtrili. "I don't believe you. Jindigar is dead. All of Kamminth's is dead."

"I'm glad that rumor is still about, but I doubt it's believed in the highest official circles. Must we stand about on the street?" twittered Rrrelloleh, strictly in character. The wings fluttered, feathers rustling.

But something penetrated Storm's armor. "By the sandpits, it *is* you!" His eyes wide, he raked Sister Marietta with a glance.

Rrrelloleh trilled, "For the moment, this is Sister Marietta, who accompanies this rich and eccentric Lehrtrili to care for his uncertain health. At my insistence, we have stopped because we recognize your dress, and wish to invite ourselves to your wedding. Afterward, we may have an interesting proposition for all of you to consider."

Storm shook himself out of his daze and answered, "Afterward . . . well, we've all agreed not to allow anything to cloud this day for us." Seeing their curiosity, he added, "I promise I'll tell you all about it, afterward. I just can't believe you're alive. It's got to be a good omen."

"Jindigar is dead until we've passed the Rashions and cleared orbit. But Rrrelloleh would consider it a wonderful privilege to join your wedding. The obligation incurred would not be slighted."

"Oh, I never . . . I mean, we wouldn't expect you to feel obligated."

"Custom is custom," answered Rrrelloleh. "Self-invitation is a Lehrtrili custom. Yours will also be honored."

Storm surveyed the street as if on a hostile planet. "Come inside, then." In the vestibule, he paused to wind the green ribbon about the outside digit on Rrrelloleh's left hand and then up the arm. "This means you're my guest. I'll get one for Sister Marietta in a moment. Come."

He led them down a winding stair into a large open room. One whole wall was made of sliding windows composed of small, transparent colored squares, heavily draped. Outside the open wall, she could see a courtyard and a large pool where the water was as still as glass. White cup-shaped flowers floated in the pool. Overhead, streamers and flowers in five vibrant colors canopied the room, forest green, yellow, bright blue, red, and rich cinnamon brown.

Lehiroh, dressed in every shade of white, styled from flowing robes and capes to tailored jumpsuits and tunics, filled the room. The only touch of color on the guests was the satin ribbons wound about their left hands and arms which seemed about equally divided among the five prominent colors.

In a moment, Storm returned with a green ribbon for Krinata, and she fretted, "I feel out of place in black."

"Oh, black is perfectly appropriate. We only selected white because Bell's family wanted it." When he'd wound the ribbon properly, asking three times if she was sure she wanted to stay, he led them to a section of the room occupied by people wearing green ribbons.

It was almost high noon, the traditional moment for weddings, so there was little time for them to meet Storm's family. They only caused a momentary stir, and then everyone was intent on taking their places.

Outside, a number of black-clad dignitaries appeared and stationed themselves in a circle on a huge lawn beyond the pool. This was some sort of signal, for everyone inside the room rushed to form up into lines, one line for each color.

It was only then that Krinata saw the other grooms and the bride, for each of them led a line of their kinsmen. The bride, she noted, was dressed all in red without even the white accessories. She vaguely recalled that red denoted the power of the life force for the Ensyvians, and Lehiroh eyes probably didn't see all this as clashing colors.

After flitting about checking on details, Storm came and dragged Rrrelloleh to the head of the green line with him, saying, "This way you won't have to move as fast when the dancing starts."

She took the place behind Rrrelloleh, mulling over this thoughtful comment and feeling more uncertain of herself. But the woman behind her didn't seem to mind being displaced, so Krinata just began scanning those opposite her for cues.

There was a burst of noise, traditional music, and the lines all began moving at once. Luckily she noticed everyone start off on their left foot. The lines wove circles about the pool, then spiraled to come to rest in a giant star formation, the grooms and bride each facing one of the black-clad dignitaries, their relatives in a line behind them.

The house, three stories high, circled the pool area with

many windows opening onto it. Each window was jammed with Lehiroh men, women, and children. A deep hush fell as the music and marching stopped.

Krinata tried not to think of the eyes fixed curiously upon her and Rrrelloleh, and listened to the rapid exchange between the black-clad old man and Storm. It was in some archaic Lehiroh language she'd never heard before.

After a vigorous question-and-answer session, repeated between each of the grooms and the bride and their confronter, there was a burst of music, and all the lines moved sideways to their left until they confronted a new questioner, whereupon the exchange was repeated.

The next time, Krinata was ready to move on the burst of music. But she didn't know what to expect after the fifth questioning session. However, it seemed perfectly natural that Storm should change places with the black clad old woman he confronted, so that now she headed their line.

The grooms and bride now formed an inner circle. They each grasped the ribbon of the one next to them, unwinding the ribbons so that they connected the circle. Meanwhile, everyone else did likewise, each joining himself to someone on the left while taking a ribbon from someone on their right. From above it would be a multicolor cartwheel.

On the next burst of music they all circled left, Krinata trying to fake the quick dance step which Rrrelloleh managed well enough. They hadn't made a full circuit before she was wondering how soon it would be polite to drop out.

She was about to ask Rrrelloleh when the music cut off with a squawk, doors flew open all around the courtyard, and Ducal troopers, many with Rashions on leashes, swarmed out to surround the celebrants, weapons lowered. The armored uniforms also appeared on the roof, and behind the people watching from windows.

ELEVEN

Riot at a Lehiroh Wedding

An amplifier boomed. "Nobody move."

The silence was so deep Krinata could hear the pool's pump, and a huge bird winging by overhead.

When the commander was certain he had everyone's attention, he announced, "You are harboring four conscriptees who were ordered to report to the Duke's forces two days ago. Not only are these four to be taken from your midst, but I am thus authorized to collect every able-bodied male here. And as many females as I see fit."

The voice and accent was human, not Lehiroh—possibly from nearby Ramussin, which was also of the Nineteen Stars.

A rustle of dismayed protests rippled through the crowd. The amplifier boomed, "Since you've violated Ducal law, no consideration will be made for Ensyvian custom."

Krinata heard a low, shivering note from Rrrelloleh. Now they understood what Storm hadn't wanted to discuss out on the street. She wasn't at all surprised when the grooms responded to the four names called out by the commander.

Armed men flanked by men leading Rashions approached the edge of the wheel formed by the celebrants. In a moment of tense defiance, the outermost people in the wheel, whose ribbons were much longer, raised them into a chest high, satin barrier before beamer proof armor.

The troopers paused, looking neither left nor right, as if they were at parade attention. The amplifier barked, "Forward!" The troopers all took a step in unison, breasting the wall of satin ribbons. For a moment, Krinata thought there was going to be a riot—or massacre.

But the celebrants dropped their ribbons. The soldiers worked

up the wedge-shaped spaces between lines toward the cente
where the four reluctant conscriptees waited.

The detachment targetted on Storm halted. "This is an un
forgivable outrage," stated Storm, his voice carrying emphasi
because of its colorless lack of passion.

"You mean," said the human squadron leader, "you didn'
expect the Duke to enforce his decrees in the most memorabl
way? Think! After this, no one will resist for any reason."

"After this," said Storm, and Krinata felt genuine regret in
his words, "no one will obey, for any reason."

The trooper made an uncivilized sound and grabbed the
Lehiroh's shoulder, propelling him back along the wedge-shaped
avenue, between lines of his men, all human.

As the last of the troopers turned to go, he noticed Rrrel
loleh. "I thought Ensyvians were too incestuous to let outsider
into their ceremonies. Or are you a convert?"

She felt Rrrelloleh stiffen, but he remained patiently silent
eyes fixed on the high distance. Emulating, Jindigar literall
was not there. This being was Lehrtrili, and Krinata knew i
so deeply that even the Rashions surrounding her could no
have found a hint to the contrary in her mind.

The officer who'd taken Storm dumped him on two of hi
men and returned to inspect Rrrelloleh.

"Answer, Lehrtrili! You're wearing a voder!" He poked a
the box on Rrrelloleh's chest.

Krinata said, "He's elderly and unwell. His name is Rrrel
loleh, and I am his nurse. I will answer for him."

The officer kept his weapon on Rrrelloleh, but eyed Krinata
taking in every detail of her costume.

Around them soldiers were culling men from the lines o
celebrants, pushing and kicking them into a bunch near th
door Krinata had marched out of. Protests were rising from
the crowd. Some of the Lehiroh men, she noted for the firs
time, had enlarged breasts. Those men were being defende
by others who insisted on replacing the lactating ones.

The women were massing, protecting the pregnant ones
She knew they were perfectly capable of tackling the arme
humans, might kill a few before the beamers cut them down

The officer inspecting her pulled her roughly away from th

Lehrtrili, noting she was human, not Lehiroh. Suddenly, she didn't like the wolfish grin she could see below his eye shields. "You're a brave one, Sister. I like that." He held his weapon to her temple, and ordered, "Farmer, sic your beast on this one. Gravitz, take the Lehrtrili." He focused on Rrrelloleh. "Now, what are you two doing here? Should I run you in for sedition—or espionage?"

Krinata's heart leaped to her throat. The Rashion crouching at her feet growled thoughtfully.

Rrrelloleh presented his leptolizer, butt first, to the officer. "My entry visa, sir, in perfect order. Walking through the park, we saw an Ensyvian groom pacing nervously in front of this house. Curious, I invited myself to his wedding, promising to abide by his customs thereafter."

The officer seated the butt of the leptolizer in a socket on his armored hip. It gave out a bleep and projected the port-of-entry seal. "This can easily be checked. If it's legal, then the charge will be espionage."

He tightened his grip on Krinata. "Now, you."

"She doesn't carry a leptolizer, only an identdisc."

"Let's have it."

Fingers shaking, Krinata fished the disc out of her belt pouch. He snatched it, turning it over and over. "Looks real. Could be forged, though." He watched the Rashion as he snapped, "State your name and your business here!"

"Marietta of the Sisters of Jacob, nurse to Rrrelloleh."

As she spoke, the Rashion's uneasy murmuring grew to a roar, and he went for her throat, teeth bared.

Several things happened simultaneously. The officer snarled, "She's lying!" A child screamed, falling from a window and landing with a sickening thud. Someone pushed two of the armored men into the pool where they sank like stones, while their buddies tried to fish them out. And Rrrelloleh clamped both hands around the Rashion's wrists, flipping him to the end of his leash and pulling his trainer off balance.

In three graceful moves, Rrrelloleh had the Rashion that had been watching him knocked unconscious, the officer and his two men tumbling in different directions. Grabbing Krinata's wrist, he ran toward the knot of conscriptees.

A beam cut a black swath across their path. Dragging Krinata, Rrrelloleh ripped off his mask, and leaped over the beam. They were heading for the most guarded door, the multicolored glass one leading into the large room. It was suicide. Yet she kept running.

The conscriptees were fighting their guards now, rolling and tumbling, some with amateurishness, and some with keen professionalism. Already two guards lay bleeding a dark bluish blood she knew was really red, human blood. The armor might be total protection from beam weapons, but it was a handicap hand-to-hand. A detached part of her mind wondered why armored men had been sent against the obviously unarmed. What did that imply about the Duke and his men? Cowardice akin to Rantan Zinzik's?

Jindigar waded through a heap of bodies to the four grooms, and snapped, "Let's get out of here! With us gone, they won't have any reason to persecute the family!"

One of the grooms, the one wearing dirt-smeared yellow, raked the Dushau-faced Lehrtrili with a glance, froze in the act of disemboweling a guard with the guard's own weapon, and exclaimed, "Jindigar! Dear God, he's alive. He's alive!"

Storm tossed an armored guard over his head and grunted, "We can't leave without Bell!"

Another kneading his shoulder where a beamer had singed his blue sleeve, leaving a rent that exposed sculpted muscles, said, "Bell's . . ." he sidestepped as one armored man charged him, "around here somewhere."

The yellow-clad groom flipped the charging trooper onto the stack of dazed men with an absentminded air as he followed blue's gesture, looking for his bride.

The blue groom heaved a trooper off another Lehiroh, admonishing, "You can't do that to my cousin!" Over his shoulder to Storm, he said, "Guard Jindigar, I'll find her."

The yellow groom exclaimed, pointing up at the roof. "They've got her!" An automatic spraybeamer was set on its tripod, aimed at the riot below. The red-clad bride was held between two burly men, standing on the edge of the roof.

The amplifier let out a blast of music followed by the commander's voice. "Surrender at once or the bride dies!"

Paralysis swept the courtyard. The only sound was the rattling of armor as the troopers picked themselves up. Many, too horrifyingly many, celebrants did not stir. Others gazed fixedly at the red wisp on the roof above them.

The yellow groom had lifted Krinata by the shoulders, out of the way of a falling trooper. Now, he gazed into her eyes, and said, quizzically, "You're human!"

Storm grunted, "Friend of Jindigar's," but his eyes were on the red-clad woman above them.

Yellow answered abstractedly, eyes on Bell, "Oh. That's all right, then." He set Krinata on her own feet.

At the next amplified command, the troopers locked shackles and tanglefoot fields onto the living celebrants.

Six men secured Jindigar, and were about to take him away when the commander ordered, "The Sister, too."

Krinata didn't know whether to be relieved or terrified.

Two huge vertical landers, with Ducal seals newly painted on their scarred old sides, swept down into the court. The entire family was packed into those riot-squad wagons. The only resistance was a bit of sullen foot-dragging. The grass was littered with too many corpses dressed in festive white, smeared darkly with blood. And now gas burpers had been brought up. Hostility would be met with an excruciatingly painful gassing that wasn't always entirely harmless.

A wall of guards and Rashions separated Krinata, Jindigar, and the bride and grooms from the others. The riot wagon was so crowded, people were unable to sit. The air rapidly filled with the stench of beamer burns, human and Lehiroh sweat, and in one case, vomit.

Storm turned to the wall, curled in on himself, agonizing over the result of defying the conscription order. "I never thought they'd do such a thing. Never!"

The blue groom gripped his shoulder and whispered, "Neither did we. We all discussed it. Everyone agreed."

"Shut up, you!" The bruised and grass-stained squad leader who had ogled Krinata now held a beamer on Jindigar.

Blue turned from Storm. Without so much as a narrowing of the eyes as warning, blue yelled, "Was it worth it?"

The fierce cheer was deafening in the confined space. Suddenly, the floor tilted, then tilted the other way, rocking them from side to side. The amplifier said, "Keep it down in there or you'll get seasick!"

But the atmosphere had changed. The guards sensed it, and Krinata saw fear in their eyes. If the entire Ensyvian population felt like this, did the Duke have a chance? Apparently, they could conscript Ensyvians, tax them into poverty, and take away all freedoms with impunity. But infringe on their religion, and whole families—even the least religious—would proudly fight to the death.

When they'd landed, they were offloaded through a chute reeking of animal dung into a huge barn jammed with lines of people being processed like prisoners. Storm whispered to Jindigar, "I wish now I hadn't invited you."

People shrank from Jindigar muttering that even to speak to a Dushau was death. But Storm and the whole family showed no signs of shunning him.

They were strip-searched. Krinata was amazed to see groups of all the other Razum species also being herded through. This was either a conscription center or a massive jailing operation. Were they impressing all criminals?

In line behind her, Jindigar muttered, "They're going to have a time stripping me." He began to pluck indigo and yellow feathers from his arms.

In the line ahead of Krinata, there was a scuffle as a trooper ripped the garment from a Lehiroh woman. The male Lehiroh in line behind her protested she was pregnant. The guard answered, *"That* can be taken care of handily."

This is not real. Please, don't let it be real. Krinata had been raised an aristocrat on one of the oldest colony worlds of humankind, amid traditions of uncompromised honor. No noble could lend a good name to such proceedings.

The feeling she'd had in the park came back. There were huge gaping cracks in the secure walls of the Allegiancy. The Empire just wasn't what she'd always imagined it to be. *Was it ever?* A nostalgic pain filled her eyes with tears.

Hearing her sniffle, Jindigar, behind her, risked muttering, "This is war, Krinata. A despot's war for power. It couldn't have happened two centuries ago. *That* Allegiancy was worthy of your loyalty . . . and mine."

With that consolation echoing in her mind, Krinata had to grasp all her courage and Zavaronne pride to disrobe before a man whose groin pulsed at her every move. He took his time stamping an ID on her belly, noticing her humanity with relish. Then he stamped the indelible number on her forehead, lingering as if he was going to kiss her. His breath was hot, but not foul. Yet she was revolted, her whole body quivering with disgust.

Jindigar, neither looking at her nor averting his gaze, stumbled deliberately. The handful of feathers he'd gathered flew into the guard's face, and he sneezed. Jindigar apologized profusely, meanwhile tangling his avian feet amid the human's boots. They both went down in a heap, Jindigar crying out a contrite apology for each new offense.

Krinata stared for a moment, then used the time to pull her robe about her. Jindigar helped the human to his feet, brushing stray feathers from the man's now dusty uniform, contriving to thrust more of them under the man's nose.

"As you can see," grunted Jindigar, "I've been trying to remove this costume, but it takes butyloline and alcohol to strip the adhesive."

The man swallowed his anger, looking Jindigar up and down. He snatched the walking stick away from the Dushau with a lurid epithet, and spat, "I know you people don't carry weapons, but this is forbidden. Next!"

At the exit line, they were issued a thin turquoise shirt and trousers outfit, cut the same for everyone and fitting no one. They wouldn't let her keep her robe even when she complained of the cold. Jindigar again claimed he needed solvent to "change clothes," but was issued an outfit with pants too short for him, and shirt too narrow. He handed them to Krinata, saying, "Two layers might help."

She gratefully donned the second layer, and whispered her thanks for helping her. He answered, "My situation could hardly be worse, so it was no risk."

Many of the pregnant Lehiroh could not wear the trousers

at all and settled for the oversize shirts that almost covered them. Then they were herded out into the afternoon sun, separated into a number of groups, loaded into surface vans, and carted a short distance to another building Krinata never saw from the outside.

They lost touch with the rest of the family, but the bride and four grooms were shoved into an underground cell with Krinata and Jindigar.

Hours later, guards came and took Jindigar away. He forbade Krinata to fight for him, and Storm held her as she lunged reflexively at the guards. When he was gone, she cried. Bell came to sit with her, offering only a warm shoulder in comfort, for it was all she had.

But Jindigar returned, cleaned and dressed in turquoise shirt and pants that almost fit, and a grave expression.

When the guard left, he said, *"Truth* has been taken. There was nothing Arlai could do, and no one aboard had his central keys, so he's behaving under Allegiancy strictures. But everyone is being ferried down here."

In horror, she imagined the session he'd gone through that had yielded those few terse sentences. Yet he showed no outward sign of the strain. That worried her.

Hours passed in which guards tromped up and down outside their cell. It was one of five force-field enclosed cells at the end of a corridor. Strangers, Holot, were crammed into the cell next to theirs, and a group of humans into the end cell. Yet the two opposite were left empty.

Then, when Krinata was sure it was late night despite the relentless bright light, *Truth*'s passengers arrived, bewildered, some still "walking wounded." Grisnilter was supported between two Dushau, his right leg dragging. The humans, Cassrians, Dushau and Holot were herded into the two opposite cells. They could see each other, but not hear.

Jindigar, though, had the answer. He questioned the other Dushau via sign language, explaining that it was a code often used in noisy environments.

Arlai, it seemed, was all right for the time being, his parting remark to them having been a pledge to keep Imp out of trouble until they returned. The authorities had assumed he was still under full Allegiancy restriction, but soon some Sentient would notice Arlai had not taken the new Allegiancy delimiting programming. Meanwhile, Arlai was determined to play it straight until he could rescue them.

Jindigar swore. "I wish I had a way to tell him to sit tight. There's no reason he has to go down with us. Why didn't he take off as planned? At least they'd be safe!"

"Ask," prompted Krinata.

Jindigar put the question and Grisnilter answered. Jindigar translated, "Because he refused to abandon us." He paced a circle, fretting, "But I *ordered* him to!"

"Maybe he knows how to get us out of this. Disobedience isn't built into him, is it?"

"He's mature. He had discretion. I hope he uses it."

"Have you ever had reason to mistrust him?"

Storm said, "Not exactly mistrust, no, but I remember the time on Dilatter when Arlai was orbiting empty while the Oliat and the entire team were encamped. He'd warned us there were hailstorms in the area, remember?"

Jindigar's mood lightened. He smiled as he said, "And we divined that none were going to hit our camp?"

Another of the Lehiroh said, "And Arlai . . ." And he gasped into silent laughter.

Another groom finished, talking to Bell and Krinata, "Arlai sent a probe into the upper atmosphere and disrupted the air currents just so one of those dratted storms drenched us when dinner was half-cooked!"

"And then he had the nerve to claim innocence!"

"He had a reason," argued Jindigar. "We'd become too complacent. But guarding ourselves against another practical joke, we set the double watch which saved our lives. Even an Oliat can't afford to become overconfident."

Storm squatted comfortably on the floor of the bare cell, toying with a thread. "I've often wondered if Arlai is psychic. Or maybe you've secretly trained him as an Oliat?"

Jindigar chuckled. "I've wished I could." He translated for those in the opposite cells. All but Grisnilter laughed. That began a marathon session of reminiscences in which Krinata submerged herself, not wanting to face where they were or what was to become of them.

When she'd long since given up expecting food, a meal of sorts arrived. It was a bucket of raw yeast-grown protein amenable to all their various metabolisms, palatable to none. It arrived on a tray via a trap in the wall, accompanied by a pile of plastic bowls—no spoons.

The five Lehiroh gulped it down willingly. Storm commented, "After two days of fasting, even this tastes good." To Bell he said, "It wasn't what I was planning for your wedding night, though."

For a moment, Krinata thought Bell's staunch good humor would hold. Then the woman broke into human-sounding sobs. *If it were my wedding night, I'd be inconsolable.*

The four grooms gathered about their bride, self-conscious. Krinata wished they could at least have some privacy, but knew that even if she wasn't there, the spy eyes in the ceiling would be active. *Voyeurs!* She made a rude gesture at the spy eyes and was rewarded with no reaction.

Exhausted, Krinata slid down the wall to slump at its base. The room was kept at a fairly amenable temperature, but she thought she'd never fall asleep. Yet she did.

The next morning, they were taken to a sanitation stall, open, public, brutal. She relieved herself and showered, wondering how she was enduring this, while knowing it was much worse for those whose cultures had nudity taboos.

By midmorning, they were taken from their cells—all twenty-eight *Truth* passengers and the five Lehiroh—to go before a magistrate where they were arraigned for espionage.

The magistrate's computer had only one entry under her name: wanted by the Emperor. Jindigar wasn't listed at all. She assumed the records showed he'd died on Cassr, meaning at least one of those soldiers had survived to tell the tale.

Krinata's understanding of Allegiancy law was worthless. Besides, martial law was in force, and they had no rights at all. All her aristocratic heritage made not the slightest impression on this Duke's magistrate. The Allegiancy may as well have never existed. *It doesn't really exist anymore.*

Remanded to the custody of a prison reputed to be impossible to escape from, they were herded into a large, windowless groundbus, fully automated so there was no driver to overpower. Rows of hard benches lined each side, with one long bench across the rear. As the door slammed and the bus began to move with a grinding roar that became a white-noise background, Krinata surveyed the hullmetal panels protecting the bus's onboard brain. It probably wasn't Sentient. But Jindigar was a circuitry wizard. Perhaps they could take over the bus. Where to go after that was the problem. She wasn't even sure where they were in relation to the spaceport.

With the Dushau clustered in the rear, ignoring everyone, she gathered the rest and started talking before she had a plan worked out. She was beyond desperation, and had to try something. The others listened, in the same mood.

"I could get us to the spaceport," offered Storm. "I grew up around here."

Bell eyed the hullmetal panel, ran a hand over it, and said, "The welds are softique, the stuff used in gross circuits. A current would melt them away in a flash."

"The light!" exclaimed Trassle, climbing onto his seat and ramming the light fixture with his closed, chitin protected hand. Dimness descended as the only light left came from the rear fixture. But Trassle pulled a live wire down. "Luckily, this bus must date from pioneer days."

Storm said they had plenty of time since their new prison was more than two hours from where they'd started. Bell went to work on the bulkhead and Krinata went to the rear to talk to Jindigar.

She was stopped by a wall of indigo bodies. Desdinda stood off to one side, arms crossed, watching something on the bench spanning the rear of the bus. Her air of bristling disapproval told Krinata she was looking at Jindigar.

Rinperee said, "Don't interrupt them."

Craning her neck, Krinata could make out Grisnilter lying on the rear seat, Jindigar seated next to him, speaking in the dreadfully kind whisper usually reserved for the terminally ill. "What's the matter with Grisnilter?"

Jindigar looked around. "Krinata?"

face, as if the woman's wildest surmise of perfidy had been triumphantly confirmed. *I must be misreading that!* Krinata pushed it out of her mind and concentrated on Jindigar and Grisnilter, kneeling beside them, rolling with the sway of the floor. She told them of her half-baked plan, ending, "So all you have to do is figure out how to scramble the onboard and reprogram our destination."

A pinched, haunted anxiety descended on Jindigar's eyes. He gazed at Grisnilter. The old Dushau showed pale teeth, holding Jindigar's eyes with his own. Grisnilter's air of intense demand was replaced by silent helpless pleading.

At last Jindigar spoke. "In the time we've got left, I can either *try* to rewire this bus, or *try* to take your impression. Grisnilter, how many lives is it worth?"

Desdinda started to say something, but was silenced by the others. Rinperee said, "All of our lives, and more."

"I'm not trained for this!" protested Jindigar.

"You've a supreme talent, though. It runs in your family, and I've seen your farfetch test," argued Grisnilter. "You'll never go episodic, Jindigar. You're too stable."

Into Jindigar's anguished silence, Grisnilter said, "You'll still be able to work Oliat. Your conscious mind will have no access until you are trained."

Krinata, intrigued but impatient, interrupted, "You can do whatever it is *after* we escape."

"No, Krinata, you don't understand," said Jindigar. "Grisnilter is dying. The strain of this ordeal is too great."

"Don't get dramatic now!" commanded Grisnilter. "It's a perfectly natural phenomenon, death. Even Ephemerals do it. But I've a responsibility. I must not die until I've passed the Archive."

It finally penetrated. *Dying*. Had she caused this attack by her anger that one time? She took the old Dushau's hand, capturing his eyes. "I'm sorry I was so rude on the refugee's ship. I didn't mean it, and I've no excuse except I was worried about Jindigar. I hope what I said didn't make you ill. I've been meaning to apologize."

"I haven't been so polite, myself, child. You may not have

meant it, but you were absolutely correct to call me down. I've treated Jindigar shamelessly."

She wanted to hug him, but instead she just patted his hand. "Rest now. We're going to get you out of this."

Jindigar, rising and steering her away through the press of Dushau bodies shielding their elder, said, "He knows it's unlikely we could steal a lander and make it to *Truth* with a semi-invalid in tow. After what he'd been through before we rescued him, that rescue itself, the affair with the seeker craft, now this—even if we got him back to Arlai's sickbay, there's a frighteningly high probability his memory will be impaired and he won't be able to give the impression."

"Impression?" interrupted Krinata.

"I told you, remember? Grisnilter's an Archivist, carrying our Compiled Long Memory. If he dies without having impressed that memory on a younger Historian, it will be lost. But I'm the only one here who has a chance of taking the impression, even though I'm no Historian."

This, the Historian's profession, was what Jindigar had been desperate to avoid all along. It might even be his reason for exiling himself from Dushaun.

"Wouldn't Arlai have a better chance of helping him than any doctors at the prison?"

"He can't make it," said Jindigar, his voice heavy with defeat. "I've fought him as long as I can. There are loyalties— like your loyalty to the Allegiancy—to one's species, to one's civilization, to life itself, that take precedence over personal loyalties."

She looked up into his eyes. *He doesn't believe that.* Yet he was pleading for her understanding without realizing that, in the bitter aftermath of her disillusionment with the Allegiancy, she was on the verge of repudiating the very part of herself capable of loyalty to an impersonal idea. She'd thought she'd understood him, with his intense loyalty to individuals who had proved their worth. She'd never been capable of that before meeting him. And now she had nothing else. Looking up into his eyes, she realized Grisnilter had called him to serve abstract, unjudgeable future generations of Dushau, not real stood before her, broken, pleading for her approval so he wouldn't hate himself quite so much for abandoning them.

His nailless fingers were on her cheek, and she knew his fear in her bones. *He doesn't believe he's immune to going episodic.* But she also knew his determination. She said, "You don't have to wire this bus for us. We can manage. Do what you must. I understand."

"I'll come to help, if I can. After Grisnilter's had his way with me. But I warn you, there might not be much of me left." Head bowed, he went back through the screen of Dushau.

She went back to the front of the bus, ignoring the grating sound of Desdinda's voice as she issued her final warning to Jindigar. It was as if the woman felt he, Grisnilter, and the others who helped them, were committing a sacrilege. Perhaps they were, but from what she'd gleaned of this whole situation, Jindigar was taking the first step toward purifying his reputation among his people. She wished she understood why he didn't want this. Certainly, it was more than the fear of going episodic. He might be evolved prey, but he didn't lack for courage, and that was something *she* had to emulate now.

Reaching the front, she called with forced cheerfulness, "Well, Jindigar can't spare the time right now, so who else has an idea how to do it?"

Trassle gave it a try, with Terab kibitzing.

A spark leaped, and Trassle was thrown back into the watching crowd. The vehicle ground to a halt. Nothing they could do after that would cause the doors to open.

The air began to go stale very quickly. The Dushau also wilted. She never saw what Grisnilter did to Jindigar, but her last memory before she passed out—sure she was already dead—was Jindigar huddled in on himself, clutching his head and moaning softly. She didn't have the strength to crawl to him and hold him as she had in the imperial antechamber.

She woke up in a long barracks building. The roof overhead was a parabolic curve. The bed under her was scratchy and hard with a lumpy contoured sag under her ribs. The air was hot. She heard water running somewhere.

Head spinning, she dragged herself upright, incuriously noting the entire complement of *Truth* laid out on similar beds spaced only arm's length apart. There were other beds, empty, marching off into the distance.

She got to her feet and essayed the long, long walk toward the running water. She found Jindigar in the shower, steam billowing around him. When the napped skin was wet, it showed the dark blue number stamped on forehead and torso. He was slumped, dull-eyed, and pale-toothed. He didn't seem to notice her. She tried to force life into her voice, calling over the rush of water, "How can you stand that!"

He turned it off, looking at her without recognition. She remembered, *There might not be much of me left.*

"Grisnilter's dead, Krinata. He was right. He must have been right. It must be that I've been wrong...."

Dear God! His mind! Her own brain still foggy, she made a snap decision, remembering how he could always pull himself together when others depended on him. "Look, *Prince* Jindigar, you made me a promise, and you're going to keep it. We're stuck in a rat trap with no hope, but you still owe me transportation to a nice safe planet where I and my progeny, if any, can live in peace, freedom and security. I need an Oliat officer to accomplish that, not an Historian!"

Her indignation, by the time she finished, was genuine.

He stood silently before her, naked, dripping, amazed. Then he threw his head back and let out a cry neither sob nor laugh. Two steps, he scooped her up and spun her around, his wet nap soaking her turquoise suit. "Krinata, oh, you are so real! Of course, I'll keep my promise. Don't I always?"

But over the next days, Krinata barely saw Jindigar. The Dushau protected him fanatically, as if he were an invalid in critical condition. Lonely as she was, she had no success thawing the others toward her. Days later she found out why. She was using the shower stall in a corner, and had turned off the water to dry herself when the four humans came in, the two women moving toward Krinata and the men away. One of the women was saying, "They think he's going to die, that's why they won't let her near him."

"If Gibson's right, and she's sleeping with him..."

"How could he be wrong, after she came out of his cabin like that?"

"Even so, Gibson oughta keep his mouth shut. Now all the Dushau know because he let Desdinda find out, and it's clear enough she hates Jindigar. Now the rest of them think Krinata harmed him. Imagine, they think a little natural could do any harm. I warrant that's what the man needs!"

"You volunteerin'?"

"Hell, no! Don't get me wrong. I couldn't care less what other kinds do, but that don't mean I'd do the same. She wants him, she kin have 'im. But I don't hafta talk to 'er."

"Still, Jindigar's different from the rest o' them Dushau. He's good folk. Solid. Don't like ta' see 'im ailing like this. I hope they know what's good for 'im."

They chattered on as they washed, and Krinata had to wait, hoping she wouldn't be found eavesdropping. She'd almost forgotten the time she'd come out of Jindigar's cabin wearing his robe. Gibson had drawn the logical and ridiculous conclusion. Without knowing the Dushau lifecycle, what else could they think? But the disapproval of cross-species fornication had frosted her already cool relationship to the rest of the *Truth*'s complement.

It was worse because Jindigar didn't acknowledge the relationship, for those who didn't disapprove didn't know how to treat her. Knowing this, she could handle it. But did Jindigar know of the rumor or was he being protected from it?

Certainly the Dushau were keeping her away from Jindigar mistakenly, when she might even help him, Krinata began to note her surroundings and plan. They were in a desert. A force dome covered twenty-five identical barracks. One building was an infirmary. Once a day they were allowed to go to a larger building where they were fed adequate but revolting food. And though prisoners in other barracks were led off to a huge, flat building to work, all they were given to occupy their time was the maintenance of their own building. This they were all forced to do with primitive tools as guards stood over them and made sure they were properly humiliated.

Even Jindigar, as much as his fellows tried to protect him, was forced to scrub floors while guards gloated over the high and mighty prince brought low. But he took it with his usual disregard for the trappings of dignity, which in itself was a kind of genuine dignity of true royalty. Krinata took her cue from this, and threw herself into her tasks with a childlike glee that soon baffled the guards into leaving her alone, calling her simpleminded.

Once, Desdinda saw her chance to strike a blow at Jindigar, and surreptitiously knocked over the bucket from which he was scrubbing the latrine floor. Krinata, working at the other end of the room, could do nothing when the guard flattened Jindigar with the butt of his weapon.

The daytime heat was crushing, somewhere beyond human endurance. The nighttime chill was enough to leave ice on the bathroom floor. She was issued extra clothing, but it hardly helped. She spent a lot of her time wrapped in her blankets, curled on her bed, shivering. Or else, she'd lie prone, waiting for the heat to abate. So there was very little time when she could pursue Jindigar.

Finally, late one afternoon, she went out onto the porch for some air, and found Jindigar sitting at last unguarded. She sat down beside him. "I hope you're feeling better."

"So do I," he replied.

At least he's talking. "I'm going to be awfully blunt and candid, but I have to know. Have you been avoiding me? Do you want me here?"

She hadn't noticed two Dushau coming out of the door behind her. They circled to confront her. "Leave him alone!"

She said calmly, "I was only talking to him."

"I said leave him alone! He is not to be disturbed."

"I wasn't 'disturbing' him!" she retorted, beginning to feel anger building. How could they talk about him as if he weren't even there?

"I say you were."

Krinata didn't even know the Dushau's name. She stood up and faced him squarely, "Don't you think Jindigar should be the judge of that?"

"He's in no condition to judge anything."

She looked down at Jindigar who was staring blankly off into space. *God, maybe they're right.* But she wasn't going to

make a scene that would put more stress on him. She made a
frustrated sound and whirled to stalk back to her bunk and
fling herself face down, trying not to cry.

Later, Rinperee found her there, and sat beside her waiting
to be noticed.

"What do you want?" Krinata challenged, wishing she didn't
sound so belligerent.

"To try to explain. I know you're important to Jindigar.
And I know you want to help him. But..."

"If you're talking about that horrid rumor, it's not true!"

After a shocked pause, Rinperee asked, as if truly seeking
information, "Can you honestly tell me Jindigar means nothing
to you?"

She sat up, crossing her legs. She had to be civil, now that
one of them was at least acknowledging her existence. "He's
probably the best friend I have left now. But I'm nothing to
him except a fairly competent programming ecologist who's a
pretty mean bluffer, too. That stupid rumor is a lie."

"Krinata, I'm Dushau. You don't have to explain the 'stupidity' of that rumor to me. But you are wrong to think you're
nothing to Jindigar but a programmer. And therein lies a dread-
ful danger to *him*. It was none of my business what he did to
himself as an Oliat, but he's an Historian now, and his clarity
of access to the Archive depends on his *not* acquiring any
emotional scars to lie between him and that spliced memory.
If he nurtures friendship for you, he will grieve hard at your
death, and lose countless precious facts Grisnilter and all his
forebears suffered so to preserve.

"That is why we guard ourselves so from entanglement with
Ephemerals. When it was just his personal memories he was
throwing away, few could intervene. Now, we all have a stake
in his well-being. And I'm the closest we have to an expert
on treating his condition. I've asked the others to keep you
away from him, so I feel I owe you an explanation."

"Explain this, then. What's wrong with him? How do you
know he doesn't need to talk to me?"

"In absorbing the Archive, he's undergone an intense mental
strain, a challenge to his ability to sift reality from phantasm

He's struggling on the verge of going episodic. Do you know what that means?"

"I'm a certified Oliat debriefing officer, and within a couple of credits of getting my field liaison rating. You may know Historians, but I'll bet I know more about Oliat."

Humor melted the stern expression on Rinperee's face. As if sharing a private joke, she bent toward Krinata and intimated, "My father, two of my brothers, and my sister are Oliat. I've no talent for it, or I would be also. I've taken a lifelong interest in it. I can't claim ignorance."

Abashed, Krinata apologized. "I have my little prides."

"And you're well entitled to them. I can't belittle what you've accomplished for Jindigar and all the rest of us. What can I say to bring you to trust my judgment?"

Krinata's curiosity wakened, and she set a test. "The Dushau unanimously deny being telepathic. If trading memories isn't telepathic, what is?"

"Telepathic, as it's commonly used, refers to perception of worded but unvoiced conscious thoughts of others. Few Dushau have such ability, and never very strongly. What Historians do in keeping the Archive—what the Oliat does to constitute and balance—have no comparison among Ephemerals. Therefore we deny the application of such concepts as telepathic or psychic or precognitive. It is simply our mode of awareness that is different."

"All right," said Krinata, chalking it all up to tangled semantics. *They're telepaths, never mind what they say.* "But Jindigar's undergone some kind of immense psychic shock of the same magnitude as losing his Oliat, and that nearly wiped him out. I know, I lived through it with him. And I helped him then. Ask him, if you don't believe me. What makes you think I can't help him now?"

"I'm neither Historian nor Oliat; I'm a Sentient psychologist. But I know enough to recognize a Dushau under an intolerable burden. Such is Jindigar. He needs time and quiet to assimilate events. You may have helped him before, in the short run. But, innocently enough, you were setting him up— now, or fifty or a hundred years from now when you must die—to take a grieving. Do you know what a grieving is? What it does to Dushau?"

"I know it's a terrible thing. But everyone grieves. One can't refrain from emotional attachment for fear of the pain of parting."

"True, parting is a normal aspect of life. A certain number of grievings must come into every life—it's necessary to the maturing process. But when a Dushau grieves, the emotions are, um, wrapped tightly like filaments, into a fibrous wall across memory. Depending on the intensity of the grieving, that wall can be translucent or opaque and unbreakable. A Dushau who has only Dushau friends will have a manageable number of grievings. A Dushau who befriends Ephemerals will have so many scars, so many mind blockages, however faint they may be, that his sanity becomes endangered. A Dushau's life depends on investing his emotions wisely, you see."

She had known all the facts, but had never put them together quite like that. The concept stunned her. No wonder Dushau seemed so aloof and uncaring; they were afraid to care.

"But I'm only one person, and he doesn't care for me."

"Jindigar has spent a large part of his life involving himself ever deeper in the affairs of Ephemerals. He may decide to change that now, and I think you owe him that chance—when he's healed enough to think straight again. If, when he's healed, he decides to throw away the Archive he's paid so dearly for and continue to develop friendships with Ephemerals, then there's nothing any of us can do. All I'm asking, Krinata, is that you have the sensitivity to allow *him* to make that decision when he's healed enough to make any kind of decision. Don't force it on him now, when he'll grab at anything for immediate relief. With this, he has become truly a prince among us. Who would, any of us, except perhaps Desdinda, give our lives for his. If he truly means anything to you, give him the grace of your absence."

Krinata could only agree. But her life became suddenly bleak and hopeless. In voluntarily giving up Jindigar, she felt she was giving up something that had cost her as dearly as the Archive had cost him. It could take him fifty years to recover, and he'd regard it only as a medium-length convalescence. She had to shut herself off from whatever had kept their prison and their hopeless future from sapping her spirit. Her days became listless, and her nights sleepless. And in the end, it was a resolve too difficult to keep.

One night, she was awake during the seventeen-hour darkness. She went out onto the cool porch. Sitting, watching the stars, wondering which was *Truth,* or even if *Truth* was still in orbit, she heard a sound.

She froze, listening, wondering if other prisoners were digging an escape tunnel. But now, the scrabbling was not furtive. She crept around the end of the building, and found a scrawny, three-quarters starved piol digging in the moist ground under the skirt of the elevated building.

As she watched, it increased its tempo frantically. Then it jerked back and came up with a wriggling something in its claws which it promptly devoured. But when Krinata made a move toward it, it scampered away.

After that, she set herself to tame the wild one, putting out bowls of water and scraps of food. Soon, she had it eating out of her hand, and figured that it had once been tame. Finally, she arranged for Jindigar to find her in the shower room bathing the piol, thinking one could love such an animal but not grieve over its death as over a person's.

And that was the beginning of Jindigar's recovery. Deciding the piol was female, he named her Rita. Each day, he fed and groomed and played with her. She soon became part of the barracks life.

Frey proclaimed Krinata a genius. Storm made her part of his small family where before he, too, had been adamant about keeping her away from Jindigar. And when Bell finally got up the nerve to ask if the rumor about her and Jindigar were true, Krinata could explain to someone who believed her. It was such a relief.

As the days passed Krinata spent a lot of time wondering why the Dushau and all of *Truth*'s complement hadn't been executed out of hand. But there were no answers.

The hashmarks she made on her windowsill showed they'd been there ten local days, though it seemed like ten years, when the rest of Storm's family was thrown in with them. They looked tortured and starved, and she was sure there were fewer of them. All they talked of was those who had died, many in prison. The survivors were hardened and proud, defending their religious principles.

Krinata overheard snatches of conversations held in tense undertones about whether the marriage was really valid, interrupted in the middle as it had been. The newlyweds maintained it was. Some of the older, more orthodox said it wasn't. The group polarized with Storm and his mates joining the *Truth* complement, and the family keeping to themselves.

Her tally of days had reached fifteen when a flurry of activity swept the camp, the guards forcing everyone to clean, polish and mend everything in sight. Rumor had it that they were about to be inspected.

Something in Krinata woke to hope again, and escape plans began to form in her mind, plans involving Jindigar. Just thinking of working with him raised her spirits.

The big morning arrived. The guards, all spit and polish in their best uniforms, paraded the prisoners outside their barracks, seeming to expect the nonmilitary prisoners to form up as if they were a precision drill team.

Then, amid imperial magnitude drum rolls, the compound was invaded by smart-stepping imperial troops, armed and armored, carrying the Emperor's banner.

Krinata's heart sank when she saw Zinzik, robes flying, crown flashing, marching amid his Honor Guard. She despaired even before he stopped in front of their ranks, singled her out, and said, "Step forward, Krinata Zavaronne."

TWELVE

Zinzik's Revenge

Quaking inside, Krinata advanced in front of her line and made a precise obeisance.

"A loyal subject, are you?" asked Zinzik, pacing, his eyes running up and down the row of Dushau until he spotted Jindigar. Abstractedly examining the prince, he added thoughtfully, "And how do you explain what you have done?"

"I thought you were simply making a mistake which you, in imperial wisdom, would soon correct. I saw no reason for loyal subjects to die because of an error."

"I am Emperor. An Emperor of the Allegiancy doesn't make mistakes."

She knew he already had her slated for execution, and wondered if he'd have her shot on the spot or saved for public ceremony. But she looked him squarely in the eye and said, "This time, you did, Excellency."

He dismissed her coldly, calling Jindigar out. "Illustrious Prince of Dushau. Come, greet your Emperor."

Jindigar remained standing, eyes focused on the distance, as if he'd gone back into that catatonic state.

Zinzik roared, "Jindigar, step forth!"

Jindigar brought his eyes to bear on the Emperor as if noticing him for the first time, gave a very unceremonious shrug, as if it were of no moment to him where he stood, and took two paces forward to present himself beside Krinata.

"Well!" prompted Zinzik.

"Well, what?" asked Jindigar.

"On your knees, Dushau!"

"Why?"

"I am your Emperor! I hold the power of life and death ove you!" Unbelievably, Zinzik was livid. She realized he clung to the trappings of power while the core of his influence erode away, support of the Kings and the Dukes lost. She glance at Trassle who was watching alertly.

As if reasoning with a simple child, Jindigar said, "I ow no fealty to any Emperor. My oath to the Allegiancy wa broken by the Allegiancy's Emperor. The power of life an death does not give one the power to command fealty. O loyalty. Or any esteem whatsoever."

That will make a marvelous epitaph. But at the same time Krinata surmised Jindigar was functioning normally.

Whereas Krinata's response had barely affected the Em peror, Jindigar's tapped a deep anger that twisted the Lehiro countenance. A moment later, the oily superiority was back barely masking ferocity. "You do not impress me, Jindigar You will be brought to heel. Publicly." The Lehiroh wer evolved predators. But Zinzik, she thought, was not so evolved Amazingly, Jindigar stood unflinching before that ferocity. Sh could hear the rapid breathing of the other Dushau behind her barely able to abort a *flee* impulse. Desdinda whimpered.

Zinzik strolled along the double rank of prisoners, until h came to Bell and her husbands. He came closer, despite th nervousness of his guards who flanked him tightly. His li curled in disgust. "Ensyvians!"

Then he glanced thoughtfully at Jindigar, still standing fron and center, impassive. He snapped to a Holot trotting alon, behind him, "Get all these aboard immediately, except th Ensyvians." He considered Jindigar's expression. "No, includ these five, but not the mob. Then get me Nodrial, and tell hin to bring *all* the documents pertaining to this case. I will knov *why* it took so long to notify me!"

With that, Zinzik stomped off amid the pomp and honor offered by the suddenly bewildered staff of the prison.

Within the hour, they were on their way offplanet. Durin a commotion started when the family members, anguished a parting, apologized to the newlyweds for treating them badly Jindigar contrived to hide the scrawny piol under his shir

There was hardly a bulge. Jindigar had lost weight since he'd carried Imp to the Emperor's audience chamber.

They were hustled aboard *Timespike,* the imperial flagship, by cargo carrier. Without g-seats, they arrived bruised and strained. They were paraded into the brig, a narrow corridor lined with four-person cells. Two extra cots had been jammed into each cell, leaving virtually no room to stand. Krinata could see the very unprivate all-species toilets in the rear of each cell.

Taking roll as they were divided into groups, Krinata discovered that all twenty-seven *Truth* passengers plus Storm and his mates were there.

The guards, three women and eight men charged with putting them in their cells, were all human. When they were lined up along the center of the brig corridor, the commander ordered the Dushau sprinkled throughout the group. Then he had them count off into two groups of six and four groups of five, deliberately separating the Lehiroh as well.

Krinata contrived to stick beside Jindigar, and ended up with him, Desdinda, Bell and Storm in a five-person cell. But when the guards tried to crowd them into the cell before them, Desdinda went wild—prey cornered. Emitting a feral scream, she leaped on the guard who stood between her and the gate at the end of the brig shaftway, tore at his throat with her teeth, and left him bleeding on the deck to charge into the Holot guards who stood beside the gate.

Before she'd gone three steps, she was dropped by stunner fire. Jindigar had charged after her, for all the world as if he'd lay down his life for her. But two human guards stopped him with crossed weapons. A little sound escaped him before he subsided.

Two guards carried Desdinda off to the infirmary, swearing all the while. Frey was shifted into Desdinda's place and forced into their cell as if he might resist also. Bars slammed across the doors, in addition to the snapfield. Power failures on battleships were too frequent to trust prisoners to force fields alone.

Jindigar stayed by the bars, watching the guards leave,

before he turned and extracted Rita from her place under his shirt. Placing her on one of the beds as if she were a decorative doll, he said, "Now there's hope."

He's blown a circuit at last!

But Storm said, "Let's not say it too loudly, though."

Jindigar eyed their bare surroundings. There must be monitoring devices; prisons always had them. But Jindigar said, "There's nobody listening now. As soon as they bring Desdinda back, and as soon as Arlai contacts us, we must be ready to move."

Afraid to accuse him of insanity, Krinata said, "Jindigar, do you know how that sounds?"

Bell said, "Insane, that's how." Krinata glared at her.

Frey was clinging to the bars, gazing after Desdinda, oblivious. Jindigar considered Bell and Krinata as if Storm, Frey and he shared a special Oliat rapport, an understanding of their environment all her ecological training couldn't emulate. Jindigar explained patiently, "I'm better now. Really I am. I can know things. The rest I can deduce."

Krinata inspected him. He was standing normally again. His teeth seemed a healthy blue, his voice resonated. Was he just pulling himself together to deal with another crisis, or had he overcome the ordeal Grisnilter had put him through? "What do you mean, know things?" asked Krinata.

"Frey and I . . . sense environment. Rhythms. Even without Oliat."

Frey turned. His eyes were haunted. "Desdinda."

"I think she's going to make it," said Jindigar.

"You *wish* she's going to make it," corrected Frey.

Krinata saw the boy's fear, and she could understand it. Desdinda had undergone the shattering of her Oliat, as Jindigar had, but Jindigar had survived. Frey's ambition had been to officer an Oliat. And now he saw the danger of it.

Heavily, Jindigar admitted, "Wish. Yes."

Into the bleak silence, Storm said, "Arlai."

Jindigar turned from Frey. "He's nearby. That I know. Knowing Arlai, I deduce he set this situation up. There was no way to get us out of that prison, except by the decree of someone superior to Duke Nodrial. Meaning, the Emperor.

Nodrial is plotting against the Emperor. I think Zinzik knows it because Arlai contrived to get word of our presence to Zinzik, making it clear that Nodrial had no intention of just handing us over to Zinzik. Nodrial is vulnerable because he's already using Rashions to control his populace. What do you think the Emperor will do?"

"Squash Nodrial," answered Krinata. "Take the Rashions for himself." She almost gagged at the thought.

Jindigar nodded, then crawled onto the bed next to one wall, cuddling the piol in his lap. "Arlai's smart enough to see that as soon as he discovered the Rashions."

Krinata said glumly, "To me, this looks like one of Arlai's spectacular failures. I'd rather spend the rest of my life in that prison than in Zinzik's grasp."

"We're in Arlai's environment now," answered Jindigar. He stroked Rita, and then turned to Krinata with a start. "I never really apologized to you for not reprogramming that bus. It was a good idea, Krinata. It might have worked."

"Leaving us in the middle of a desert."

"We might have been able to reprogram without setting off all the alarms. And the spaceport . . . I don't know. We could have improvised something."

"Look. I think I understand why you had to do what you did. We may yet make it, now that you're back with us."

He hugged Rita, then handed her to Krinata. "Can you sit down a moment? I want to move this cot."

Awkwardly in the packed room, he unfastened his cot, moved it closer to the bars, and climbed back onto it. "You all may as well try to get some sleep. I'll watch for Desdinda. Nothing will happen before she gets back."

Krinata was sure she couldn't sleep with the lights on. She sat staring at Jindigar and Frey who gazed fixedly up the shaftway. At intervals, Jindigar pointed to the overhead spy eyes, indicating they were active. After a while, Frey motioned to them first, apparently having learned how to detect observation. She watched them, noting very little difference in the way he treated Frey and the way he treated her, except he didn't teach her anything but piloting.

Since they'd entered the cell, Jindigar had behaved toward

her like his old self. Was she really doing him irreparable harm by responding? It had been his choice, after all. And she couldn't find it in her not to respond. Even though their situation now was far worse than before, she suddenly found her energy and optimism returning. But was it selfish to cling to him because it made her feel good? There was no way to resolve the dilemma, and so she fell asleep gnawing on it, the warm piol curled in her lap.

She dreamed she was prisoner on a transparent spaceship. All around her, messages flew on clouds of energy contained in pipes in the walls, and she could feel their pulse. She could hear the angry buzz of hostility, the languid ache of sickness, the coarse celebrations of troopers primed to blood lust and held in check by respect for a superior blood lust. But the situation was transparent in time, as well, and behind it lay many, many similar occasions. Dream turned to nightmare as setting after setting spun into the center of her consciousness and away, leaving her unsure which situation was current.

Smothering in the rising fear, she was jolted back to reality by the slap of marching feet and cries of protest. The cells were open and they were being paraded in the shaftway again. This time, they were taken to decent showers and given comfortable, well-fitting ship's issue clothing. Then, two abreast, they were marched through miles of corridors.

Krinata had thought *Truth* a large ship. *Timespike* held the cubic of several city blocks, and Krinata was soon totally lost. Yet, she realized where they were going scant seconds before they arrived. The Emperor's audience chamber.

The room was as huge as a hangar deck, but decorated in expensive fabrics, textured walls, and imperial crests. Four exotic bird sanctuaries filled the corners with color and a pleasant background sound. The floor appeared to be polished wood, though she knew that couldn't be. Not in space. The throne on which the Emperor sat was a replica of the one in the palace. The imperial leptolizer stood ensconced over a disguised holostage, giving him direct access to his Empire.

This time, though, the room was not filled with the court delegations. A regiment of troops lined the walls in smart dress satins, but carrying real weapons. With a thrill of goose bumps, Krinata thought she recognized some of the troopers' faces from her nightmare. But then she forgot that as she stifled a cry at the sight of Rashion trainers and their charges stationed about the throne.

Krinata and Jindigar were in the lead. She'd seen Desdinda join them, looking pale-toothed yet ambulatory, hanging back as far from Jindigar as she could.

Zinzik gestured negligently at Jindigar as they were brought up to the throne steps. "One more chance, my Prince."

Jindigar remained standing. So did Krinata. But she heard a rustle behind her—some of them were kneeling. She didn't want to know who.

Zinzik stood and walked down the steps to look Jindigar in the eye. "No?"

"No," stated Jindigar mildly.

"I see. Well, we shall find your weakness. And when we do, we shall stage a public confession. You see, you've become some kind of a symbol of the Oliat system, the last remaining Oliat officer at large in the Allegiancy. The rumors magnify you out of all proportion. But I can use that. At your news conference, held just before your execution, you will reveal all the vile details of the Dushau plot that has brought the Allegiancy to these dire straits. Your loyal testimony will re-unify the Allegiancy behind the rightful Emperor."

So he is in trouble with the Kings!

"If I were going to die anyway, why would I lie?"

"Thousands of years old, yet innocent as a babe." His expression hardened. "Because if you don't do as I want, someone precious to you will be dismembered, by a predatory carnivore, right before your eyes. While if you do as I want, not only will they be spared, but I will have you transported to Dushaun, alive and well. I even might send along all of your friends, alive and well. If I'm especially pleased, I could add wealth even a prince would appreciate."

Because of the memories he now carried, Jindigar felt an obligation to survive even upon the deaths of others—as much against his nature as that went. He also needed to return to

Dushaun to be trained to unlock those memories, despite all his reasons for not wanting to return home.

"A prince," answered Jindigar thoughtfully, "can not be bribed or blackmailed, especially not by an Emperor who has broken faith with him." Krinata heard the unspoken finish to that, though Zinzik appeared oblivious. *No matter how much he wants the bribe or fears the threat.*

Krinata's admiration leaped like a flame, while she recognized the pride motivating him. He was being asked to destroy the reputation of his species before civilizations yet to be born in the galaxy, as well as the integrity of the Oliat. There was probably some Aliom principle stiffening his spine, but his pride in his adherence to his ethical, moral, and legal codes shone forth.

On the other hand, she knew the tattered shambles of his nerves left by his experiences of the last few months. Zinzik had designed bribe and threat to tear Jindigar apart along the very axis already unendurably stressed: loyalty to his people versus loyalty to his friends. Not for the first time, she regretted her friendship with Jindigar which, as Rinperee had predicted, might do him more harm than good, though in a totally unexpected way.

How much could he take before he broke? Would he watch a Rashion tear her throat out, and still hold to his principles? Despite what Rinperee had said, she didn't think he cared more for her than for his principles. But if he broke, would he die of insanity, unable to cooperate with Zinzik's demands, thus losing any chance of saving the Archive? Or would he stage the confession and be sent home, thus saving the Archive so his feeling for her could be said to force him to do what Grisnilter and Rinperee wanted him to? It was a decision only Jindigar could make, and Krinata wasn't kidding herself. His values were not human.

All of this flashed through Krinata's mind as Zinzik circled Jindigar, as if able to see right through his calm facade. Then, grinning confidently, Zinzik snapped his fingers. "Richter!"

One of the Rashion trainers trotted over with his charge. A woman came with him: Lehiroh, tall, slender, dark, and hard-eyed with a cruel twist to her lips. Krinata told herself not to interpret other species by her human biases. But she didn't believe it this time.

She was right. As the Emperor stepped back to perch sideways on his throne, as if about to enjoy a good show, the woman pulled out a screenboard, propped it against her waist with one hand while she punched up data with the other.

"Ready, Richter?" asked the woman.

"The beast is ready. He's one of the prize—"

"Enough! All right, Jindigar. Which of these companions means the most to you?"

Jindigar's stared fixedly as if he didn't hear.

"We'll kill them all, one by one until we get a rise—"

The Rashion whimpered and tugged at his leash. The trainer went with him, first to one then another of the *Truth*'s complement. The protosentient seemed confused and frustrated as he came to Krinata, whuffled at her feet, then started around again.

"This is getting nowhere," declared the trainer. "He seems to regard them all equally."

"Nonsense. Start with—" The Lehiroh woman spun about looking at the motley bunch, and chose Bell. "—that one. Strip her. Bring her around front here so everyone can see."

Bell's guards shoved her up front and removed her clothing. Jindigar watched in that unembarrassed way he had that made it seem she was still properly clothed even when she fought exposing her vestigial mammary glands. "Now," said the Lehiroh woman, who obviously held the same contempt for Ensyvians as the Emperor did, "is there a Lehiroh guard who'd like a little fun with an Ensyvian bride?"

Every Lehiroh male guard in the room stepped eagerly forward. "You!" she chose one. The male came forward, leering. As if on a mutually arranged signal, all four of Bell's mates lunged forward ripping themselves loose of their guards and charging the volunteer tormenter. As they rolled on the floor, guards converging from all sides to put a stop to it, the Rashion made confused noises deep in his throat.

Despite the fact that a Rashion had attacked her with what seemed intent to kill, Krinata wanted to gather the poor creature up in her arms and soothe its pathetic cries. She wondered if the training methods were so brutal that the dimwitted creature was terrified of failing a command.

At last, peace was restored. The woman consulted the trainer and sent Bell away, pulling Krinata out in front.

Suddenly, Krinata wondered if that screenboard contained an account of Jindigar's defenses of her. If Nodrial were as thorough as a Duke should be, and if he were actively cooperating with Zinzik now, those two incidents, at the wedding and in the stripsearch barn, were surely on record.

Jerking her off balance, the guards positioned her and methodically removed her clothing. Zinzik held up a hand. "Stop. Let me admire this." He rose and sauntered down the steps, circling Krinata, eyes drinking in every detail of her human anatomy. He poked her belly, pinching the sparse roll of fat there, feeling the hard muscles tensed against him. He ignored her tiny breasts, for they did not spell female to him. Other Lehiroh would consider him a pervert if they interested him. He ran his soft hands across her back as if she were a pedigreed animal for sale. He noticed the scars Arlai hadn't had time to remove from her upper arms.

"Not bad," he declared. "She seems to have survived a remarkable number of adventures relatively unscathed. Surely there's a human present who'd like to play with her?"

There were a great number of them, but Zinzik chose a very, very large human male, asking, "Don't you think she might be too small for you?"

"Humans like it that way, Excellency."

"She might not."

"Does that matter?"

"Of course not. She's yours."

All during this, Zinzik was balanced on his toes, ready to dance out of the way if Jindigar should somehow get loose of the four guards now on him and charge forward. Jindigar was staring devoutly at the artwork decorating the ceiling.

The immense human handed his weapon aside, and began to shed his light armor. Jindigar still refused to acknowledge what was happening. Zinzik approached the Dushau warily. "I'm not going to stop him, you know."

The Rashion still fretted confusedly at Jindigar's feet. Did the Dushau have such mental control that he was emitting nothing the Rashion could read? If so, Krinata hoped he could keep it up. She hoped he didn't care a bit for her because if she were the cause of his mental breakdown and death, she couldn't live with herself. Then she saw Trassle and his wife trying to protect their offspring from the sight. *What am I going to do?*

She looked at the hulk now stripping in a businesslike way. He was already showing signs of enthusiasm. She had to do something, and soon. Though they had the upper hand, she'd begun to develop a genuine contempt for Zinzik and all those he'd brought to power. If it would get Jindigar home and save his Archive and his sanity, she'd gladly endure worse than this, or even die. *He* was worth all she had and more. Zinzik and what was left of the Allegiancy weren't worth the cost of destroying. *But what can I do to help Jindigar?* It was the first time in her life she'd been a totally helpless victim, too scared to think.

She caught a glimpse of Zinzik watching her. Disgust welling, she squeezed her eyes shut until she saw red. *Oh, Jindigar, what am I going to do?*

Suddenly, eyes still closed, she saw Zinzik reflected in a decoration on the ceiling, and simultaneously, she saw him directly. She had read descriptions of Lehiroh male excitation but had never seen it. Now, she recognized it with the total familiarity of an Emulator's identity with the species. With a shudder, she recognized his attitude as characteristic of a practice she considered a perversion.

Trying to shake the fantasy while cursing her imagination, Krinata forced her eyes open and looked at the Emperor. The strange split perception remained overlaid above what she could see. Her own eyes brought her no suggestion of what her imagination told her. Those odd echo visions shifted, as Zinzik turned to the Lehiroh woman who had set this up. From his glance, she imagined Zinzik often had the woman set up such tantalizing sights for him.

Unable to tolerate the vision, she eyed the hulk again. He

was watching the Emperor familiarly. He'd done this before, and was awaiting a signal. She had no doubt the Emperor's contrived shows usually went to conclusion.

Even with her eyes focused on the brute, she was aware of Zinzik teasing his Lehiroh female. And she perceived the Emperor's wakening pleasure from the other's pain. She began to understand Zinzik, and thus what must come next. Her part was to be terrified and be brutally overpowered. That would hurt Jindigar, who would also be aware of the pleasure Zinzik took in her pain—as if Zinzik himself were raping her.

Instantly, she knew what she had to do.

But she couldn't. She twisted to glimpse Jindigar. He was still staring at the ceiling, at Zinzik's image? Frey had crept up beside him, his eyes fixed on the throne. As her gaze lit on Jindigar, he turned midnight eyes on her. They widened a bit; the vaguest hint of a shocked recoil struck her. Abruptly the overlaid awareness snapped off.

The sudden emptiness almost took the starch out of her knees. Alone in that echoing void, slammed into the stark reality of what was about to happen to her, she caught her breath, and faced what she fervently hoped was the ultimate test of her life. Did she have the nerve? *For Jindigar? Yes. Of course I can do it. I have to. I'm alone in this. Jindigar can't help me. He can barely help himself.*

On Zinzik's cue, the brute began his assault, grabbing her hair and pulling her head back to tilt her face to his. Everything in her said, *Bite his lips!* And she almost did, but then swallowing her gorge, she summoned a smile she hoped was seductive, and forced her body to melt into his grasp.

It had been a long time since she'd had a man, and while her mind squirmed and screamed, her treacherous body noticed how awfully good masculinity could feel, how enervating it could be to the will. His clean, brown skin was soft, tufted with sharp curly hairs. A clean man-scent engulfed her. But suddenly, as if recalling where he was, he tightened his grip painfully. "The Emperor wants you to resist, woman. Put up some fight!" He shoved her away and hit her across the face.

She went sprawling, stifling a yelp, gathering all her courage and refusing to scramble away and run for it. The deck was hard and chill, but she gathered herself into a seductive pose, noting with horror that hitting her had roused him more. She smiled. "I see you're ready. Come on and tumble." *Can I go through with this?*

The brute stalked after her, readier than ever. Any symptom of arousal she had felt was washed away in sheer terror. Gritting her teeth behind her smile, she raised one hand to fondle him intimately, trying to seem admiring and welcoming while she'd rather emasculate him.

In the moment she knew she couldn't go through with it, in the moment she faced her crumbling courage and knew she could not stifle her scream if the man grabbed her arm to pull her to her feet, Zinzik cried, "Enough!"

The brute looked up, wounded. He was throbbingly ready to do his Emperor's bidding. Bewildered, he asked, "No?"

"Later," commanded the Emperor. "You may leave now. Sign out for the rest of this watch."

Naked, he stood to attention, bowed formally, and said, "Yes, your Excellency." He gathered his clothes and left.

Krinata told herself she must not collapse now or she'd lose her tiny victory. Her role called for her to stand up, legs braced, hands on hips, chin up and challenge any other man in the room to a tumble. But she stayed on the floor, trying not to make it so obvious that her legs were curled to hide her nakedness.

"I've a much more interesting idea," said Zinzik with the air of one about to pull off a final coup. "That one! The female on the end!"

Two guards brought Desdinda forth. She struggled, still weak from the stunner, but the guards dragged her out and threw her onto the deck beside Krinata. She went skidding.

"Surely," said the Emperor, "there's someone here who's had a yen to try a Dushau female?"

There were many volunteers snapping crisp, eager salutes to their Emperor. This ship, Krinata belatedly realized, was manned by the Emperor's own, hand-picked, elite personal guard. They were accustomed to this very private game of his. While the Emperor selected his volunteer, Krinata tried to offer the woman some advice.

The Dushau looked at her as if she were half a worm found in a fruit. There was a wild look to her eyes, and a peculiar purple paleness to her teeth. There was nothing left of the poised Oliat officer they'd rescued from the exploded ship. This was a broken personality, and though it was a desperate tragedy, Krinata's only thought was not ever to have to see that look in Jindigar's eyes.

As an athletic-looking Holot separated from the guards and stalked toward Desdinda, the Dushau scrambled to her feet and whirled to face Zinzik. Krinata saw Frey lunge forward as if to forestall Desdinda's move, but Jindigar caught his arm and held him squirming. She was sure that Jindigar intended to take that lunge in Frey's place, but just then Desdinda called out, "Stop! *I* will provide your confession. I, too, have been Oliat."

Jindigar froze. Zinzik stood, raising his hand to stop the approaching Holot, triumph lighting his eyes. She was sure Jindigar had stopped breathing, but then she heard his inarticulate cry of anguish, frustration and defeat.

At a snap of Zinzik's wrist, six guards closed in around Desdinda. She was snatched off the floor and pushed along to a chorus of lewd remarks. Their guards gathered them into marching order, Krinata and Jindigar bringing up the rear this time. As they were about to pass out of the audience chamber, Krinata glanced back and saw Zinzik take a beamer from one of his guards. She snatched at Jindigar's sleeve, making him turn so as not to be shot in the back.

But the Emperor aimed the weapon nonchalantly at the Rashion who'd failed to spot Jindigar's favored friend and drilled him neatly through the lower abdomen.

The creature screamed and fell writhing. The trainer clenched his fists, but remained unmoving. One of the other guards asked, "Excellency, shall I finish it off for you?"

"I didn't miss my shot!" replied Zinzik, offended. "Let it die, serving as a lesson."

"Yes, Excellency."

Krinata noted the man didn't ask at whom the lesson was aimed. She, too, was afraid she knew. *Hate is unbecoming in a Zavaronne*. Her mother had always told her that with pride. This was the first time in her life she wanted devoutly to disobey her mother, and she wasn't sure she could refrain from it much longer.

That's not an Emperor. That's a lowlife!

As they were being herded back to their cells, Krinata and Bell forced to walk naked, clutching their clothes, ogled by every passing male, the Dushau attempted to reorganize so they would be grouped together instead of scattered one to a cell. But as they entered the brig corridor, the guards insisted they regroup with the same cellmates as before.

In the confusion, Krinata saw Rita slinking along the bulkhead and back into their cell. A scurry was just emerging. The scurry put out an ocular to inspect the creature, then rolled around it and went on its way. *Oh, if they take her away from Jindigar . . .*

When the guards were satisfied, they were herded into their cells. Krinata suffered a pinch on the rear from a human male who leered when she jumped and squealed. But then the bars closed between them.

As the guards withdrew, Krinata stood holding her breath, waiting for her heart to calm down. But her native armor crumbled, strained beyond tolerance, and she flung herself onto her cot, curled up in a ball and gave in to gut wrenching sobs.

She wanted to become wholly mindless, obliterating all the reality about her, but she was aware of Frey watching in helpless dismay, Storm comforting Bell. Jindigar asked something, and Bell replied that she didn't know how to help. Krinata was human, and an aristocrat.

Jindigar said; "Some things are universal."

His whole life has been compromised, and he wants to help me?

The beds, jammed against one another, jiggled as they settled themselves. Krinata didn't even have the strength to fling a cover over her bare back. She buried her streaming nose and eyes in a bunch of sheet and took an orgasmic satisfaction in uncontrolled weeping, wallowing in the shame of such weakness. There was no point in being strong. All was lost anyway.

Jindigar moved onto the cot behind her and began to knead her back. Tentatively at first, and then with more assurance as she didn't shove him away, he went after the knotted tension with a medic's precision. The soft, napped skin of his hands felt warm, not pasty soft like the Emperor's nor caloused like the soldier's. The hard fingertips, lacking nails, were perfect. There was no trace of human masculinity about him.

Gradually, she felt the eruption had spent itself, and she knew she couldn't impose her hysteria on everyone else like this. She held her breath against the hiccups and at last could say, "Thank you. I'm sorry."

"For what?" asked Jindigar in a whisper.

She turned and saw Bell asleep across Storm's lap, Storm sitting with his head propped against the wall, eyes closed.

"Bell's so much more . . . that was just ridiculous of me."

"Are you embarrassed?"

"Yes. And it's all for nothing."

"I don't understand. You did the only thing—" He stopped, his eyes going to the ceiling, and he put a finger over her lips. She figured the spy eyes were working, though she could detect no sign of them.

A few seconds later, the eye went off and Jindigar said, "I'm sorry they caught us like this. Krinata, would it help you to know that in another moment, I'd have broken?"

Suddenly, she really was embarrassed. She'd never felt so with him. "I would have, too. Besides, what good did it do? Now Zinzik has his volunteer!" The bitterness choked her. "Damn that woman!"

Again he put a finger over her lips. "No. Poor Desdinda. She suffered so from the destruction of her Oliat. It was her first Oliat, and only her second office. And then, in the midst of that nightmare of loss, she fell into the clutches of the most perverted fiend in her private mythology, an Invert. She couldn't accept help from me, and there was no one else, so she gradually lost touch with reality. Then she had to watch her pet fiend perform the ultimate perversion: sullying the sacred Archive. From her point of view, everything Dushauni has been wholly soiled and her confession is to a much lesser crime.

That I was opposed to giving Zinzik what he wanted makes it logically obvious that it's the right thing to do.

"We can't blame her, Krinata. Desdinda perished the day her Oliat died, because she'd been installed in an office far, far beyond her meager talent. It's not her fault."

In that weird state beyond hysteria, Krinata's mind replayed the fragment of overheard conversation with Frey. Now, the young Dushau was in an upper bunk, curled up facing the wall, trying to ignore his awareness of Jindigar. She didn't know how she knew, she just knew. "Jindigar," she asked very softly, "who did you mean to insult that time you told Frey that I had as much talent as Desdinda?"

Puzzled, he asked, "You heard that, too? I'm sorry." He gazed at his hands, awkward and embarrassed. And then a peculiar look suffused his face, and he glanced over his shoulder at Frey. Frey shuddered and drew in on himself. "No. No, it would never work." Another shockwave passed over him, and the look of wild surmise swept back to Krinata. "How did you know cooperating would make Zinzik stop it?"

"It was the most peculiar thing, but then I have this wild imagination. I suppose years of imagining such things coupled with the strain must have—"

"What things?"

Now it was her turn to be embarrassed. She tried to evade, but he pursued until she explained how she often imagined she was an Oliat officer. "Under stress, I guess my mind was playing tricks on me, trying to escape reality. Human minds do come up with intuitive solutions to impossible problems while trying to escape into fantasy." Increasingly embarrassed, she told him of every nuance of her experience evaluating Zinzik. "I must have put it all together from some unconsciously noted details around the palace."

That was the standard explanation, and Krinata felt he was about to deny it when Rita, chittering and puffing, dragged an object over and deposited it on Jindigar's lap, then sat up and preened herself, expecting a reward. Jindigar looked at the oblong box blankly. Then his whole demeanor changed, his eyes lit, and he grabbed the box. Then he saw the piol, set the box in Krinata's hands, and swept the piol to his chest, murmuring reassuringly.

Krinata turned the thing over and discovered it had a screen on one end. *A comunit!* Gradually, it came to her, and she wrapped a fold of sheet over it. "Arlai!"

The unit came to life. "I can't see anything. Krinata, is that you? Jindigar?"

Jindigar tucked the piol under Krinata's pillow and swept the unit around to face him. "Arlai, listen." And he reprised their situation in a few terse words. "I'd estimate we have no more than six or seven hours before Zinzik has what he wants of Desdinda and kills her."

"Kills—" started Krinata.

Jindigar waved her to silence. "You didn't think he meant any of those lavish promises, did you? How could he turn loose somebody who'll repudiate every word of that forced confession? Besides, imagine what awaits on Dushaun for anyone who'd make that recording for him!"

She hadn't thought of that.

Suddenly, Jindigar leaned forward, his head coming down on Krinata's shoulder as he made a hissing sound.

Krinata froze, and a moment later realized it must be the spy-eye check. Jindigar was hiding the instrument from them. She surreptitiously checked to make sure Rita was asleep under the pillow with all her limbs covered.

A moment later, Jindigar straightened hastily when Storm said, "Uh, I must have dozed. What's going on?"

Jindigar explained, ending, "Come, you too, Frey, listen to Arlai."

Engrossed, Krinata didn't even notice that the Dushau had invited a very humanoid male to share her bed when she was stark naked. They huddled over the comunit, discovering that Arlai had appropriated one of the scurries belonging to Spindrift, *Timespike*'s Sentient, fabricated this unit in *Timespike*'s lab and tuned it only to himself. They were private, as long as the spy eye was off.

As Bell slept peacefully, Arlai told them, "My orbit intersects yours every ninety-three minutes, and in six hours twenty minutes, I'll pass within easy thruster-suit distance. That will be more than halfway through *Timespike*'s night, and the duty crew will be lax."

"Can you open these bars?" asked Jindigar.

"Well, that's the problem. Spindrift is young, passionately dedicated to the Emperor. I got the scurry by a ruse. He doesn't know I've got it. But if I use the scurry to open the cells, he'll know, and trigger all the alarms."

"You could block that, take over—"

"Jindigar, do you want me to destroy Spindrift?"

Surprisingly, Jindigar thought hard. Krinata saw Storm glance worriedly at him. But Jindigar said, "No. No, Arlai, we'll find another way. Let's assume we get out of the cells. Where are the thruster suits stored?"

Arlai threw a schematic of *Timespike*'s interior on the screen and showed them the route.

Storm said, "But look, this is shorter—to the hangar bay. And not all of us are checked out on thruster suits."

Krinata had been suppressing an urge to yell, *No thruster suits!*, telling herself not to allow a stupid phobia to develop. Now she seized the rational excuse. "What about the children? Does a battleship carry Cassrian child-sized thruster suits?"

Glumly, Arlai said, "No, but—"

"So what about the hangar bay?" asked Storm, "It's so close, and time's our worst enemy in this kind of operation. Those in the other cells will be caught by surprise when we move, and we'll have to drag them—"

"Storm," interrupted Arlai, "that bay contains the Emperor's own yacht!"

"So?" asked the Lehiroh. "After what he's done, stealing his yacht seems a mild form of justice. I hope his favorite art objects are aboard!"

"You don't understand," argued Arlai. "It's a rebuilt seeker craft, with a class-one Sentient. You'd never be able to get aboard, let alone break the security seals."

"Arlai, you've got that yacht's modified schematics," said Krinata. "Surely—"

"He does?" asked Storm. He looked to Jindigar.

"He does. But he's right, that Sentient is programmed for absolute security. And the Emperor's own yacht's Sentient— there'd be nothing to do but enthrall it."

Krinata saw Arlai's simulacrum don a stricken expression. "Jindigar," he pleaded.

"What do you mean, enthrall?" asked Krinata with a sickening feeling she knew. Bogey man stories out of the Corporate League's downfall came to her: Sentients run wild, fighting among themselves and for various factions.

Jindigar examined his hands in his lap. She could feel the bed vibrating under them with his suppressed emotion, but she couldn't divine what that emotion was.

Arlai asked for the unit to be turned so he could get a better view of Jindigar. "Krinata, is Jindigar shaking?"

Jindigar said, "No," as Krinata said, "Yes."

Without warning, the screen went blank.

The carrier beam was still there, for the thing emitted light. But Krinata felt a surge of panic and had to strangle back a cry of despair. Then Arlai returned, apologizing. Very formally, he said, "I, too, feel a sense of urgency. The technicians have just broken into my starboard inrational circuits. They're working from my original schematics, mapping the modifications as they go. They've already done considerable damage, but when they reach the Oversee-and-Command branching, they'll mindwipe me and mechanically reimplant Allegiancy conditioning."

"Oh, Arlai," groaned Jindigar.

"Your troubles are by far worse," said Arlai staunchly, "but I tell you this so you may understand why—Jindigar, I wouldn't—I don't want to—if there's any other way—" He stopped, as if realizing he was sounding most un-Sentient. "Jindigar, if you order it, I'll enthrall the yacht's Sentient. But don't ask me to sear-out Spindrift."

"I kept you out of the wars, Arlai—" started Jindigar. But then he seemed to recover, weighing alternatives. The shaking became worse as he came to a decision. "All right, on my responsibility, at my command, enthrall. But do it carefully. Don't harm."

Storm chewed his lower lip, regarding Jindigar warily. But

Krinata thought he was evaluating the Dushau's remaining strength, not fearing him as anyone else might after hearing such an order. Storm asked, "We still have the problem of getting out of these cells."

Jindigar put his face in his hands as if to wipe away something vile, then faced Arlai squarely.

Softly Frey said, "Jindigar, no."

The older Dushau looked at the younger, and an immense chasm opened. "We can't do it without you."

Frey's eyes went to Krinata. "She hasn't agreed."

Fixing Krinata with his eyes, Jindigar asked, "Arlai, could your scurry insert a message in the food delivered to the other cells?"

Comprehension dawned on Arlai, who nodded and asked, "Could you? With just three?" Krinata was bewildered.

"If Frey agrees and Krinata is willing to try."

"What?" asked Krinata at last, sensing that the test she had just undergone was by no means ultimate.

"Zinzik is driving us all to the brink of the unthinkable," said Jindigar. "If there's any hope of saving Desdinda and, and, everything, then this is the least immoral of our options."

"What?" demanded Krinata.

THIRTEEN

Predator

"Krinata," said Jindigar, twisting his long fingers together and contemplating the tangle, "the insights you experienced into Zinzik's attitude and function were no fantasy. I didn't realize . . . I don't know how I could have missed it. But I did. It was very unprofessional."

She put her hand on his knee. "Jindigar," she prompted.

He searched her eyes. Storm and Frey watched silently. "I didn't feel you tie into us. Please believe, the first I knew of it was when you looked directly at me—something about weighing relative values. I don't know what you were evaluating. Right then, I sliced it off. I wouldn't endanger you, certainly not without your consent." He broke into some obscure Dushauni self-condemning invective.

It finally dawned on her. *Not imagining that? It was real? It was the Oliat experience?* But there was no time to think about it now. Jindigar had a plan to get them out of here, and he was disintegrating before her eyes. She gripped both his hands firmly, calmly.

"Jindigar, that little vision you gave me saved my life. I couldn't have—I *couldn't*. I'm sorry my cowardice put Desdinda on the spot, and I'm sorry she couldn't brazen it out. But being sorry won't get us out of this. Your plan—however wild—might. I'm willing to try anything. You can only die once, and I don't want to be meat for Zinzik's perverted tortures. I'd rather go down fighting."

"You don't know what you're asking. Every time you've done something for me, you've nearly gotten killed in some gruesome way. This would be the worst of all."

She tried to be hard and commanding. "Let's hear your plan

224

and let me judge whether I'll go for it. And let Frey judge whether he'll go for it. You're not our elected conscience, you know."

The Dushau looked at her strangely. Frey shrugged, a beautiful rendition of the gesture, that said Krinata had just made self-evident all the arguments against the scheme. "Jindigar, you can't be serious. No Ephemeral ever—"

"Do you know how many things I've done in my life that had never been done before?" asked Jindigar rhetorically. "Besides, she's right. We've nothing to lose but integrity and self-respect, and Zinzik will snatch those before killing us." He looked to Frey, leaving his hands in Krinata's possession. "You have the most to lose. You understand part of the theory, and some of the risks. Are you willing to become an Invert? It's a long life ahead of you, boy—"

"Not if I don't risk it." He returned Jindigar's look with a sudden fright. "You're only planning to invert a triad subform, aren't you?"

"Well, Desdinda *could* invade and tetrad. With her monumental lack of ability, that could leave us all insane. I doubt she even understands subform theory, let alone—"

"With Krinata as our weakest leg, that—"

"Krinata would be our strength in that case. She'll crumble if we drift, and she'd be especially vulnerable to disruption—remember how your first duad was? And if either of you get anywhere near the Archive, you'll be lost forever. I don't want to catalogue all the horrors. If we've decided to do it, let's not dwell on failure. There *is* one, narrow, path to success. Let's concentrate on that alone."

"That sounds sensible," agreed Krinata. "Now—"

"But first," interrupted Jindigar, "I must be sure you realize you're risking not just your life, but your sanity, your health, and your reputation—not to mention ethical principles—or endangering your immortal soul. . . ."

"We don't have all night. Just tell us what we're doing!" demanded Krinata. She shuddered at the visions of horror he conjured. Nothing like that was going to happen. "You're acting as if you're seducing me into black magic!"

Jindigar flinched. "Allowing for cultural and species differences, yes, you could put it that way."

It was Frey who told her. "He's going to be anchor for an Inverted Triad. That's a subset of Oliat Offices used to affect the environment, not just perceive it. I've only done a few triads. I'm not at all well trained in it. I've never Inverted. You'll have to be Focus, of course—that's an Inverted Outreach—"

"No," said Jindigar. "She wouldn't last three seconds. She has a bit of talent, but has never balanced. She didn't invade and triad us, Frey, she was leeching us. Unchecked, she'd have had both of us episodic in a matter of minutes. *You* will have to Focus. If I can hold you steady, you've the strength to carry the energies, and you've experience as sub-Outreach. Krinata's a natural Conceptor."

To her, he explained, "That's an Inverted Receptor. The basic talent is a vivid visual imagination. You will conceptualize—*imagine*—the snapfield fading, the bars retracting. Frey will take the image, plus the raw energy I provide as Anchored Invertor, and focus it externally, making it happen. It's a terrible thing to do to him—"

"Not as terrible as letting Zinzik have his way," answered Krinata, finally beginning to understand this bogeyman they'd built up. And just as she'd thought, there was nothing to it. It was a form of group psychokinesis, something that some people could do under laboratory conditions, and a few species could do in the field. It wasn't any kind of magic, especially not "black."

"You're both determined, then?" asked Jindigar.

When they assented, he turned to Storm. "It will be like an Oliat that's lost its Outreach. You won't be able to communicate with us, and you'll have to protect us—Krinata most of all—from anything that might disrupt her concentration. If she wanders, she'll go down and we'll all go down. As soon as the doors open, I'll attempt to shift offices to Dissolver, that's an Inverted Protector, but that's what it takes to dismantle one of these triads. I'm not sure if I can do that on the move. You four will have to get us moving and keep us moving. Carry us, if necessary, all the way to the landing bay. If I can do it, we should be dissolved when we reach the yacht. If I fail, we may all be dead. If Desdinda invades..."

"We're not dwelling on negatives, remember?" interrupted Krinata. "When do we start?"

They began preparations, Jindigar arranging every detail. While the Lehiroh studied the route to the yacht, Jindigar entrusted Rita to Storm's care, composed messages to send to the other cells, gave Arlai specific instructions on enthralling the yacht's Sentient, woke Bell and briefed her, made Krinata get dressed and stare at the array of cells they could make out obliquely from their own until she could see it with her eyes closed, and gave Frey some exercises.

"All right, now," said Jindigar grimly, "let's see if we can work a proper subform: Krinata as sub-Receptor; you as sub-Outreach; me, sub-Center. We must know when the others get the messages. All the cells look just like this one. You know who is in each cell. Krinata, you're going to see for us, what is going on among the others."

He had them settle down, himself supine, one leg crooked, one arm thrown over his eyes. Frey sat against the wall, his legs arched over Jindigar's feet, and Krinata curled up by the snapfield, where she could see a bit of shaftway and other snapfields. Presently, she felt a slight pressure on her forehead—no, Jindigar's arm on his own forehead. Then there was a field of indigo darkness—no, Frey seeing the cell lights through closed eyelids.

Rinperee, and Trassle with his children were sleeping. Terab sat beside the snapfield, glumly contemplating nothing. In another cell, Trassle's wife, and two Dushau, were sleeping. One of the human men and one of the Lehiroh were playing with improvised dice.

Unaccountably, that cell was interesting. She stayed there until gradually, her perception began to shift, narrowing to the dice. They weren't just bits of chipped stone with numbers carved on them. They were dancing masses responding to the laws of probability. But those laws were warped around the two men. An idea nudged its way to her. She could make the dice fall a particular way.

She visualized the highest score. On the second try, it worked.

And again, and again, regardless of who won. Until the only way they ever fell was high-score. The human accused the Lehiroh of cheating. But the Lehiroh denied it, abstractedly contemplating the dice. Then he scanned the ceiling, the walls, and his eyes came to rest in Krinata's direction. Stunned, he muttered an awed expletive. Then, as if she were standing beside him, she heard, "Jindigar?"

The impulse to answer came, but she couldn't. The Lehiroh deduced what Jindigar's group was doing, however, explained quickly to his companion, sure they had a plan. As he was waking the others, the panel in the wall opened and produced their dinner, plus a read-once message capsule.

The scene shimmered as she became aware of the aroma of food. The cell around her became substantial, the awareness of two other views of it remaining. It wasn't like looking through Dushau eyes; her brain wouldn't be able to interpret the wide-angle, multi-image messages from Dushau eyes. Rather, she was aware of their understanding of their visual fields, and acutely aware of the focus of their attention.

"Adjourned," announced Jindigar with a sigh. He sat up, grabbing Frey. "Do you realize what we did?"

"Inverted," he said dully, but there was resignation in it, not horror. Then he said to Krinata, "You're good."

They ate because they knew they'd need the strength. Then Jindigar reassembled them, saying, "Krinata, just like with the dice. Sit here, see the shaftway, and imagine the cells clear of fields and bars."

She felt as she once had waking from a severe fever: things not quite real; eyes too lazy to focus; mind not wanting to concentrate. But she asked, "If you can do this 'adjourning' why do you have to shift positions and dissolve us before we get clear? It'd be safer to run like this."

"This effort will take much more energy. It's different. Believe me, Krinata, I know what I'm doing."

"Oh, I do." Despite the spaced-out, aching stretch of a burning fever, the detached bemusement that prevented her from really enjoying what was happening as she'd always dreamed she would, she knew she'd treasure this memory forever as the highpoint of her life.

When they'd settled again, she knew those in the other cells were prepared now. She leaned back against the wall, and let herself into a fever-dream where the fields faded and the bars withdrew, freeing them all. She even remembered to open the gate at the end of the brig shaftway. The guard there had to be asleep at his post. The surveillance crew manning the spy eyes were more interested in a game where the stakes were the first chance to rape the prisoners.

She set up the entire scenario with loving detail as if it were one of her favorite dreams.

Then it happened. The sizzle of the force field disappeared. The bars retracted into the bulkhead.

But Krinata wasn't aware of it as more than a minor annoyance. She was into her dream. She saw Jindigar get to his feet and wander out into the corridor, and she followed with Frey, Storm at her heels, tucking Rita inside his shirt. Bell clambered over the rumpled beds and tumbled after them. People were emerging all around them. The three of them remained floating in a silent communion. The group moved.

A scurry rolled into the brig corridor and reversed in place, leading them. Arlai said, "Follow me," from the comunit. *It's his scurry*, imagined Krinata.

The brig security barricade at the end of the hall was also retracted, and two Holot drowsed at their station.

Everyone filed by silently, except the Cassrians, whose chitin clicked on the deck surface.

Twice during their silent wending through shaftways, crewmembers marched by. Krinata imagined they didn't spot the ragtag line of escapees. Then, just after a detachment of armed guards swept by, Jindigar wilted into Storm's arms, gasping, shaking. The edges of her perceptions blurred, twisting into nightmare shapes—Desdinda's face, but she imagined it away. They were safe, surrounded by their four Lehiroh Outriders. She'd seen them fight once. They went on. Finally, they came to a hatch with a pressure-seal light over it. The scurry signaled it open, and they started in. Two of their Lehiroh dealt with the duty guard expediently. Krinata became aware this wasn't a dream. The other two viewpoints, the fever weakness and ache were fading.

With a rhythmic rattle, a wall of bright armor appeared between them and the yacht lying in its cradle. Imperial armor, imperial emblems seen from *four* separate viewpoints swam hypnotically in her mind. She tumbled back into dream, but now it was not under her control. It was nightmare.

She could only see one thing at a time, and could not by any force of will lift her attention from that thing.

Beamer fire crisscrossed around them, flashing off deck and bulkheads. Krinata appreciated the beautiful pattern with only peripheral awareness that it was deadly.

A Lehiroh sent an armored man into a graceful cartwheel, to land in a heap. Krinata stared helplessly at him while he tried to rise, only to be smashed by the body of a comrade whirling down on top of him.

A swath was cleared through the armor, and Desdinda was there, seated in a chairmobile, the fourth viewpoint, distorted, blackened around the edges.

As Jindigar staggered to Desdinda, Krinata saw his face coming toward herself, twisted into a feral deathmask. Frey cut off the view, grabbing Krinata by the shoulders, capturing her eyes. *We've been invaded, distorted into a tetrad. We must rebalance. Trust Jindigar.* It was her own thought, not Frey's; she was absolutely certain. But she could not have thought at all had he not been there.

Yet Frey was more frightened than she, looking to her for courage. And she found it. Grabbing his wrist, she pulled him forward, their four Lehiroh moving with them, keeping them in a box free of the squirming, scrambling dogfight all around them.

They enclosed Jindigar in their zone of peace, and Krinata began to drag Desdinda's chair and Jindigar with them toward the yacht. Miraculously, the entire fight went with them. She went back to imagining *Truth*'s complement winning through to the yacht entry, leaving unconscious troopers behind them.

Trassle stole a beamer, cutting down six troopers before he was stopped by a Holot. Their own Holot tackled that trooper and grabbed his weapon. Combined fire made the remaining troopers hit the deck as the *Truth*'s complement scrambled for the yacht, Jindigar dragging Desdinda.

Then it happened. The world flipped inside-out. The four viewpoints overlapped and spun out of control. The refugees shriveled into twisted horrors, mere caricatures of people. They dripped ichor and babbled in garbled screams. Everything they touched steamed as if sullied by acid.

Krinata felt her own body covered with ugly growths that oozed puss. Her hands became instruments of torture to the one she touched—Desdinda. And Desdinda was the only pure thing, the only salvation for them all. They must touch her, yet dared not for it destroyed her.

Paralyzed in this vision, Krinata was stunned when something hard and smooth crashed into her and sent her spinning. Dazed, she rose, surprised to find her body returned to normal. Troopers had broken through the Lehiroh defense. Teaming up, two by two, the Lehiroh turned on the guards, tossing them about like dolls with the fury of their outrage. One trooper landed on top of Desdinda. Six others cut through and swept Desdinda and their comrade away. One enterprising trooper, noting how weak Jindigar was, gathered him into a fireman's carry and lunged for freedom. But Storm tackled the man and dragged Jindigar loose.

Simultaneously, one of the Lehiroh collected Frey from where he'd been tossed as another pulled Krinata up, tilted her over his shoulder and ran for the ramp into the yacht, followed in close order by all the rest of the escapees.

By the time they had taken out the yacht's onboard guards, Jindigar was on his feet, leaning heavily on Storm. No one had spoken to the three of them, had barely looked at them, making no attempt to communicate with them, as if they were a constituted Oliat.

Jindigar led them to the bridge, panting, bleeding from a shallow cut over one eye, limping slightly from a wrenched muscle. Gathering the triad, one hand on Krinata's left shoulder, one hand on Frey's right, he caught their eyes. Krinata felt an odd dizziness as she looked into their eyes and into her own from theirs. But it closed a circuit, and her breathing calmed. Horror receded.

Gradually, awareness of looking into her own eyes faded, and she was herself looking at them. "Adjourned," said Jin-

digar. "Best I can do right now." His head drooped, and he le
go of Frey to hug Krinata. "I almost lost us. I'm sorry." He
hugged Frey. "I wish I had your talent!"

All business, then, he stumbled toward the control stations
tumbled into a chair and surveyed the instruments. Trassle wa
already working over a board, next to Terab. As Krinata foun
the captain's chair, Rinperee slid into a navigating station.

"Arlai?" asked Krinata, scanning the controls.

"I have her. It will be as if you were at my helm, Krinata."
But his voice sounded strained.

While the passengers secured themselves, Krinata studie
the controls with rising panic. "None of this looks familiar."
She'd learned *Truth*'s boards, but had never studied piloting.

Jindigar said, "I studied the schematics, remember?" Hi
voice held a burr of tension, and it seemed to echo in her mind
He leaned across Terab's station and flipped switches in fron
of Krinata. "Arlai? Ready?"

"Do you see the vacuum telltale?"

"It's on. We're tight."

"That's what my reading says. No time for a full check
They're trying to grab control of the bay doors back from me."
The bay doors opened, and they swooped out into space. Tera
and Trassle cheered. Jindigar drew his knees up to his chin
visibly shuddering. Krinata felt as if gun muzzles were traine
on her back.

"Twelve minutes," said Arlai. "I'm moving out of orbit t
track and lock on. We'll detime in tandem. Rinperee?"

She'd taken a board behind Krinata. "Stand by."

Krinata shivered as the hairs on her neck stood up. Jindiga
raised his head to watch her as she worked with Arlai to se
the course. "I'm sorry I couldn't make the Dissolution. I wi
as soon as we're clear."

It was as if she were touching the fields of a magnetic bottle
Her skin crawled. "Krinata, don't lose your nerve now. It'
just a leakage—"

"*What's* leaking?" Her voice shook.

"Joint awareness. I judge they're preparing to fire on us
That's logical."

"Confirmed," said Arlai. "Beamcannon coming into focus. They've got enough juice to take out a seeker." Then his voice changed. "We've got trouble. The human male left as helm watch onboard *Truth* just woke up and discovered I'm active. He's attacking my circuits." There was an anguished cry, "Jindigar, help!"

Krinata's heart leaped, as if it would tear holes in her chest, her whole body wanting to lunge to Arlai's aid. Jindigar straightened, then drove his fingers over the board before him, pulling up an image of Frey somewhere back in the yacht. "With me! We've got to take out the guard onboard *Truth* before we get there, or Arlai will have to do it!"

Krinata saw Frey swallow hard and agree. Jindigar turned to her, and when their eyes met, she tumbled back into nightmare, three diverse scenes—a fourth lurking darkly as Desdinda fought back to consciousness somewhere—and she said, hearing her voice echo oddly, "What can we do?"

"Imp," said Jindigar. "A mad piol is a match for most men. Imagine the look on that man's face if a bundle of claws, teeth and fur attacks him." His voice echoed oddly, too, but even after he stopped, the idea flowed through her mind in vivid pictures.

She knew *Truth*'s bridge, knew how Imp would find the man sprawled as Jindigar had, legs protruding from an access panel, probably wearing green polka-dot pajamas. She saw the whole thing as Imp, fed up with this intruder, worried at the man's bare toes until he crawled out to bat at the pest. Imp went for the throat. The man threw the spitting ball of fur across the bridge to land in the captain's chair. But Imp launched himself again, and the man ran for a weapon.

Arlai slammed emergency bulkheads shut, herding the intruder while Imp harried his heels all the way. At the last, Imp threw himself on the man's back, and the man careened into a wall smashing Imp hard. The piol slid down limply as the man, bleeding now from several superficial cuts, opened the hatch marked WEAPONS and stalked into the dark, tumbling head over heels into the aft refuse bin. Arlai had changed the label just in time..

Her daydream was shattered when the deck bucked under her. "Screens up!" said Arlai in his business voice, then added, "Imp isn't seriously hurt, and I've only lost a few sensors." In another tone, he added, "Jindigar—"

Krinata felt the multiawareness fade as Jindigar adjourned them again. He answered Arlai, "Not now." He folded in on himself, groaning. In a sidewise flash, she saw his teeth were paling.

The next shot rattled them hard, but shields held.

"I've taken a hit," announced Arlai, and coolly produced a damage report of which Krinata understood not a word.

Krinata heard herself, but didn't believe her own words, nor the sudden icy calm in her voice. "I'm going to have to fire these guns, Arlai. Can I do it? Maybe it will keep them from firing at us long enough to get away."

"I'm not permitted weapons, Krinata, nor is your onboard programmed into them," answered Arlai, and she detected true regret in his tone. "Your fire control is on manual. But Jindigar's at that board. Targeting is by digital calculators and non-Sentient live-tools."

She had to try. She locked her board to Arlai and scrambled around to Jindigar's station. The big Dushau was huddled with his feet on his seat and his head buried between his knees. He was shaking violently, as if in a fit. She could feel a ragged blackness eating away at the periphery of her awareness. It had Desdinda flavor, a mad distortion, growing with every passing minute.

"Arlai, show me what to poke when," demanded Krinata.

A display lit on her board, the orange light turning Jindigar a sickly color. One of the switches on the display began to flash. "This is your fire-control rack. One, Three, and Five are armed. Aim by centering this screen mechanism." Cross-hairs appeared over the image of *Timespike*, and the centering controls lit up. Any idiot could do it.

"*Timespike* is recharging and maneuvering for advantage. You have eighty seconds before they can hit you six times with their beamers while sending three more missiles after me. The yacht will buck when you fire—it has lousy gravity control. You've got seeker missiles, Krinata—three hits could totally destroy that battleship, which carries a crew of six hundred. I've taken another hit. Rinperee, give me those numbers quickly or I won't be able to program them. I've got onboard fires."

Rinperee's voice began to drone numbers.

They had to have Arlai if they were to live through this, for the seeker craft could barely accommodate them packed in like sardines. But to fire on that ship was to strike at the heart of the Empire.

She could see Zinzik leering, feel his hand on her back, smell the breath of his minion as he undressed her, and was amazed that she found herself hesitating.

Jindigar: custodian of a living memory longer than human history; a true prince of his people; a man who could be inwardly ripped to shreds by the torments of others; a man of loyalty and honor such as her father had always called worthy of an Emperor's respect; a man the Emperor had tortured by the choice between his loyalty to his friends and his honor-bound duty to his people and all the civilizations yet to come in the galaxy. The thought of what had been done to Jindigar was almost enough to make her strike.

She thought of Trassle's proof that Zinzik had taken the throne by a ruse. There hadn't been time to be sure the evidence was solid. She felt it was, but she had no proof.

Jindigar put a hand on her wrist. She looked at him, seeing a silent battle there. *He's holding Desdinda out of our triad. He can't keep it up much longer.*

A side monitor screen lit showing the *Timespike*'s bridge. Zinzik was there, in full ceremonials, leaning toward the pickup. Desdinda, once again in a chairmobile, sat behind him. "Surrender, or be destroyed," he decreed, as if it were of no moment to him which they chose. But there was a light in his eye that seemed familiar. He enjoyed pain, preceded by as much torment as possible.

It was the same expression she'd seen on his face when he disposed of that poor Rashion. His eye roved their bridge

contemptuously until he saw Jindigar. "So you survive again
Well, not for long." He grabbed a weapon from one of his
guards, the ugly smile broadening as he pointed it at Desdinda's
head. "You think I don't remember what happened when Fe
deewarn died? Bring that ship back to its docking bay—gently—
and maybe you won't die as your Oliat did."

She felt the impact of those words on Jindigar, like flin
shards coated with acid, driven deep into the half-healed wound
of mind. The pain blinded her. She couldn't breathe. Couldn'
move. But she could see Zinzik's face, the same twisted lee
as at the moment he'd shot the Rashion.

As his eyes narrowed, and his hand tightened on the grip
of the beamer, she summoned every last ounce of strength in
her, and slammed her open palm down over the row of switches
firing all weapons on the flagship of the Empire.

Simultaneously, their ship recoiled, and she grabbed at Jin
digar to keep from falling. Jindigar screamed, "No!" The world
went crazy, color blotches smearing, sounds expanding and
contracting, and that horrid smile loomed closer and closer
filling her mind. But the smile was on Jindigar's face.

Eyes squeezed shut, she denied that perception with all her
soul and clung to the warm napped shoulders as he clung to
her. He had lost the battle to keep Desdinda at bay.

Then he pushed Krinata away, shaking her.

She stared into Jindigar's swirling, haunted eyes. The two
of them—the four of them—the two of them. Perception os
cillated as he tried to cut them off from Desdinda and Frey
But he couldn't shatter what he had built. His sense of panic
at what was to come hit her.

The screen display went fire bright, and she hid her eye
against the top of Jindigar's head. She didn't feel his grip
tighten as they were both swept away into a vortex of intens
pain. Hot lances of fire entered her eyeballs and pierced to the
back of her brain. An explosion of fear turned to ravening
panic.

She couldn't breathe. Her skin prickled. Her eyes felt too
big for her head. Her mouth fell open so wide it almost spli

her cheeks and she screamed. It went on and on and on until she felt the universe lost, and she was tumbling into hell to remain forever at the outer brink of sanity.

And then, with a snap like a bone breaking, it was over. She was on the deck, Rinperee bending over her as Storm eased Jindigar from his chair onto the deck beside her.

Arlai announced, *"Timespike* has been destroyed. Stand by to detime, eighty-three seconds."

Terab scrambled to Krinata's helm station.

"Three seeker craft astern," announced Arlai. "They're ranging, and we're pursued by *Timespike*'s missiles, but we can't take evasive action now."

Trassle stepped over Jindigar and took the weapons station. "Arlai, how do we fire stern missiles?"

Arlai instructed him, then reported, "You got one! Another's chasing one of my landers." Then, "Detime!"

The screens went gray. Krinata pulled herself up using Rinperee. She could make out a tiny white blip accompanying them. "That's got to be Arlai," she said.

Rinperee looked at her with new hope. "Yes, it's Arlai." She turned to Jindigar. "We're away free, that is, if you are—"

"We'll be all right," he managed. When he spoke, his voice didn't echo, and she saw only through her own eyes now.

Krinata breathed a deep, shuddering sigh. It was over. They'd made it. All the horrors he'd predicted hadn't come to pass, though the horrors that had were worse. *I killed the Emperor— maybe the whole Allegiancy.* But, no. She'd seen for herself; the Allegiancy was dead already. And the man she had killed was certainly no Emperor, and the crew of his ship no better than he. She regretted their deaths, but didn't feel like a vengeful murderer.

She knelt beside Jindigar, embracing him to still the tremors that swept both of them now. The warmth helped chase the *amputated* feeling away. In a few days, they'd be at Phanphihy, a new world and a new life. There would be nightmares, but they'd fade. They were free.

The smell of smoke and singed fur intruded, and suddenly

Rita was prying her way between Jindigar's legs, licking his face. A patch on her back was still smoking, and she whimpered pleadingly for Jindigar's attention.

The tremors lessened. He uncurled, gently taking the piol into his lap. He looked up at Krinata and smiled. "I hope Imp likes Rita."

He's interested in life again. He'll recover, too.